KING OF HARLEM

A tightly woven enigma around real and interesting characters, *King of Harlem* makes for a gripping read. Jones is a bright new light in the mystery genre.
    —Clive Cussler, author of *Raise the Titanic!* and *Trojan Odyssey*

With a clever cast of three-dimensional characters, Steven Philip Jones has done more than write a wonderful whodunit. He has managed to successfully mix fact with fiction in highly entertaining fashion. I hope to see more of Sassafras Winters in the future.
    —Phillip Tomasso, author of *Adverse Impact* and *Third Ring*

King of Harlem is a fun read that gives one the feel of the PI novels from the past with perhaps a softer edge than some of the more hardboiled books.
    —Lorie Ham, author of *Deadly Discrimination*

Titles by Steven Philip Jones
Published by Mundania Press

King of Harlem

Talismen—The Knightmare Knife
By Steven Philip Jones and Barb Jacobs

KING OF HARLEM

STEVEN PHILIP JONES

Mundania Press

King of Harlem
Copyright © 2005 by Steven Philip Jones

All rights reserved under the International and Pan-American Copyright Conventions. No part of this book may be reproduced or transmitted in any form or by any means, electronic or mechanical including photocopying, recording, or by any information storage and retrieval system, without permission in writing from the publisher.

This is a work of fiction. Names, characters, places and incidents either are the product of the author's imagination or are used fictitiously, and any resemblance to any actual persons, living or dead, events, or locales is entirely coincidental.

A Mundania Press Production

Mundania Press LLC
6470A Glenway Avenue, #109
Cincinnati, Ohio 45211-5222

To order additional copies of this book, contact:
books@mundania.com
www.mundania.com

Cover Art © 2005 by Christopher Jones
Titling and Layout by Stacey L. King
Book Design and Composition by Daniel J. Reitz, Sr.
Marketing and Promotion by Bob Sanders
Edited by Bob Sanders

Trade Paperback edition ISBN-10: 1-59426-110-5
Trade Paperback edition ISBN-13: 978-1-59426-110-7

eBook edition ISBN-10: 1-59426-111-3
eBook edition ISBN-13: 978-1-59426-111-4

First Edition • August 2005

Library of Congress Catalog Card Number 2005920385

Production by Mundania Press LLC
Printed in the United States of America

10   9   8   7   6   5   4   3   2   1

The First Chapter

So you want to know about Orson Welles and me.

It started one early February morning. I was still sleeping when my grandfather bellowed all of six inches away from my ear. "Phone, gundamnit."

My eyes shot up, tugged window blinds. *Sixty-five years old and he has the lungs of a baby.* "Who is it?" My voice cracked as I tried to crank up my brain.

"Don't know. Think they're callin' from Canada. They try to reverse the charges, ya' tell 'em to go screw themselves. Hear me?"

"Right." I fumbled out of bed and shuffled towards the wall phone in the cracker box kitchen. "Go screw yourself."

"Not me, gundamnit! Them! *Them!* Tell *them* to go screw themselves, gundamnit!"

I was steering on automatic pilot when I put the receiver to my ear and spoke into the mouthpiece, "Hello. Go screw yourself."

"Canada Lee is not amused."

"Canada!" was one of my oldest friends. As kids we ran loose in the same gang of scalawags, Canada my first Negro friend. As adolescents we worked together as stable hands. For me it was just an afternoon job to raise money for ball games and egg creams, but Canada, who never grew taller than five feet five, took advantage of the opportunity to learn how to ride. As adults I wormed my way to Chicago while Canada toured America's jockey circuit. Later he lighted on New York City to study boxing, eventually winning an amateur lightweight title. "Is that you?"

"Who else would be using Canada Lee's name except for us?"

"And who else talks as screwy as you do? How are you, buddy?"

"Canada is fine. Why did you tell us to go screw ourselves?"

"Oh, that was Governor's fault."

"He has a peculiar way of demonstrating his affections we think."

"Tell me about it. I've got to live with him. Why are you calling? You in town? Fighting, maybe?"

"Canada no longer fights nor rides the ponies. Sometimes he screws, but not himself."

"Don't beat a dead horse."

"We wouldn't have been much of a jockey if we couldn't. Canada is in New York City. Harlem, to be precise. We have heard you retired from the sissy game of baseball to become a private investigator."

"How did you hear about that all the way out on the east coast?"

"Canada Lee keeps tabs on all of his old friends. You would not believe some of the things we know about Abe Borodkin, Max Pilzer, Chauncey Morehouse..."

"All right, I get the point. So what are you doing if you're not riding or fighting?"

As it turned out, chance had turned Canada Lee into an actor. The Federal Theatre Project was WPA chairman's Harry Hopkins latest strategy to help get unemployed Americans off the dole by offering government-sponsored jobs. A unit was established in Harlem, a district whose show business enthusiasm was legendary, but where opportunities to perform professionally were few. Hallie Flannagan, the Project's chairwoman, announced that only ten percent of any unit's ranks could consist of professionals who had been receiving relief. The remaining ninety percent had to be made up of amateurs. The Harlem Unit of the Federal Theatre Project allowed hundreds of starry-eyed Negroes a chance to pay the rent and fulfill life-long dreams, all at government expense!

After nearly fifteen years of battering his body, Canada decided to try out for *Macbeth*. He was good enough to convince its first-time director, a twenty-year-old protégée named Orson Welles, to give him the part of Banquo. Canada was ecstatic, grateful for the job, but his director now found himself in trouble. Canada was calling me to ask if I would hire on with the Harlem Unit as Welles' bodyguard.

"There is a chapter of the Communist Worker's Party here in Harlem," Canada explained. "They are convinced Orson wants to insult Negroes with a Williams and Walker version of *Macbeth*. The Communists are trying to turn the borough against Orson."

"Are you doing blackface?"

"Of course not."

"Then tell the Communists that."

"We have. They will not listen."

"Let 'em watch you rehearse."

"Our producer presented the Communists with an invitation, but they declined. Sassafras, things are growing ugly."

We had seen some ugly things growing up, so I knew, contrary to the way he expressed himself, Canada was not given to hyperbole. "How so?

"A growing population of protestors pickets the Lafayette, our theatre, around the clock. They average two hundred a day, working in shifts. And we have begun receiving death threats against Orson's life. Most are primal screams, nothing more. Very few, but still a few, are serious and coherent."

"How are you receiving the threats?"

"Most are mailed. Some are slipped under the exit doors. We receive an average of ten a day."

Yep. That sounded ugly all right. "Have you notified the police?"

"We have. Patrols have been stepped up, but that is all."

"About all they can do, really."

"No one worried about our *Macbeth* before the Harlem Communists stirred them up. Canada believes if people see Orson is under watch, no one will strike at him. Once the reviews come out and people read our efforts are sincere, this discontent will disappear."

"I hope you're right, but it sounds like wishful thinking," I said.

"Perhaps. But Orson is determined to see it through, and so is our Unit."

"I appreciate the offer, but why do you need me? You're better with your fists than me. You're quicker. You're colored so you won't stand out in the crowd. Hell, Canada, you've got a lot more riding on this than I ever could."

"What you say is true, but there are places you can go with Orson that Canada is not allowed. Besides, serving as Orson's bodyguard would take Canada away from his rehearsing. So he recommended you to Miss Flannagan, as Canada owes you for favors past due and has heard you need the money."

Strange way of paying me back, pal. I thought it, but I kept my trap shut. I knew what Canada was trying to say as I rubbed the thin scar along the back of my neck. "How much?" I asked.

"Thirty dollars a day, plus expenses incurred on the job, room and board."

"When's opening night?"

"In two months on April 14."

Oh, good. A guy can get a lot of contusions in ten weeks. I thought it, but I didn't say it. Poverty tends to make a body keep a tight rein on his sarcasm. "Okay. I'll give it a go. For the rent. I owe Governor about a year's worth."

Arrangements to bring me to New York had already been made and a suite was reserved for me at the Cosmopolitan Hotel, two blocks north of Orson's apartment. Before I could honestly appreciate the responsibility I was assuming, I was on the job.

❧❦

Six weeks later I was sitting slumped in an overstuffed and under-upholstered chair in an apartment on 123rd Street in Harlem. It was three thirty in the morning, and all around me a Saturday night rent party was coasting along at full steam. All I wanted to do was go back to my hotel and catch some shut-eye. But I couldn't do that. I had to watch over Orson Welles, and he insisted on being the guy who turned out the lights at any party he graced.

The tenement consisted of four rooms linked by a narrow hallway, one of which, the main bedroom, had been locked to bar uninvited guests. The other bedroom was reserved for folks playing poker or rolling dice. I was in the living room, converted into a dance floor by removing most of the furniture and storing it in a neighbor's flat. I could have maybe grabbed a stool in the kitchen, but since that room was little more than an extension of the living room I opted to stay where I was.

Every lamp around the dance floor had had its white lights replaced with red bulbs, and at least seventy-five people were jitterbugging to the Lindy Hop. Keeping an eye on a hyperactive young man like Orson under these conditions was nearly impossible, but the party did provide me two allowances.

First, although Orson and I weren't the only whites in the place, there weren't many others and most of them were beat cops, who had come up to tell us to pipe down then stuck around for the party. Better yet, Orson was probably the only other person at the party besides me who couldn't hoof, try as he might on the dinky dance floor.

The poor boy was too pathetic to look at for too long, so I started watching the vigorous musicians holding court in the living room. There was a stride piano player, a drummer, a guitarist, and some clown on a trumpet. These last three were playing free of charge, and, in a sense, so was the cat on the keyboard. The original pianist, hired through an agent, Libby Boyette, had moved on hours ago to another parlor social. He had been displaced by Abba Labba, a popular nightclub musician since the 1920s, who had outperformed him in a feral cutting that had sent everyone screaming "Break it down!" or "Get in the gully and give us the ever-lovin' stomp!" The loser was the only musician walking away from this party a sawbuck or two richer than when he arrived, but it was the man who captured the piano stool who came out ahead in what mattered most. In Harlem you weren't a jazz musician if you couldn't cut at a rent party on a Saturday night. Abba Labba held on to his professional reputation by performing here for free, as he would at some other function next Saturday, and the next, and so on until the day he or Harlem died.

A burst of light, like a Photoflash lamp, flickered outside the kitchen window. A sedentary brownstone across the alley blocked my view of the night, but it was clear there was lightning in the sky. I assumed customary grumbles of thunder followed the fireworks, since there was no way I could hear anything outside over the din of the rent party. For twenty-four hours a southern storm had perched along the New England seaboard, repeatedly dousing a cold rain on New York City. More than a few of the showers turned into downpours, two or three even threatening to become deluges, but despite the lightning the storm was acting sluggish, as if it had finally played itself out.

There wasn't a drop in sight. Like my grandfather was fond of saying, "Looks like ol' God's gonna have to knock down a couple o' more barley pops 'fore this mother can kick in again."

His memory made me smile. It also made me sad, which startled me. This was hardly my first sojourn away from my hometown or Governor, but for some reason all of a sudden I felt homesick.

"What'cha thinking about, shamus?"

I looked up to see Ben Kanter, a member of Orson's WPA cast, talking to me. Cream-skinned with a nose better tailored to a Hibernian than a Negro, Kanter could likely have passed for white if he had ever felt the urge.

"Nothing of practical use," I said. "How are you doing?"

"Can't complain. I've wanted to ask you something though. Some of the guys in the crew swear you're that Sassafras Winters who pitched with the Chicago Cubs a couple years back. How about it?

Oh, great, I thought. *Just what I needed.*

"Guilty as charged," I confessed.

Kanter smiled, nice white even teeth. "Cool deal, McNeil!"

"Thank you. Go away."

"Hey, I'm not going to razz you! Tell me, were you a real Dillenger, a Dracula, or what?"

Kanter might as well have been speaking Greek until I realized he was tonguing jive. "You want to run that by me again? I can't lay your racket." I was hoping I told him I didn't jive.

"Oops. Sorry. Been waxing native all night."

"It's cool. I used to be able to hold up my end of the conversation, but it's been awhile since I was here last. I've gotten old. Forgot too much."

"Yeah. I can see what you mean." Kanter slipped me a good-natured wink. "Well, what I was asking was, were you hot? Were you good? Did you make the grade? Could you play, damn it?"

"I can play. I shored up Malone and Root when I had to."

"*Pat* Malone! *Charlie* Root? You were on the '29 club?"

"I said I could play. You saw us that year?"

"Oh, gosh, yes! I was in Chicago with my papa that July on a Sunday when your team played the St. Louis Cardinals. I remember that old man the Red Birds have got managing them, Hornsby, knocked one right out of left field onto Addison Avenue for your guys. Or was it Clark Street. I forget what those roads are called."

"*Old man?*" Hornsby? In 1929 that old man Hornsby pelted 40 dingers over a variety of fences throughout the National League. He also batted .380, drove in 149 runs, hit 229 times, and scored 156 runs. He was the quill of a damned fine litter that included Kiki Cuyler, Lewis Robert "Hack" Wilson, and Riggs Stephenson. During the July Kanter's dad brought him to Wrigley Field, the Cubs won 24 out of 33 games. By season's end we captured the NL pennant by 10 ½ lengths.

1929 was a great year. But it could have been better.

Having pitched middle relief in the Cubs' final regular season game, I went out with some of my teammates and got plastered for the last time in my life. One of two reasons for my going on the wagon can be blamed on us losing the World Series that year to the Philadelphia Athletics when we should have clobbered them. It hurts to think maybe we celebrated too soon for our own good. As for the other reason, it has nothing to do with my baseball career so it doesn't matter right now.

The Cubbies and I lost one more World Series in '31, this time to the New York Yankees and Babe Ruth, and by 1936 most of my teammates were out of baseball and on their own. These days a new roster was sitting in Wrigley's home dugout, led by Phil Cavarretta, a Chicago boy born and raised. His team had already played in their own October Classic in '35, but didn't finish any better than my class. Suddenly it dawned on me that I hadn't seen any of my fellow veterans since retiring in '34, and I was damned close to turning thirty-five years old. So was Hornsby, "The Rajah." We were all getting long in the tooth. Getting old fast with nothing to show for it but two bungled World Series.

"Yeah...Addison. Listen, Ben, I'm beat. Can we jaw tomorrow at rehearsals?"

"Sure. Hey, I understand. Orson's been running us all ragged. We'll slide your jib later."

I watched as Kanter weaved his way back into the mainstream of the postage-stamp sized dance floor. Just like I figured, he wasted no time seeking out Rose Ramsey, the gal throwing this shing-ding at a buck-a-head admittance.

Rose was the Lady-in-waiting in *Macbeth*, but on 123rd Street, a hop, skip, and jump from the A-train stop-off, she was a singer who had been watershedding and throwing social matinees to pay her rent since the stock market crash. She was tall but stout, with caramel-colored skin and a teddy bear face. More than once I had noticed Rose and Kanter talking to each other during rehearsals or spotted them together around the borough, and you didn't have to be Sherlock Holmes to deduce each thought the other was swell.

The young couple struck up what seemed a familiar conversation. Nothing exciting was going to happen there so I glanced away to scan the crowd, something I figured bodyguards did from time to time.

Just under half of the hundred and more folks jostling inside the tenement were quailed from *Macbeth's* cast and crew, the majority consisting of truck drivers, tradesmen, housemaids, laundry workers, seamstresses, porters, elevator operators, and shoeshine boys. Standing out in the crowd, dancing like a madman with a beauty a head taller than himself, was Canada.

He somehow sensed me staring at him, turned his rugged cherub's face at me and waved. I waved back, then glanced at Abba Labba's impromptu quartet again as a vocalist joined them. It was Rose. I searched for Kanter to see if he was watching her, but didn't spot him anywhere as Rose began belting out an old Ethel Water's tune.

I closed my eyes for a moment to yawn, stretched my arms and legs until the sinew threatened to pop, then did something unforgivable. I fell asleep.

When I felt the rap on the side of my head it was nearly dawn. Dusky orange sunlight permeated the air outside the kitchen window. Anyone awake was either content with doing the monkey hunch on the dance floor, talking, or eating what remained of the fish and pig's feet. Dozens of bodies lay helter-skelter about the living room, sleeping where they had fallen. The place looked as if somebody had gassed the Savoy. I had to blink a couple of times before I could figure out Canada was standing next to me.

"We have an uninvited guest," he said.

I followed Canada's gaze across the room towards a bullish middle-aged white man hastily cutting a wary path through the unconcerned congregation. The stranger's coat and conservative seersucker suit were ruffled and his cheeks unshaven. His round hound dog face, drooping mustache, and round spectacles reminded me of Teddy Roosevelt. He didn't look like a leftist radical, but I riveted my gaze on him while I asked Canada about, "Orson."

"He is fine."

"What do you think? Is this cat after him?"

"Canada doesn't know. The Philistine flashed a dime store police detective's badge and pushed past Rose to gain entrance."

"The guy looks like an aardvark left out in the rain. He's no cop. My guess is he's a private dick."

"Canada will defer to the expert. Shall we escort the gentleman outside for questioning?"

"No. Let's give him some rope and see where he goes."

Canada pointed at Orson, passed out in a corner, an arm draped over the shoulders of a statuesque Negress, an enviable smile on the young man's face. I thought about Welles' wife, Virginia, back at their apartment, probably waking up around now to get breakfast ready for her husband and faithful companion. *Twenty is too young to get married.*

The stranger paid no attention to Orson. All he cared about was making a beeline for Rose's back rooms. Nothing else in the flat mattered to him.

I stood and my knees cracked, complaining, like two cars backfiring one second after the other. My back bitched that I was making it do too much too soon. I ignored the pansies. "You coming?"

"Canada Lee wouldn't miss it."

We went after the peeper, arriving in the narrow hall leading from the kitchen in time to see him kick in the door to the bedroom facing the alley. I heard metal snap, saw part of a bolt fly out into the hall, then lost sight of the dick as he charged into the bedroom.

Canada and I ran after him, storming into the bedroom right behind our quarry. The place was a mess, as if the dick had managed to toss the room in the whole three seconds he had been alone in here. In that time he had found his way to the window overlooking the alley two stories below. It was open. The stranger held a standard .45 revolver in his hands, aiming it at something or someone down in the cul-de-sac.

"I got him. Call the cops, boys."

"Who the hell are you?" I asked.

"My name's Andre De Shields. I'm a private investigator. Now call the cops!"

I still didn't know what was going on and momentarily lost my train of thought, something I had a bad habit of doing when pitching in pressure situations, to the disgust of my managers. Canada brought me back when he touched my shoulder. "Sassafras, there is blood."

True enough, beads of moist crimson ran from the open window back to a vanity at the other end of the room. A broken bottle of cold cream marked the start of the trail.

"What the hell is going on here?" I asked. People from the party were beginning to mass in the hall outside the door, whispering among themselves.

"I said call the cops!"

I moved to the window. "Why?" I glanced out and down. Framed in the 45.'s sights was Ben Kanter. He was frightened, standing beside an uncovered manhole, hands dirty and smeared with rust, one assumed from having removed the sewer's plate now lying at his feet. I could hear rainwater rushing through the nearly overflowing street pipe. The pavement of the alley was wet and slick from the storm.

"One last time, just what the hell is going on around here?" I asked.

"I've been looking for a fella named Norton Denbrough. I tracked him here, but I do believe this nightrunner killed him before I could get to him." De Shields was grinning, almost as if satisfied that he had been too late.

Clipping from *The Brooklyn Chronicle*, March 15, 1936:

MANHATTAN BANKER MURDERED AT HARLEM PARTY

WHITE FINANCIER WAS IN LOVE WITH NEGRO ACTRESS, POSSIBLE VICTIM OF LOVERS' TRIANGLE

A Harlem negro, Ben Kanter, was arrested today on suspicion of killing a white Manhattan man, Norton Denbrough, during a rent party on 123rd Street.

Kanter, 32, is suspected of killing Denbrough during a lover's quarrel over Rose Ramsey, the party's hostess and a negro actress with the WPA's Federal Theatre Project.

Denbrough, 30, lived in Gramercy Park West and was employed at Manhattan First National Bank in the investment branch. The bank fired Denbrough last December for dating Ramsey.

According to Andre De Shields, a private investigator, Denbrough had been living with Ramsey for several weeks.

"There's no doubt Denbrough was romantically involved with Ramsey," De Shields said. "So was Kanter. I saw Ramsey and Kanter together around Harlem plenty of times."

The victim's mother, Claudette Denbrough, hired De Shields after her son started spending long periods of time away from home.

"She wanted to know what her kid was up to," De Shields said.

Denbrough was last seen alive just after dawn this morning by De Shields. Apparently Kanter killed Denbrough during a fight in Ramsey's bedroom, carried the body down a fire escape, and disposed of it in a sewer in an alley behind Ramsey's apartment building.

Violent runoffs in New York sewers from Saturday night's thunderstorms have made it impossible to begin a search to recover Denbrough's body.

"We might never find it now," a police spokesman said. "We'll try, but it's unlikely. Not that it matters. We've got the killer. That's what counts."

Chapter Two

It was after two o'clock before the police let Orson and me see Kanter. He was being detained in a holding pen in the Harlem precinct's basement, along with any stray cat or drunk the bulls picked up the night before. The drunks would be released at sundown. Kanter would be staying until the judge pronounced his bail at the Hall of Justice Monday morning.

The basement was humid from steam pipes, damp from bad plumbing, and reeked like a slaughterhouse in August. Six and two would get you four that when they flushed the toilets upstairs all the waste came down here, along the walls, coagulating on the floor.

"How are you doing, buddy?" I asked Kanter after the cops left us alone, Ben and his cellmates on one side of the bars, Orson and me on the other.

"Oh, sure," Kanter said, trying his best to smile, "now you want to talk."

"Exactly what is going on?" Orson interrupted.

"I was hoping you two were going to tell me."

"How do you mean?"

"All I know is they arrested me on suspicion of manslaughter. The bulls think I killed some cat named Norton Denbrough. I thought the cops might have said something more to you guys while you were waiting."

I shook my head. "I did talk to De Shields for a second. Got him to agree to talk with me more later over a free beer. All he'd say right now is Denbrough's mother retained him to find her wayward son. I guess they live over on the west side. Real upper-crust blue-blooded family."

"So how come the cops think I killed him?"

"Because you were in the wrong place at the wrong time. De Shields swears he saw Denbrough in Rose's bedroom window this morning just before he crashed the rent party. Now there isn't a sign of Denbrough anywhere."

"The guy got up and left. Big deal."

"A *very* big deal, if he isn't found. Rose's bedroom door was locked from the inside. Canada and me will have to testify to that. We watched De Shields break the bolt to get in. Nobody said they saw anybody going in that room all night, and Rose swears she locked it shut just before the party started."

"Then De Shields is seeing things. If Rose said she locked the door, she locked the door."

"Rose locked the door from the outside," Orson pointed out. "What the police need to know—what we would like to know—is why the door was bolted on the inside and who bolted it."

Kanter didn't have any answers and didn't bother wasting time admitting it.

"Anyway," I said, "De Shields was the only person in the bedroom when Canada and me got there. Whole place was a mess, like somebody rifled it trying to find something. Plus there's some blood running across the floor to the window. You don't appear to have any cuts. De Shields doesn't have any. Where did it come from?"

"There is one thing I don't understand," Orson said. "How can Ben be accused of murder if there isn't a body?"

"He's being accused of manslaughter. There's a difference. Suppose someone did dump Denbrough into the sewer behind Rose's this morning. The runoff from that storm we just had probably swept his body all the way to the East River by now."

"So they don't need a corpse to convict me?" Kanter asked.

"Not if it's reasonable to suppose Denbrough's body won't ever be found. All the court needs to justify setting a trial date is a motive and an opportunity on your part, as well as evidence that a crime was committed. After that all a prosecutor has to do is prove beyond a reasonable doubt that you killed Norton Denbrough."

"But I didn't kill him! Denbrough has to be alive! All they've got to do is find him."

"Just because you didn't kill him doesn't mean Denbrough hasn't assumed room temperature," I said. "Don't forget about that blood. And you told the police the manhole cover was already off the sewer when you found it in the alley."

"Sure. I was trying to slide it back over the hole when that fat private dick started yelling and waving his gat at me."

"Didn't you see anyone else?" Orson asked. "Someone who might have come down the fire escape from Rose's window?"

"No."

I asked, "What were you doing in the alley this morning?"

"Why?" Sparks of comprehension flashed behind Kanter's eyes an instant after he asked the question. "You guys think Denbrough was in that window. You think I killed him!"

"No," Orson stressed. "But how can anyone help extricate you unless we know all the available facts."

"Screw the facts! Some two-bit peeper tells everybody he saw this

Denbrough cat in Rose's bedroom window, and now you all think I'm some kind of green-eyed monster! All the evidence the cops have is circumstantial. So why is De Shields' word better than mine? Huh? One white man says the nigger killed another buckra man and that's good enough to round up a lynch party!"

"Ben, all we want to know is what were you doing in the alley."

"You're saying a stranger was in Rose's bedroom! You're saying Rose is some kind of mama! A pink's whore! She's the best woman I ever met! How could you think that way, Orson?"

Orson jerked as if he had been slapped. His brown eyes drooped until he was staring at the floor. His expression reminded me of a child being scolded by his mother. "I promise you, Ben, I hold Rose in the highest regard. My only concern is for you and the Unit."

"You're only 'concern' is for *Macbeth* and keeping the Communists from getting their hands on any bad publicity! To hell about what happens to me!"

"Goddamnit, now that ain't fair!" I shouted. "Something happened in Rose's bedroom today. The bolt, the sewer, and the blood prove it. Maybe it was murder, maybe you were made a cuckold, I don't know, but something's rotten here. Things have gotten out of hand and you've been left holding the bag. In short, you are in serious trouble. You could go to prison for manslaughter. Do you hear me? If you don't start cooperating and answer some questions, you could go to prison for a long time."

Kanter's anger deflated. He desperately shifted his eyes between Orson and me. Time and again he seemed ready to tell us something then bit his tongue. Finally he turned around and walked to the back of the cell, slumping down on the only available chair, the lidless toilet.

Orson asked, "Ben?"

"I've got some thinking to do." Kanter's voice was barely a whisper. "Leave me alone, please."

"Ben," I said, "we just spent six hours cooling our heels to talk with you."

"Please. Just leave me alone."

Kanter slouched on the toilet, acting confused and defeated. The only thing he seemed sure about was that he wasn't going to say anything more.

I, on the other hand, was seething. As far as I was concerned Kanter was behaving like an ungrateful brat. I stomped to the exit and hammered on the door. Orson stayed with Kanter. When an officer unlocked the exit to let us out I said, "Orson. Let's go."

He waited a moment. "If you need anything, you know you just have to call."

Kanter nodded his head and waved once with a flap more than a gesture.

Orson came away from the cell slowly and followed me out of the basement.

We hailed a cab outside the precinct. I wasn't supposed to meet with De Shields until four, but with nowhere else to go I told the driver to head for the Astoria Café then gruffly settled into the back seat with Orson. My companion nursed his thoughts and didn't say a word until we were halfway to my destination.

"Ben's hiding something from us, Sassafras," he concluded.

"No fooling."

"But what is it?"

I told Orson I was sure I didn't know.

"If Ben's innocent, why was he so defensive?"

The cleverest response I could think of was an exasperated sigh. "My gut tells me Kanter was in Rose's bedroom this morning. He might even be the guy who bolted her door. That doesn't mean he's the person who took the plate off the manhole. He had a lot of rust and crap on his hands, but he could have got that climbing down the fire escape from Rose's window. Rather or not he killed Norton Denbrough, dragged the man's body across the bedroom floor and dumped it in the sewer, I can't say."

"Would it do any good to speak with Rose?"

"I ain't sure I want to talk to De Shields much less Rose after the way Kanter treated us."

Orson started visibly. "He needs our help! Ben's not a killer! Besides, the Harlem Unit honestly has had enough headaches as it is without something like this adding to our problems."

The cab was pulling over to park in front of the Astoria. I glanced at Orson, who pleaded with me with lost puppy eyes. I hated it when he did that.

"Okay, okay," I conceded as I climbed out of the cab. "I'll meet you at your place by six." I gave the driver the address to Orson's 14th Street apartment, watched the cab drive away, then stepped inside the café.

I spent the interval waiting for De Shields sitting at the bar, sipping on sarsaparillas and listening to the radio. When Andre De Shields arrived, ten minutes late, I ordered two bottles of Drerys Beer and led him to a back booth.

"What can I do for you?" he asked, tipping his bottle back and downing half of its contents in one gulp.

So much for getting him drunk, I thought. I waved for the barmaid to bring over another Drerys. "I was wondering if you might fill me in on what you told the bulls about this Kanter business."

"Don't you mean '*Denbrough* business'?" He polished off his bottle in another gulp and considered my request. "What the hell? The book's all but closed on this one. If you want to underwrite a few rounds here, I'll be happy to share a thing or two. What'cha after?"

"How about you start talking, I'll keep buying beers, and we'll see rather your constitution or my wallet gives out first?"

De Shields smirked, a far less pleasant smile than Teddy Roosevelt's. "Never could pass on a dare. You're on. Let's see. Where to start? I was hired by this old dame, Claudette Denbrough, up in Gramercy Park West. Seems she's a widow with two kids. Beatrice, who's twenty-three, and Norton, who just passed thirty. The father, Leonard, smoked a Webley back in '29 on Black Wednesday. The family managed to keep the lights burning after that, but that was about all and that's only because of Norton. Leonard may have played the buckets on Wall Street, but his son was a crackerjack investment banker in upper Manhattan. Norton's weekly paychecks have been what's kept the Denbroughs in the family estate these past six years and more. The dynasty lives on, so to speak.

"Now for the juicy stuff. Just before last Christmas, Norton started acting queer. Started coming home later and later every night. Beginning the middle of January he didn't bother coming home at all between Monday and Sunday mornings. Told his mother the bank was busy with year-end business and he had to burn the candle at both ends to keep his head above water. Instead of fussing with a long train ride from Manhattan to Gramercy every night, he decided to save some time and fare and spend nights with an uptown friend.

"As time passed Norton started losing weight. He got paler. His clothes got more and more wrinkled and his hair wasn't parted perfectly down the middle anymore. Little things only a matriarch would notice. Claudette started to worry. Except for Norton's overtime things were looking up for the Denbroughs. Beatrice is engaged to marry Dell Joyce-Armstrong, the rubber magnate's son. It's a marriage of convenience. Everybody knows it. The Denbroughs need the financial transfusion and Dell's daddy wants his eldest son married to a pretty girl of breeding. Sort of makes you sick, when you think about it."

"It's how thoroughbreds are made," I said, but De Shields' abrupt contempt took me by surprise. It didn't seem to fit his character, at least what I'd seen of it up until then.

"That's as good an explanation as any, I suppose. So…anyway…the old lady hires me a couple of weeks ago to find out what her son is really up to."

"She didn't believe his story?"

"Doesn't seem like, does it? I can always use the easy money so I took the job. Only it don't turn out to be that easy. First thing I did was skedaddle to Norton's bank, Manhattan First National, and see for myself how hard the poor boy was slaving away. Imagine my surprise when I found out Norton was fired just before Christmas."

"Why?"

"I think they had to wash their mouths out with soap after they told me, but it seems word had come around that Norton was in love with a colored woman."

I asked if it was Rose Ramsey, but I knew the answer before De Shields could nod between his second and third Drerys. Despite the way Kanter had acted in his cell, I couldn't help feeling sorry for him.

"What did his mother say when you told her?"

"I didn't tell her. Not right away. I didn't have any evidence, and you don't drop a bombshell like that on some unsuspecting matriarch unless you've got something to back it up with. It's plain as day there was no uptown friend Norton was staying with, so I started snooping around Harlem. I talked with Ramsey's neighbors and found out Norton has been living with her since January."

"Did Kanter know?"

"Probably, but I can't say for sure. The police will have to get that out of him. I do know that during the last eight weeks or so Ramsey has been seen quite a bit around Harlem with either Denbrough or Kanter."

I shook my head. Rose had seemed like such a nice lady during rehearsals for *Macbeth*.

"Hell," De Shields said, "maybe Ramsey loves Kanter and was taking advantage of Denbrough's affections. Plenty of Harlem gals have got rich white daddies with a taste for smoke footing their bills."

"Maybe, but then why bother taking Norton in after he was fired?"

"Can't say for sure, but I've got a couple of theories. First, let's say Ramsey has a heart of gold. Norton was fired because of her, so the least she can do is give him a crib to eat and sleep until he screwed up the nerve to tell his family he'd been sacked."

"Nothing personal, but I don't buy it," I said.

"Neither do I, so here's the second. Beatrice gets hitched to Dellboy this June. Obviously no money changes savings accounts before then, but after the rings are exchanged the Denbroughs strike pay dirt. Ramsey knows this, so she offers Norton a place to stay while he tries to land a new job. That way he doesn't have to tell his family he was fired, he just received a better offer someplace else. All he'd have to do in the interim is con his mother about working overtime at the bank while working odd jobs to pay the family's bills. Anyway, Norton might have been so grateful to Ramsey that she probably would have been set for life come June. Now I can't claim I like this theory better than my first one, but it agrees with my faith in human nature."

Mine, too, as much as I disliked admitting it to myself. Either Ramsey had been playing Norton Denbrough and Ben Kanter for suckers, or Rose and Kanter had been using Denbrough. Either way, it stank.

"So what exactly happened this morning?" I asked. "How did you happen to see Denbrough in Rose's window?"

"Because, to tell the truth, I could never get my damn hands on Norton! Every time I thought I had him tracked down so I could prove he was hiding out at Ramsey's, he managed to slip away. He was worse than a fish. The man must have made some friends during his stay in Harlem, because folks had to be tipping him off whenever I strayed too close. I tell you, this borough takes care of its own. Harlem is a world unto itself and strangers are not always welcomed."

"Tell me about it." I was thinking about Orson.

"Anyway, last night Claudette Denbrough decides she has to know everything I knew. Or thought I knew. So I told her. She wasn't happy. It suddenly became imperative that she speak with her son as quickly as possible. No waiting until Sunday morning. Now. I knew Ramsey was throwing the rent party, so I came to 123rd Street and waited in the alley behind her building hoping Norton would show up. It was the only thing I could think to do."

"You hid in the alley all night? In the rain?"

"Yes. In the lousy rain. Sometimes I can be a stubborn idiot. Just between you and me, my pride is going to get me killed one of these days. It was all worth it, though, when I looked up this morning to see Norton Denbrough staring back down at me through Ramsey's window. Problem was, he was scared. Awful scared. I'm sure he knew who I was and why I was in the alley, but I do think he was going to plead for help."

"Help from what?"

"I don't know. A person, I suppose, since someone yanked him away from the window before he could shout anything."

That caught my attention. "Who? Ben Kanter?"

"That's my guess, since Kanter's the boy I found down in the alley when I looked out the bedroom window."

"What was Ben doing when you first saw him?"

"Not much. Just standing in front of the manhole, staring down into it."

"'Staring'? Not going around it or walking away or even putting the cover back over the manhole?"

"He was staring down in the sewer, all right? I know what staring looks like. He was watching something down in the sewer, more than likely Denbrough's body making like Johnny Weissmuller."

All of a sudden things were getting confused inside my head. "Let me get this straight. You saw someone pull Denbrough away from Rose's bedroom window this morning? Then, when you broke into the bedroom and looked out the window for yourself, you saw Ben Kanter staring down into an uncovered manhole?"

"I like it, ace."

"But you can't be absolutely sure if you ever saw Kanter together with Denbrough this morning? Before or after you crashed Rose's rent party."

"Nope. You've got me there. Not for certain." De Shields nonchalantly swallowed another gulp from his fourth bottle.

"Do you know if the police have found any evidence that Denbrough is in or was ever near the sewer?"

"The police can't start dragging operations until the runoff empties out of the sewers. That won't be for another couple of hours. They did find some socks and a shirt that belonged to him in Ramsey's wardrobe. Hell, you saw how her room looked when I broke in. My bet is Kanter tried to cover his tracks by grabbing anything he could find of Denbrough's in the bedroom and flush it down the sewer along with the corpse."

"That theory requires two trips," I said. "One for the body and another for the clothes. How long did it take you to reach the bedroom from the alley?"

De Shields paused to recollect the morning's activities, running a mental stopwatch alongside his memories. "Ramsey got in my way a little bit. That's why I risked flashing my Crackerjack box police badge. She wouldn't let me in otherwise. I suppose...maybe...two minutes. Tops."

I didn't say anything, but in my addled brain I seriously doubted if anyone, even Johnny Weissmuller, could make two trips up and down a fire escape carrying a dead body then an armful of laundry in less than two minutes.

"You got any more questions?" De Shields asked.

Do I? I thought. Nothing came to mind. "I guess not. Not right now, anyway."

"Fine. How about I ask you a thing or two, just to help flesh out my final report to Mrs. Denbrough." De Shields pulled out his wallet from his breast pocket, flipped it open, and removed a gelatin-silver print of a handsome brunette man with porcelain skin in his mid-twenties. The young man was wearing a mortarboard and gown, smiling broadly and holding a diploma scroll in one proud hand. The photograph itself was weary, its corners cracked and edges rubbed and faded from riding around in De Shields' wallet for two weeks. "This young fellow is Norton Denbrough. Did you ever spy him at the rent party?"

"Hard to say. I wasn't looking for him. Off the top of my head, I think not."

"When's the last time you remember seeing Kanter last night?"

"Around three thirty, I guess. I'm not proud of it, but I've been putting in some long hours the last six weeks. I fell asleep a few minutes after that."

"Nodding off while on the clock, eh?" De Shields said, grinning his not-wholly-pleasant grin.

"Hey, my job right now is to bodyguard Orson Welles," I said, my hackles bristling. "There were plenty of cast and crew members from *Macbeth* with me there last night. He was perfectly safe. Besides, it was your job to corral Norton Denbrough, and he's the guy who's dead right now, not Orson."

De Shields' grin collapsed. He dutifully put Norton's picture back into his wallet and his wallet back into his breast pocket. "Yeah. You've got me there. Take a little friendly advice, though, pal. Do yourself a favor and keep close tabs on your client. At least until this Denbrough business gets settled."

"And why's that?"

"I got the feeling at the station the cops don't appreciate the WPA getting the jigs in Harlem all stirred up again. Kanter killing Denbrough didn't improve the situation any."

"What do you mean, 'stirred up again'? Stirred up about what?"

"I thought you spoke kinda funny. You ain't local?"

I shook my head.

"Figured as much. Listen, they had some riots here in Harlem last year. The last one was the worst, too. About six cops wound up in the hospital when a crowd of nightrunners started stoning them. No police were killed, thank goodness, and things have been mercifully peaceful since, but now the natives are getting riled again because of the WPA and your buddy Orson Welles."

"That's not fair. The Communists are inciting them, not us."

"Well, now, I don't think the cops care all that much about who's inciting who. All they know are tempers are rising and another riot might bust out. Who knows? Maybe worse than the last one. Maybe this time some cops get killed. And over what? A play. John Law doesn't see where Shakespeare's so special he's worth losing life and limb over."

Neither did I, to tell the truth. But since the cops weren't signing my paychecks I kept my opinion to myself. Instead I peaked at the table. Five empty bottles of beer were standing in a row in front of De Shields. As usual I hadn't bothered to touch mine, so I slid it across the expanse to my colleague and stood up to leave. "Here. Thanks for the tip. No hard feelings, I hope."

"Thank you. And, nope, no hard feelings. I may be pigheaded, but I stopped holding grudges after I reached fifty. Life's too short. Besides, I got five free beers off you. Well, make that six." And he saluted me with the bottle I had just given him. "Tell you what, Winters. You hear anything interesting about this Denbrough mess, give me a jingle and we'll have another chat. I'll even buy the beers."

That did it. He got me to like him. "You don't miss a trick."

"Try not to."

"Sure," I agreed as I walked out the Astoria's front door and hailed a cab to take me to my hotel. God, I was tired.

Chapter Three

I was watching Carole Lombard. She was dressed up like Little Red Riding Hood, with the cape and basket. You know what I mean? Only she was also wearing shorts. Real short shorts. Carole Lombard has great legs. She was carrying her picnic goodies through a Hollywood set designer's idea of the Black Forest. I was laying in wait for her behind a papier-mâché tree. I was the Big Bad Wolf.

Then somebody shook me awake.

"Huh? What?"

"Hello. It's six o'clock." It was Orson.

I felt blood in my cheeks. "I wasn't doing anything."

"I didn't say you were."

"Of course you didn't. Because I wasn't."

"You were sleeping, Sassafras."

"Of course I was."

He grinned a know-it-all's grin, his left eyebrow arching so far up on his forehead it looked like a question mark. "The dream was that good, eh?"

Change the subject, Sas. "What are you doing here? I told you I'd meet you at your place. And how'd you get in?"

"Bellhops are always ready to use their pass key to assist anyone claiming to be a guest who has locked himself out of his room...especially if there is a big enough tip included. And I figured you'd be napping."

The sun was low, its frail rays barely able to gleam through the drawn blinds in my living room. On Sundays this meant time for supper and then off to the Lafayette.

"Christ, Orson, what if something had happened to you?" Not waiting for a reply I sprung up from the couch, sprinting in my stocking feet for the head. I spent a few moments performing the usual chores before brushing my teeth. I was unwrapping the gauze paper from one of the cadre of glasses on the bathroom counter when Welles called out, "Did you find out anything interesting from De Shields?"

"Hold on, damn it. I'm rinsing." I gargled what water I could get into the tiny glass, did what had to be done with it, then came back out to the living room. Back home Governor and I shared his three room flat with a bedroom each to ourselves and a tiny kitchen furnished with an ice box, stove, table and chairs for eating and company. That's it. We shared the bathroom down the hall with eight other tenants in our building. Here I had a bedroom with a closet the size of my own room, a private bathroom, and a very spacious living room with a fireplace and wet bar complete with electric refrigerator. I never had it this good even on road trips with the Cubs. My only complaint was I couldn't get to sleep on the too-comfy bed. Fortunately the couch served in a pinch-hitting role.

Hitching up my suspenders as I sat back down, I tossed my blanket to the other end of the sofa. Welles had grabbed a chair near the fireplace and gone to the trouble of rekindling the flames I had stoked up before taking my nap. *Ah, Carole, where are you now?*

"This suite is great," I said. "I'm thinking about buying it and applying for statehood."

"Can we get back to what De Shields said about Ben?" He sounded impatient.

I told him everything, and Orson was shocked to find out Rose had been playing off Denbrough, Kanter, or both. "I never would have given her credit for something like that," he said.

"'Credit' ain't the word that springs to my mind. I stopped off at her brownstone on the way home and talked with some of her neighbors. They all back up De Shields' allegations. A white man whose description matches the picture he showed me of Norton Denbrough has been living with Rose since the middle of January. Whenever Denbrough was gone, Rose was entertaining Ben."

"So what will happen to Ben now?"

"The judge at the arraignment tomorrow will probably decide that Ben's case should proceed to trial. Bail most likely will be high because of the nature of the crime. Probably too high for Ben to post."

Orson considered something silently. "Can anyone pay the bail?"

"Sure."

"We need Ben in *Macbeth*. The Porter is too important a role to dole out to someone with only one month between now and opening night."

"The trial probably will begin during your run. I think you would be better off in the long run replacing Ben now."

"No. I want Ben. Besides, it's the unexpected that makes theatre exciting. Can you go to the Hall of Justice after dropping me off at work tomorrow and post his bail?"

Making his Broadway directorial debut at the age of twenty wasn't enough for Orson Welles. The boy genius also worked at CBS radio where he was an in-demand contract actor. Unfortunately this meant that I was stuck at CBS six days a week, from nine in the morning until seven at night, when Orson finished performing on the *March of*

Time. I often felt my presence as a bodyguard inside the studio's security building was, to use one of Welles' favorite words, superfluous, so I told him I couldn't see why not. "After the way Ben treated us this afternoon, don't expect him to be grateful."

"Who wants gratitude? He agreed to appear in *Macbeth* in exchange for a paycheck. We've been paying him, so he can just bloody well hold up his end of the bargain. I'm posting his bail for the good of the show, which brings us in a roundabout way to you."

"Me?" My heart skipped a beat. I didn't like this. "I don't have anything to do with your play."

"What are you talking about? You're one of the crew, just like me! And as such I would like you to investigate Norton Denbrough's disappearance. Ben was correct about one thing. As long as he is accused of killing Denbrough, it will only give the Communists more ammunition to throw against our production."

De Shields' advice echoed in my ears and I shook my head. "I don't think that's such a hot idea, Orson. I'm not saying you're jumping to conclusions, but I really think I should stick close to you, at least for the next few days."

"For heaven's sakes! Why? You have no qualms about abandoning me tomorrow morning."

"That's not the same thing. I'm leaving you inside a security building in the middle of Manhattan."

"And you believe I will be any less secure inside the Lafayette?"

He had a point. The formidable cast and crew of the Harlem Unit of the WPA were nothing less than loyal to their director, a fact Welles often used to his advantage during rehearsals, not to mention against me right at that moment.

"So while I'm at CBS," he continued, "or in the Lafayette, or safely tucked away in bed at home, you could be tracking down the elusive Mr. Denbrough or any corpus delicti, if in fact he is dead."

It certainly sounded more tempting than twiddling my thumbs all day, but before I could say anything one way or the other we were interrupted by a knock on my door. Orson immediately stood up to answer it, greeting a bellboy holding a telegram. Accepting the message and tipping the boy, he closed the door and returned to his chair, opening the envelope and reading its contents along the way.

"I believe that's for me," I said.

"The bellboy didn't say who it was for. And, besides, I paid for it."

I waited somewhat impatiently as Welles finished reading. "Who's it for?"

"It's for you."

"Oh, that's nice." *Putz*. "Can I have it?"

"Certainly," and he handed me the telegram. "If you still have any reservations, why not have your assistant watch over me while you're investigating the mystery of Norton Denbrough?"

"My 'what'?"

"Your assistant. The man who sent you the telegram. The Chinese fellow."

"Chinese?" *Oh, no.* I hurriedly read the telegram:

> TO SASSAFRAS WINTERS
> FROM CHINAMAN
>
> GRANDFATHER HAS INFORMED ME OF YOUR
> POSITION STOP AM MOST IMPRESSED STOP
> HAVE JUST RETURNED FROM SABBATICAL STOP
> WILL JOIN YOU IN APPLE STOP

"Aw, nuts."

Orson looked at me queerly. "What's wrong?"

"This ain't my assistant."

"It's not?"

"He ain't even Chinese."

"Then who is he?"

"He's half the reason I don't drink anymore."

Orson shook his head. "I don't understand."

"Never mind."

"All right. Then what is your decision regarding Ben?"

I bowed my head, sighed, and weighed it all. "If you agree to stay inside the Lafayette or CBS when I drop you off, then okay. But no promises. I only got my private investigator's license last year. I've never done anything like you're asking me to do before."

"Don't worry about it," Orson said with a wink. "I wrote five detective stories back in 1932 for *Black Mask* magazine when I was living in Morocco. It was a breeze. If you have any problems, just come see me."

"Yeah. Sure. Thanks."

❧❦

By the following morning I was having second thoughts about leaving Welles alone, but in the end I decided to go ahead and at least pay Ben's bail. Seeing Orson to the security desk at CBS, I reminded him to stay inside the building until I returned.

"If I hear that you so much as poked your head out of a window for some fresh air while I'm gone, I'll pinch it off for you at the neck. Got it?"

His reply was an eighth grader's wink and a curt British salute.

"Don't screw with me, Welles." I tried to sound stern.

He handed me a blank cheque with his signature, the amount to be scribbled in after the judge's decision was announced.

"If his case goes to court, Ben's bail is likely going to be pretty steep," I reminded Welles.

"That's okay. I'll have the WPA reimburse me later if necessary."

"What if the government figures the tax payers shouldn't have to foot the bill for one of your actor's bail?"

"Then Virginia and I will starve and die."

"Sounds fair."

"How long will this take?"

"Depends when Ben's case comes up on the docket. If I'm not back by six, go grab a bite in the commissary then do your evening broadcast. I won't be any later than that."

This itinerary didn't sit well with Welles. "Sounds peachy."

"I don't have to go at all, you know."

"Go! Go. Only call if you are going to be later than six."

"Yes, mother."

I hitched a cab to the Hall of Justice. Inside I found out Kanter's arraignment would be deliberated by the Right Honorable Martin St. Anthony in room 'B'. To my ear 'B' sounded like second class, but you couldn't tell it by the courtroom. The place was huge, like an opera house, with an auditorium of polished redwood pews facing the stage. I was surprised nobody from the rent party was in attendance, especially Rose, but delighted to discover the actor's case had already made it to the docket.

St. Anthony was seated center stage behind a gray marble altar of a bench, listening to the prosecutor. The judge, who bared a passing resemblance to Woodrow Wilson, seemed only mildly interested in the proceedings, his face relaxed and posture comfortable. But his eyes gave St. Anthony away. They were intent as the judge dictated every word spoken to memory with the accuracy of a stenographer's pencil to pad.

Removing my hat, I grabbed a seat near the back and glanced over at Ben. He was sitting at a table to my left, spine stiff like a beefeater. I had no doubts that the police had been none too kind interrogating Ben, and despite his harsh words the day before, my heart went out to him. I have never felt a rubber hose laid across my back, but I have seen its results. There wasn't a mark on Ben's face, however, his aquiline nose a target the bulls had prudently resisted.

Then it hit me. I was so caught up with the proceedings and sympathizing for Ben I had failed to notice he was sitting alone at the defendant's table! There wasn't a lawyer or a prayer anywhere near him. Only the obligatory uniformed officer standing six paces away, the keys to Ben's handcuffs in the guard's back pocket.

What in the hell is he doing? This was suicide. If he thought this ploy was supposed to make him look innocent Ben was wrong. All it did was make Ben look stupid, an opinion the judge seconded when he delivered his post-deliberation decision.

"After considering all the evidence in this matter available at present, I have no choice but to go ahead and set a trial date whereupon I will hear arguments on whether or not Mr. Kanter is guilty or not guilty of manslaughter. I therefore instruct the clerk to notify the police that Mr. Kanter is to be hereby formally arrested on this charge." Here the judge paused before speaking directly to Ben.

"Mr. Kanter, I can appreciate how you may have been caught unawares in the rush between your arrest yesterday and this arraignment only twenty-four hours later. However, I can only tell you that appearing before this bench without proper council by your side, when such was made available to you, shows a lack of appreciation on your part to the seriousness of the allegations being brought against you.

"The prosecution has ably presented its arguments to me in which they've proven there is a probable motive on your part, adequate opportunity for you to have committed such a crime against Mr. Denbrough, and sufficient evidence that a crime actually has been committed. I must say that in the short time allotted to the prosecution that they have done an excellent job of preparation. I can only recommend to you with all the authority at my disposal that you acquire an attorney and follow the prosecution's example in your own behalf and properly prepare yourself for your trial.

"My judgment is that a trial will be held beginning Wednesday, April thirtieth of this year, nineteen hundred and thirty-six, in this court room starting at nine a.m.. Since there is no attorney representing the defendant to request bail, I will go ahead and announce that bail will be set at three thousand dollars. This arraignment is now adjourned. Bailiff, please call the next case."

St. Anthony's gavel came down with a CRACK!, its finality reverberating within the walls of the courtroom. I started to stand and approach the clerk about Ben's bail when a spectator seated in the bench directly behind the defense spoke up. Even Kanter turned around in surprise when he heard "Your honor, I'd like to pay this man's bail for him."

The judge dourly appraised the stranger. So did most people in room 'B' familiar with an ambulance chaser. From the faded spats on his shoes to the dingy white wool suit and up to the light green Adams hat on his head, the Samaritan exhibited all the markings of a pettifogger.

"That is your choice to make, sir. May the court inquire if you are a lawyer?"

"I don't see where that matters, your honor."

Two deep wrinkles ruffled St. Anthony's brow. "Consider my words carefully, Mr. Kanter, and also act as cautiously when choosing that council." With that the judge would have no more to do with idiots and went on about his business.

While the shyster was being directed towards the clerk, I grabbed my hat and headed outside. Commandeering a taxi, I waited for Ben and his newfound friend to come out of the Hall. Kanter was looking sick, his wounds suffering him, and the man in the green hat had to support him until they could flag down their own cab.

I had my driver follow the pair uptown, where I expected their first stop to be a hospital or a private practitioner. We weaved our way through mid-morning traffic until we came to an impressive new skyscraper on the six hundred block of the Avenue of the Americas. Paying my driver I tugged down on the front of my hat brim and tailed Ben and the shyster into the lobby. Although the actor was in no condition to look around and recognize me, I pointed my face towards the directory, watching them out of the corner of my eye as the pair stepped onto an elevator. Nobody else boarded with them, so I waited as the arrow climbed to the 12th floor and came to a stop. When the elevator returned directly empty I climbed in and rode it back up.

I disembarked at a small lobby decorated in a Victorian motif, the wallpaper a dim orange and the choice pieces of furniture antiques. The place oozed provincial education, and the double oak doors to the offices that monopolized this floor would have looked just swell on the threshold to any private wing of any library in Harvard, Dartmouth, or Yale. Embossed gold-plated lettering proclaimed that this was no physician's waiting room, as I had first supposed, but the anteroom of Anderson, Anderson, Myers & Watson, Attorneys at Law, Jervis Anderson, Senior Partner.

And what's on the rail for the snail? I had to ponder. *This just doesn't make any sense.*

Determined to see that it did I stepped out into the skyscraper's stairwell and took up a post. Propping the door open with half of an old toothpick I found decaying on the landing, I sat down on a step and peered through the thin crack between the threshold, waiting for Ben to reappear.

The time was just shy of eleven o'clock. The temperature outside was brisk but the sunlight had made the mid-March day feel warmer than it actually was, so I had left my coat at CBS. Inside the stairwell there was no sunlight and this section of the building was unheated.

From the crushed fags and wrapper debris, not to mention the dust that coated the seat of my pants and my sinuses, I could guess that the stairwell was used but seldom cleaned. Throughout the day I occasionally heard people above and below me opening and closing doors on their way from one floor to another. I overheard glimpses of disembodied conversations, some rather tantalizing, only I would never get more than a thin slice of the middle.

No one walked past me going up or down all afternoon. Everyone who had business with the attorneys used the elevators. The offices officially closed at four o'clock, and since none of the employees took advantage of the stairwell, my eyes never left the double oak doors. Even though my hams were nearly frozen to the stairs I opted to hang in there, making friends with a cockroach who was a pest at 11:23 but was rather charming by 3:36. I named him Dog.

By six o'clock even Dog wanted to throw in the towel. My hands were numb, the skin something that belonged on a drowning victim and not a living person. With the chill evening air settling in the well I was starting to risk catching a bad cold if I stayed any longer. More importantly Orson would be getting off the *March of Time* soon, and I figured I had better call him before he decided it was safe to light out for a bite on his own. The only thing dissuading me was the fact that neither Ben nor the man in the green hat had even bothered to step out of the attorneys' office for a smoke during my vigil.

Maybe they never went in? I wondered. It was possible. There were no lights peaking out underneath or sounds of movement from behind the double doors. Nevertheless, just to play it safe, I skipped the elevator and used the stairs to leave.

Escaping into the lobby, I spent a few minutes rubbing my hands over one of the radiators before I stepped into a phone booth, dialed CBS' switchboard and asked for Welles, who reported Kanter had telephoned him just after lunch.

"Ben said he was out on bail, that he wasn't up to attending rehearsals just yet but that he should feel better in a day or two."

"Did he tell you where he was when he called?" I asked.

"Just that he was at his lawyer's office. I assume it was some public defender's private cubby hole."

"He didn't mention a name?"

"No. Should I have asked?"

"It might have helped. I'm not sure. As far as I know he was leveling with you. Did you tell him anything about what I was up to?"

"No. Ben said his lawyer arranged his bail, so I assumed you two must have missed each other somehow, and I didn't see any reason to tell him anything about you."

"Good. Let's keep this investigation between us for now. There's something peculiar going on." I quickly filled Welles in on what had transpired at the Hall of Justice and after.

"Can you be certain they went into the Andersons' offices?" Orson asked.

"Not with them never coming out. No. Could be this is all a ruse. They maybe spotted me and managed to give me the slip. Maybe they sneaked down the stairs while I was riding up the elevator after them, though I really doubt Ben is up to that kind of hustle right now."

"If that were the case, then why would he have bothered calling me?"

"Search me," I said. "It might be worth a second trip to come back here tonight and rummage through the Andersons' files."

"You know how to burgle?" Welles sounded delighted by this revelation. "I thought you were new to the detective shtick."

"I am, but I'm an old hand at being a delinquent.
"Are you coming to CBS now?"
"Yep."
"Do me a favor? It'll take you to Harlem."
"I'll never make it to Harlem and back before your dinner break is over."
"Thank you, Sassafras. I was unaware of that. Nevertheless I would prefer if you could stop by Rose's and ask her if she feels up to attending rehearsals herself tonight. She doesn't have a phone."

Rose hadn't attended Sunday night's rehearsals, still too shook up over that morning's tribulations. I would have judged her to be made of sterner stuff, but one never knows.

"All right. You're the boss, God help us."
"I'll be sure to put in a good word for you with Him since you're being so obedient."
"Thanks, heaps." *Jerk.* "See you later."

I walked out to the street. Taking the A to Harlem was the cheapest way to Rose's, but at this hour the train would be crowded with bad tempered people heading home from the first work day of the week. That didn't appeal to me, so I hailed a cab. After all, I still had a blank cheque in my wallet. I didn't see how a couple of bucks were going to break Orson.

Chapter Four

Anymore, all brownstones look the same to me.

Rose's building was just like any other brick three-story I have ever seen in Bedford Stuy or here in the Apple or even a thousand miles west. Back home. Going inside and up the stairs, I took out my watch and looked at the time. About now Governor would be putting away the last of the dinner pots while his old friend, Roland, was shuffling the cards for cribbage. Life goes on.

The night was growing cooler, but kitchen stoves were heating things nicely inside so doors to most every apartment were open to let the excess heat escape. Indifferent to my presence on the stairs, the tenants went about the business of cooking, cleaning, or just sitting around and letting time slip away. It was their right. The conversations drifting out through the thresholds were as familiar to my ears as the tenement was to my eyes: "Didn't we have this last week?"; "It's too goddamn hot in here"; "I don't know what I'm going to do about work, I really don't"; "Look at this in this paper! Just look at this nonsense, will'ya?" And, somewhere in here, just out of sight, somebody had to be putting away pots while a good buddy was getting the cards ready, waiting patiently for the host to finish with the dinner chores.

Rose's door was closed, and she was talking to someone inside. Someone she didn't sound very happy to be with. I was surprised when I recognized her visitor's voice.

What do you do now? This could look awkward.

It seemed stupid to waste Orson's money, so I went ahead and knocked.

The voices dimmed and Rose opened the door. By the way she glared at me I could tell she wasn't overjoyed that I had dropped by unannounced.

"Yo', too?" she asked sarcastically.

All I could do was shrug. *I knew it.*

She sighed and shook her head. "Come in, Sassafras. Shut de door behind yo', fo' all de good et's doin'. Yo'r friend's over here."

I did as she told me. Her place looked different, mainly because her furniture had found its way back from her neighbor's to her living room. Seated in the overstuffed chair I had fallen asleep in was "De Shields."

"Great minds think alike, eh, buddy?"

Rose faced us with her back towards the kitchen door, arms crossed over her breasts, eyes and lips straight stern. "What can Ah do fo' yo', Sassafras?" she asked, trying not to sound polite.

"Orson asked me to check and see if you were attending rehearsals tonight."

"Ah plan on bein' dere." And that was all she was going to say.

"Well, I can see you two have a lot to chat about." De Shields stood and put on his hat. "Maybe we can talk some more later, Miss Ramsey."

"We'll see."

De Shields tipped his hat to her then winked at me as he left.

Maybe I should have shoved off right away, but I was curious about why De Shields had come to see Rose. "Mind if I ask what he wanted?"

Nothing.

"If something's the matter...if De Shields has something on you...maybe I can help. If you tell me what it is."

She scowled at me. "Why do yo' haf to think Ah did somethin' wrong?"

"I don't. I'm only offering help if you need it. Just in case."

"Help?" Rose was spitting mad, but she was also awful quiet. "Dat's bardacious! Haven't yo' already helped me enough already?"

"I don't understand." And I didn't.

"Ah come home one day last week an' mah neighbors tell me some private detective was askin' about me and mah private life. Come home again yestahday, neighbors tell me 'nother guy sounds a lot like yo' dropped in an' did de same thing all over again. Police come in here after mah party, tearin' up de alley, lookin' fo' dead bodies. People Ah haf to live wit' doan know what to think about me anymo'. Dey're mah neighbors, fo' Lord's sake, Sassafras! An' yo' say yo' want to help me?"

What do you say to that? Not a damn thing. You just stand there.

"De men Ah see is mah business. Et ain' yo'rs, an' et ain' dat fat fool's jes left mah house. Ef yo' needed to know so badly, yo' might haf come an' asked me yo'self. Ef Ah'd wanted yo' to know, Ah would haf told yo'. But dat wasn't de idea, was et?"

I still didn't have any answers.

"No. Didn't think so." She walked into her kitchen.

Get after her, I thought. *Don't let her get away with this. Press her about why she didn't come to Ben's arraignment. She should be sweating. Not you.*

But I couldn't do it, and I didn't. Not then. Later. There would be time later.

I didn't say anything when I left. I figured a closing door was the only noise Rose would appreciate.

Nothing in particular was running through my mind as I was walking back downstairs. Good thing, too, since I have a habit of thinking out loud when I'm flustered, and De Shields was waiting for me in the foyer. He winked and jerked his head a couple of times to indicate he wanted to talk outside.

"I was halfway to the cab stand before I decided to come back," he said when we were on the sidewalk. "Figured I didn't owe you anything for those beers yesterday. I paid for them with information. If I told you anything more, you'd end up owning me another round."

I wasn't sure what De Shields was getting at. "So am I going to owe you another Drerys?"

"No. Finally figured out I did owe you. After all, if you never asked me one question at the Astoria, I wouldn't know what I know."

His conversation was making me dizzy. "What was that?"

"About how long it took me to haul my kiester from the alley to Ramsey's apartment Sunday morning."

"I remember. You said it took two minutes."

"About that, I guess. You remember I said Ramsey did her best to keep me out of her place? The more I thought about it, the more it seemed to me that she wasn't so much trying to keep me out as keep me busy."

"How do you mean?"

"I wish I knew. Now, sure, Ramsey had to know I'm the guy who's been snooping all over this borough for Norton. And she probably knew I wasn't going to go away when I was so close to getting my hands on that slippery son of a gun. But one moment she was acting like a mother bear protecting her cubs, and the next she just folded her tent and stepped aside."

"I hear you," I said. "You think Rose was trying to stall you long enough for Norton to escape through the alley."

"Maybe. Or maybe she was stalling for whoever I saw yank Norton away from that bedroom window. Either way, all of this got me reconsidering rather the book was closed on this Denbrough business or not. So I decided to keep on snooping, only this time put a little extra effort into it."

"Did you get lucky?"

"Luck had nothing to do with it, son. I hit every tavern and salon in Harlem. Waved some lettuce and asked the hungriest people I could find if they knew anything about poor Norton Denbrough I hadn't heard already. I spent a lot of patience, and it cost me big. Hell, if it weren't for this damned Depression I don't think anybody would have dared told me anything for any amount of money."

"But someone did?" For a minute I didn't think De Shields was going to tell me, but then he went ahead.

"As it turns out, your Miss Ramsey wasn't only keeping company with Messrs. Kanter and Denbrough these last few months. She's also been seen around with the star of your play. Jack Carter."

From De Shields' smirk I assumed the expression on my face had been worth spilling the beans over.

"Maybe now," he said, "you can appreciate some of the trouble I went through scrounging up this information."

I nodded my head. It was all I could do. I was speechless.

Jack Carter was more than Orson's star, although he was a fine actor whose credits included originating the role of Crown in *Porgy*. He was also very popular with the Negroes in Harlem, none of who cared that Carter palled around with the local mob. It was even public knowledge that he had served a ten-year sentence for murder, not that it mattered. The idea of anybody in Harlem snitching on Jack Carter seemed preposterous to me, but apparently De Shields had proved me wrong.

"Finding out that Ramsey was ducking out with Carter is one thing," De Shields said. "My problem is, what do I do with this information not that I've got it? Sure, Carter ain't Owney Madden. Madden's been running the Harlem rackets from the Cotton Club since Charlie Lucky got shipped off to Hell's Gate. Carter's no gangster, but he has plenty of buddies who are. One word from him and I'll be taking swimming lessons from Claudette Denbrough's baby boy before you can say hash house."

"So what were you doing just now with Rose?"

"Being sociable. Explained to her there were no hard feelings, that I was only doing my job Sunday. Asked her if there was anything I could do for her during this difficult time. All that sort of twaddle."

"In other words, get her thinking you know something without coming straight out and accusing her."

De Shields winked again.

"If what you heard is on the level, you're playing a dangerous game."

"No worse than playing a pepper game with Charlie Root." De Shields grinned, pleased to catch me off guard. "Don't look so surprised. How many Sassafras Winters are there in the world? I recognized you right off when you told me your name at the precinct, but I figured you didn't need me telling me who you were."

I told De Shields I appreciated that, and he smiled. The sly smile of a loan shark on the prowl.

"You look like a man who has something on his mind," I said.

"Now that you mention it, I was wondering if you might do me a favor. Not that you owe me or anything."

"Of course not." I pegged him right yesterday. He didn't miss a trick. "Could it be you would like to know what Rose and me were talking about after you left?"

"If you're so inclined."

"Uh-huh." *Like I can refuse after what he just told me?* "We didn't talk. That's the problem. She chewed me out then threw me out."

"Too bad." He was genuinely disappointed. "But, you know, you could tell a guy if you spot Ramsey or Kanter or Carter doing anything peculiar. I mean, after all, you see them all practically every day down at the old Lafayette."

"I suppose I could do that...*if* that guy fills me in on anything else he digs up involving the same people."

"Hell, yes," he lied. I didn't mind. I would probably do the same thing if I had the chance.

"Tell me something first. Do you really think Rose could have played both Denbrough and Ben for patsies?"

The left corner of De Shields' lip curled. He looked like a kid who had just swallowed a spoonful of castor oil after being told it was honey.

"It's probable. Dames can always play us guys for saps." He paused, swallowed, and then started up again. "Given the right incentive, I'd even bet Carter could have been a sport and lent her his expert help. With his background, something like this is right up his alley."

"What kind of incentive? What in the world does Rose have to offer that would interest Jack Carter?"

"Who knows? Maybe her boot is really voot. I do know one thing, though, buddy." De Shields pointed an index finger at me and tapped me once on the chest. "Incentive is motive, and motive leads to evidence. All we have to do is keep doing our jobs and we'll find all our answers. I'll talk at you later."

De Shields walked away. He didn't offer to share a cab with me, but I probably wouldn't have accepted if he had. We were both going to different places.

An A groaned to a halt a couple of blocks away and I hurried to catch it before it pulled out.

Chapter Five

While on the A, I decided to detour by the Cosmopolitan. A change of clothes was in order for my return trip to Ben's lawyers, and with the night getting chillier it wouldn't hurt to pick up a jacket.

When I unlocked my door, the lights were on. Damned sure I hadn't left any bulbs burning when I left that morning, I reconnoitered. It didn't take me long to see that the place wasn't right. Things had been tidied up. The poker and thongs were back in their stand next to the fireplace. Glass rings had been scrubbed off the end tables with care. Baby Ruth wrappers no longer littered the carpet.

Maid service?

Nope. I specifically requested no maid service when I checked into the hotel. Always do when traveling. Having a stranger clean my room is an invasion of my privacy, and for over a month my orders had been religiously obeyed.

So who did it, Winters?

The telltale clue was the black camelhair redingote draped over the chair Orson sat in when he read my telegram from...

Chinaman. I called out his name.

He stepped out of the bedroom a moment later, like the character of an evil twin during the second reel of a bad melodrama. As usual he was togged in his working clothes, his butler's suit steamed and pressed to a razor's edge as always. His pepper hair was slicked back in its pompadour, and the white skin of his large schnoz reflected the light from the chandelier like a dance hall mirror ball.

"So good to see you again, Mr. Winters," he said, smiling pleasantly.

"Hi." *Shmuck.*

"I was just taking the liberty of making your rooms a bit more presentable. Hotel help is notoriously unreliable. As a matter of fact, even though the bed is made, the sheets refuse to hold a crease. They seem not to have been changed in some little time."

"I wouldn't be at all surprised..." A shudder ran rampant through the depth of my soul as I glanced at the couch. Its cushions had been patted down and smoothed out. "Oh, god*damn* it!"

"Mr. Winters?"

"I spent a month breaking in these cushions!" I leapt onto the fray and tried to smoosh the familiar dent back into the sofa. But it was useless. Chinaman had done his job too well. "Great."

"Am I to assume you've slept only on this divan since your arrival in New York?"

I moaned.

"Shall I get the Dover's powder?" He sounded sincere. He always did.

"Did I tell you to straighten my digs up? Huh? Did I?"

"I was merely performing my duties as your gentleman's gentleman."

"Yeah. Right." There was a time I argued with Chinaman that he was not really my valet, but I had long since learned the folly in that. I was a letterman back in college, but the Big C had been president of his alma mater's forensic team.

"Are you hungry perchance, Mr. Winters?"

"Oh, no! Don't try to weasel out of this by bringing up my stomach." Honestly, you would have had to be deaf not to hear my gut rumbling then.

"Of course. I was only going to mention that I made a cold plate and put it in the refrigerator. I thought you might want a snack. My mistake. Now, if you'll excuse me, there are some rather nasty things in your bathroom I was about to dispose of."

Cold plate? Chinaman makes a great cold plate.

He turned to get back to his chores. I lay on the couch, pouting, and listened to his footsteps as they padded away. Hey! I'm no sissy. I waited until I could hear the water running before I got up.

A few minutes later I told Chinaman I had to leave and pick up Orson at CBS. To my surprise he insisted on tagging along. "Okay, but just until we get to the Lafayette. Welles doesn't like outsiders at rehearsals. He doesn't even let his producer watch a practice if he can help it. So you're only going for the ride. Got it?"

"Absolutely, Mr. Winters. It'll be an honor simply to meet Mr. Welles for only a few minutes."

I switched into a turtleneck and grabbed my jacket, a cap stuffed into its pocket for later. Chinaman slipped on his redingote and we left to catch a cab. Fifteen minutes later we were at CBS. I made the introductions.

Welles tended to be shy around strangers, but he did make a half-hearted attempt to be polite. Chinaman, meanwhile, could barely conceal his pent up excitement. "This is a tremendous honor, Mr. Welles. Oh yes, a very great honor." The Big C's Boston twang warbled like a jew's harp.

"Thank you." Orson was flustered and tried to regain the upper hand. "So you're the reason Sassafras doesn't drink anymore, eh?"

"Half the reason. Yes, sir." Chinaman was very proud of this.

"I don't suppose you'd care to fill me in on some of the more personal details about that?"

Oh-oh. He's going for the double play, trying to tag out Chinaman and me.

"Oh, that wouldn't interest a man such as yourself, sir." *Nice break up, Chinaman.* "I must say that I've wanted to meet you ever since your debut at the Gate in *Jew Suss* back in...let me think...oh my! Five years ago. That was a long time ago, wasn't it? And look how far you've come! I'm most impressed, Mr. Welles. Most impressed indeed."

One out on Orson by virtue of the infield-fly rule.

"You read the review in the *Times*?"

Chinaman shook his head. "I'm sorry. I'm afraid you misunderstood me. I was in the audience on the very first night you ravaged poor Miss Betty Chancellor. It was a magnificent debut."

Orson actually gasped. *Game called on account of rain.*

By mid-March I had spent enough interminable hours listening to Welles the *wunderkind* talk about himself to know what effect Chinaman's confession had on him. After all, it was only after a series of improbable incidents that Orson stumbled into his acting debut at the age of sixteen at the Gate Theatre in Dublin.

Back in July 1931 a war of the wills was declared between Orson's guardian...his late mother's physician and suitor, Dr. Maurice Bernstein, who insisted his ward call "Dadda"...and Welles, a recent graduate of the Todd School for Boys in Illinois. The battle was over money. Specifically, how Orson should spend his inheritance. Dadda wanted the boy, who he considered a prodigy, to go to college. Orson wanted to invest his jack in the theatre. It was the classic case of the wind hitting the rock.

On the showdown's third day Orson, who suffered from asthma, was overcome by hay fever. Worried about his ward's health, Bernstein turned the attack to his advantage and used it to stave off their feud. He suggested Orson go somewhere far away until pollen season was over. Orson fell for it in the P.T. Barnum tradition, and by August he was on a donkey cart riding west from Galway, ready for the adventures of a walking and painting tour of Ireland.

One month later Orson was busted and hiking to Dublin to wire for more money. His love for the theatre led him like a diving rod to the Gate, where Orson caught the eye of Hilton Edwards, the theatre's co-director. Edwards had almost given up hope of finding the right actor to play Karl Alexander, the Duke in *Jew Suss*, but the pale, raven-haired boy was everything the director had envisioned.

Edwards took a risk with Welles and it paid off. Orson's debut left Dublin head-over-heals over the Gate's American discovery, and critics in newspapers as distant as the *New York Times* unanimously applauded the young Yank's performance.

Orson remained in Ireland long enough to appear in a few more productions at the Gate, then jumped on a steamliner for the States, confident his glorious reviews would pave the way for his Broadway debut.

But his dreams were dropkicked in New York by a Shubert's Agency office boy, who assured Orson that nobody at his agency had ever heard of the actor in *Jew Suss* and none of their agents wanted to talk to Welles. Dejected, Orson Welles, darling of the Gate Theatre, returned to Dadda and Illinois, still nearly a half-decade away from his debut on Broadway. Not as an actor, but as an unprecedented young director. Quite an accomplishment, but I could tell by the way Orson had recollected the Schubert incident to me that that no-account brat's insults still haunted him. Chinaman's compliments must have been a salve from Heaven.

"Surely you're joking! Why...why...this is inconceivable. Absolutely inconceivable!"

"Astonishing to say the least," I said. You tend to get used to these sorts of coincidences if you stand near Chinaman long enough.

"Oh, it's not so incredible, sir. There was a very large audience at the Gate that night. Don't you remember?"

"Yes, in a way. I didn't notice the audience at all during the play, you see. I was completely wrapped up in my performance and quite nervous. Your applause rather took me by surprise. I'd actually forgotten where I was! I also had a crush on Miss Chancellor, and getting the chance to ravage her, as you put it, even off scene, had monopolized my concentration."

"Oh, she is a beautiful lass, isn't she? You should see her, Mr. Winters."

"That's true enough," Welles chimed in, still obviously smitten. "She is one of those absolutely black-haired girls, with skin as white as Carrara marble, you know, and eyelashes that you could trip on, and all that. An absolute joy to rape!"

"Yes," I said, "we'll all have to get together and ravish her some night real soon."

I don't think I was ever so overjoyed to see the Lafayette in all my life, but I had seriously underestimated the impression Chinaman made on Orson. I could not believe my ears when Welles broke his own commandment to invite Chinaman inside! "I'd be very interested in hearing your opinions of this production as compared to *Jew Suss*. You may want to know, Hilton Edwards has had a tremendous influence on my directorial style."

"Oh, has he? Well, that would only make sense, wouldn't it? He is quite a visionary, isn't he?"

I groaned. There was no alternative but accept my fate.

It was nine fifteen. As the cab pulled in front of the curb I was grateful to see only twenty die-hard protestors rambling on our sidewalk, packed together under the marquee in an attempt to share body heat. It was like watching a forty-legged-sign-carrying-chant-crying ameba unable to make up its mind which way it wanted to move.

I hadn't got around to telling Chinaman about all my duties for the WPA, but the small crowd's hungry eyes were enough to warn him that Welles wasn't their favorite person. We each took a position on either side of the director, ushering him into the Lafayette. I was glad to see Canada Lee waiting at the doors, holding them open.

"Is everybody here?" Orson asked brusquely, all business.

A familiar voice intruded before Canada could answer. "Yes, Orson. We're *all* here."

Welles grimaced as if he had busted his tooth on a jawbreaker. He knew without looking that the velvety, determined voice belonged to the Federal Theater Project's producer, John Houseman.

"What are you doing here at this hour, John?" Orson, in spite of his tone, was Houseman's friend and theatrical collaborator, and had been for several months. It was Houseman, an immigrant gentleman in his early 30s, who had talked the WPA into hiring Welles.

"I am here at the behest of Ed Perry."

"Perry called you? Why?" Edward Perry was Orson's associate supervisor. His duties, among other things, included opening the theater and getting it ready for the actors, musicians, and technicians before every rehearsal. Perry was a reliable and trustworthy person, not given to making hasty decisions. "What's wrong? Did the Communists break in and vandalize the sets?"

"Nothing so tragic. When he opened the Lafayette tonight a reporter managed to push his way inside. Ed tried to ring you at CBS, but you never came to the phone, so he had to call me to attend to the chap."

"I was busy on the air! So what did you do with the newshound?"

The man in question answered for himself. "I'm right here, Mr. Welles." A middle-aged man with a vulpine face and a buzzard's teary eyes came out of the amphitheater into the lobby. "I'm Gary Groth with the Brooklyn Chronicle." Groth shoved his hand at Orson to shake, a gesture the director ignored. "I was hoping you'd answer a couple of questions about your lover's triangle."

"My what?"

Houseman explained. "Ben Kanter, Rose Ramsey, and the late Norton Denbrough. Surely you've heard of them. They've been in all the papers."

Apparently Orson didn't read the newspapers. "Have they?"

Everyone in the lobby, except Welles and Chinaman, dutifully nodded our heads.

"Oh, my."

"That's yesterday news," Groth said. "The Chronicle wants to get the inside scoop on what really happened. The juicy behind-the-scenes stuff. 'Jilted Negro actor kills white society dude over colored mama.' It'd make great publicity for a bloody play like *Macbeth*, don't you think?"

Canada and Houseman couldn't help laughing, but Orson appeared to be dumbstruck for the second time that evening. *I didn't think it was possible! It's a miracle!* Fortunately the producer was there to pick up the slack.

"Mr. Groth, our production of *Macbeth* is a *cause celebre* unto itself. If it weren't for our notoriety, you wouldn't be here haranguing us."

"Oh, come on, Mr. Houseman. A show can always use more publicity, eh?"

Welles found his voice. "Not this kind of publicity!"

"Maybe we should escort this gentleman outside?" Canada suggested.

"Now settle down, shorty," the reporter said, unimpressed with Canada's bravado. "Don't get in an uproar."

That didn't set well with my old friend. As quick as I could I cleared my throat and said, "Excuse me, but maybe I should introduce you two. Mr. Groth, this short guy is Canada Lee."

"Hey, s'that a fact? There used to be a pretty good boxer by that name. You guys ever heard of him?"

"We are him," Canada said.

The light bulb went on over Groth's head. "Well, maybe I should be going now."

"We think that would be wise."

"Of course, if you change your mind about an interview, Mr. Welles, just get on the horn and let me know. I'm at the Chronicle."

Orson said he would try to remember.

After Canada conducted Groth to the door, Welles asked a second time if the troupe was all present and accounted for.

"Rose isn't here yet."

Orson glared at me, and I shrugged my shoulders. "She said she'd be here. That's all I know."

"Fine. She'd better get here soon. Now let's hop to it. First things first. Canada, do you know if we're ready to begin sacrificing the goats?"

Chinaman's expression was priceless.

⊱⊰

While Welles scurried about the Lafayette, doing his best to pretend Houseman wasn't following him on his rounds, I tried to explain what was going on to Chinaman.

When Orson agreed to become the Shakespearean director for the Federal Theatre Project's Harlem Unit, he was confronted with an obvious problem. Since the "Bard of Avon" hadn't written many roles for Negroes, which of his plays could be performed by the Unit's all-black cast?

Virginia Welles saved the day when she suggested transplanting *Macbeth* from Glamis Castle to the Citadel of Henri Christophe. It made perfect sense, Orson loved to point out, because the exploits of the mythical thane and the Haitian slave-turned-despot were practically identical blow for blow. When presented with the idea, Houseman proclaimed Virginia's idea as utter genius.

Harlem's reaction, however, was mixed. Everybody was happy Shakespeare was coming to the borough but, as Canada told me that first day, a lot of folks were suspicious the WPA's *Macbeth* was going to poke fun at Negroes. And they had reason to think that way. Not just because Orson was twenty, white, and had never directed professionally before, but because a tyrant like Christophe was hardly a role model.

The musical unit of the Harlem Unit eased tensions somewhat when its first production, *Walk Together Chillun!*, opened to acceptable praise on February 5. But doubts continued to linger about that "little white boy's mumbo-jumbo," which most people along Seventh Avenue had started calling *Voodoo Macbeth*.

Chinaman was astounded by the orderly chaos going on inside the Lafayette. There were hundreds of costumes, ranging from trim Napoleonic uniforms for the king's soldiers, to gnarled and hairy hides for the witches. The sets, designed by Welles, were real eye-poppers. The moors of Scotland had been pushed aside for a new backdrop, a lush and claustrophobic tropical jungle. Virgil Thomson had whipped up a moody score spooky enough to make Bela Lugosi's blood run cold. And for a dash of authenticity...a detail Welles was fanatical about...a troupe of five African drummers had been hired to sit in with Thomson's orchestra.

The leader of the troupe, Asadata Dafora Horton, was a pip to talk to with his impeccable Oxford accent. Horton's four companions knew very little English, but that didn't keep one fellow, Abdul, from becoming the percussion section's number one personality. Abdul was an honest-to-goodness, real-life witch doctor with diamonds inlaid in every one of his teeth, each tooth cast in gold.

As I went on filling Chinaman in on what went with what and why, Orson and his producer stopped to look over some lighting changes with Abe Feder, the technical director. After that we trotted over to the orchestra pit where Thomson was having a go-around with Asadata about the music. The Africans had just laid down a chant that was supposed to accompany the rhythmic beating of their drums during one of the witches' scenes. Thomson had been less than impressed.

"May I hear it?" Welles requested.

The Africans obliged, and Orson exchanged unsatisfied glances with Thomson, who asked, "Are those chants really voodoo?"

"Oh, yes. Yes, indeed, Sirs. That is absolutely real, authentic voodoo."

"They don't sound wicked enough," Thomson said.

"Sirs, I..."

"Sometimes for the theatre you have to exaggerate."

"I am sorry, Sirs. You can't be any more wicked than that!"

"Asadata," Houseman asked, "just what are the chants? Really."

"Well, Sirs, what they are...they are strong spells."

"Spells for what intended purpose? To conjure up demons?"

"Oh, no, Sirs!" Asadata was horrified. "These chants are to ward off the beriberi, not encourage it. We dare not call upon Baron Semadi. He might come!"

Thomson slapped his palm against the top of his podium while Welles sighed and tugged on his right ear.

"Yes, I can see your problem, Asadata," Orson said. "But we need something darker. Can't you give us something a bit moodier if not as potentially apocalyptic? I'll take the responsibility for anything that happens."

"And I as well," Houseman added.

Asadata stared at his director and producer as if he had heard few braver if not less intelligent words. "We can try, Sirs."

"Thank you. And Virgil?"

"Yes, Orson?"

"Try to take care of your own problems from here on. Music is your department after all." We strolled swiftly away, Thomson's palm popping the podium again and Welles grinning mischievously.

As usual Orson checked in with the principal actors last. Gathering them together he introduced them to "This rather charming fellow. Calls himself Chinaman. Works with Sassafras."

Chinaman had already met Canada Lee, Welles' cigar-chomping Banquo. Then there was Edna Thompson, who played Lady Macbeth. Miss Thompson, a genteel fixture of Harlem theatre, was returning to the stage from a two-year absence after a near-tragic automobile accident. Getting her to perform in *Macbeth* had been one of Orson's early ambitions, her presence a signal to his peers that this was going to be a quality production.

Welles introduced the Macduffs, "Maurice Ellis and Marie Young. Then there's Hectate, Eric Burroughs, a graduate of the Royal Academy of Dramatic Arts. Jack Carter is Macbeth."

Like Miss Thompson and the absent Kanter, Carter was a light-skinned mulatto. All three actors, in fact, had to wear make-up on stage to darken their complexions. Carter's tastes ran to bespoke shoes, custom-made English suits, and alcohol. Too much alcohol. Drinking had driven him into an early retirement after *Porgy*. Orson was determined from the get-go that the talented and popular Carter would play Macbeth, however, and the director's persistent coaxing finally landed the actor. Judging from what De Shields had found out, this might not have been such a wonderful break, particularly for Ben Kanter.

"Pleased to meet you," Carter greeted Chinaman, the pink of courtesy. "You know, we don't get the opportunity to meet many strangers at rehearsals. How did you manage to wrangle an invitation out of Orson here?"

Chinaman blushed but said nothing, and was saved by Miss Thompson's brief, "Hello," then, "Orson, I have to talk to you about the goats."

"Don't worry, Edna. They'll be out of your way soon."

"That's my point. Some of the girls in the cast, myself included, would rather not watch the butchering."

"All right. Go down to the dressing rooms and I'll let you know when Abdul is finished with the sacrifice."

"But we'd still hear the poor things bleating."

"So what would you have me do, Edna?"

"I'd just as soon you not have them slaughtered at all. You should see their eyes, Orson. They're so cute. One of them looks like you."

Welles didn't seem to know if Miss Thompson was complimenting him or insulting the goat.

"We need the goat skins if we're going to have authentic voodoo drums," he said. "Authenticity is essential. You can understand that."

"Certainly. But do we have to remain in the theatre and listen while those animals are having their throats slit?" Miss Thompson shivered.

"You want to leave? The theatre? You and the cast?"

"Only some of the women. Well, there were a couple of men who mentioned to me that they would prefer giving up their seats."

"We're starting a long rehearsal tonight. You all knew that!" Orson was not at all happy. "I can't have half my cast running around loose right now. Edna, please!"

Before she could speak, Carter put in his two cents. "Now, Orson, the stage is going to be occupied while Abdul and his friends make the Lafayette into an abattoir. Where is the harm if the cast takes a couple of hours to get themselves in the right frame of mind for the long row ahead?"

"You mean let them get tanked up at the nearest joint, Jack Carter, that's what you mean." That was precisely what Carter meant, but Welles knew he had lost this argument.

Orson went to the orchestra pit, followed by Houseman, where the two men prattled for a few moments with the Africans. It reminded me of a players' conference at the pitcher's mound. Coming to an agreement, the director and producer took over center stage and called for everyone's attention. The cast and crew listened while Welles announced that anyone not interested in watching the goats sacrificed may leave the Lafayette until midnight.

"By that time Abdul assures me he will have completed the ritual and the goats shall be skinned. But be forewarned." Here Orson seemed to slip out of his director's character and into Lamont Cranston, the hero he played once a week on *The Shadow* radio series, somehow getting his voice to sound as if he were whispering into a bucket. For added effect he tucked in his chin so his forehead blocked the overhead lights and cast his eyes in shadows. "As professional actors I will hold each and every one of you accountable for your actions. Any of you who do not return by the stroke of midnight, or who do so in an inebriated condition, will find yourself in a predicament like Cinderella's. That is to say, you will be unceremoniously sacked, which will put you one rung lower than the goats if you stop to think about it. That's all. I'll see you at the witching hour."

Welles exorcised Cranston and led Houseman away to other matters. I decided take advantage of Chinaman's presence and grabbed him by the arm to lead him out to the lobby.

"Look," I said, "I'm stuck with you here, so I want you to do some good for once."

"Your gratitude has always been my remuneration, Mr. Winters."

"Yeah. Right. Listen, I have some business to attend to downtown. You may have noticed that our protesters do not react kindly to Orson. He should be safe inside the theatre, but I want you to keep an eye on him. Make sure he never steps foot outside of the Lafayette until I get back. Can you do that?"

"As you request. And when should I expect you to return?"

"Oh, jeez, not until after midnight. Good God, I don't want to see those poor goats with their guts spilled out all over the stage. Ugh! Icky!"

Leaving Chinaman to tend to his duties, I made tracks through the lobby and the front doors. Behind me Asadata and his band were working on their new chant. I wasn't sure but I could have sworn, mixed in with their black magic hymn, were the words "Meester Houseman...Meester Welles..."

Chapter Six

Outside the Lafayette, just for the hell of it, or so I told myself, I rubbed the "Tree of Hope."

"Tree" might be an exaggeration. It was a knarred and skinny growth, but somehow over the years the borough's actors and musicians had come to believe it was Seventh Avenue's own touchstone of good luck. Personally I would have chose a sequoia, not a six-foot twig any healthy sneeze might cut off at the roots, but in Harlem you learn to make do with what you've got.

I flagged down a taxi and gave the driver the Andersons' address. When we pulled in front of the skyscraper on the Avenue of the Americas, I paid the driver and put on my cap as I stepped out of the cab. I paused outside as the taxi drove away to listen to faint organ music as it echoed through the concrete canyon. Rockefeller Center was only a couple of blocks away. What I was hearing were the whispers of a skater's waltz, and in my mind I could picture pretty women in short skirts pirouetting beneath Prometheus on the artificial ice.

"Ah, New York," I said to no one as I entered the office building.

I hummed the waltz melody as I climbed the stairs to the twelfth floor. The tune put me in a good mood. I stopped humming when I saw that the toothpick I had used to prop open the stairwell door was still in place.

"Damn it, Dog, I thought you were going to get that."

In the lobby I put my ear against one of the double doors to listen. Nothing. *All gay! Olly, olly, oxen free.* I bent to one knee and removed my wallet, where I cached a variety of lock picks for such emergencies. The way was breached in less than five seconds. *Go figure it. They blow two year's worth of wages for an average Joe on a couple of doors, but they won't spend more than forty cents on the deadbolt.*

Inside, the layout reminded me of the lobby with its fancy wallpaper, thick carpet, and antique furniture. I suppose high muckamuck lawyers need such crap to impress their clients. Who knows? I tiptoed from room to room, making sure I had the whole place to myself before I seriously started invading their privacy.

First order of business was to find out if Ben Kanter had ever really been here. The best place to start seemed to be the Andersons' colossal collection of filing cabinets. Good choice. I rummaged around inside the appropriate drawer and soon found, in its proper place, a very thin file with "Kanter, Ben" typed neatly on its tab.

The width of the file promised slim pickings, so I wasn't too disappointed with what little I found. There was a page of notes about Ben's arrest and arraignment, dictated by someone named Herman Bogart. *The man in the green hat, I presume.* Probably, although I had trouble picturing him working in these posh digs.

The other items in the file were some preliminary notes about Ben's case handwritten on legal paper by the senior partner, Jervis Anderson.

"Why would the firm's big boss get involved with this case?"

I didn't know, just like I didn't know why there were no carbon copies of an arrest report or the stenographer's record of Ben's arraignment in the file.

I can see the latter, I thought, *but the arrest report? Even the prosecuting attorney had a carbon this morning.*

After I slipped Ben's file back home, I played a hunch and began to scrounge through more files to look for...I don't know what. Something was screwy, that was for certain, and it wasn't just the delinquent police report.

As far as I knew Ben Kanter was like any other poor bum from Harlem. Nothing special about him. So how could he afford lawyers like the Andersons? Why pick these lawyers in particular? And what the hell did Mr. Green Hat-cum-Herman Bogart have to do with respectable lawyers? He had hardly impressed Judge St. Anthony. Finally, why lug Ben all the way up here after the arraignment, instead of getting him to a doctor? Even an umpire could see Kanter needed tending to this morning.

While I was making my brain whirl trying to strain these questions through my underdeveloped noodle, I kept searching the files for a name. Any name. I wasn't picky. I also couldn't think of anything else to try.

I began with Welles, since you could never be too sure about him. Nothing.

"Well, I guess that's a relief."

I checked out the producer's name, but came up empty. Since it was close by I looked for Hopkins, but the WPA's chairman was absent.

"Who next, Sassafras? Roosevelt?"

I peaked, just in case, but struck out.

Next I checked under crew names and cast names. One foul ball after another. I even glanced in the "*W*"s again to see if I was in there, but wouldn't you know it?

"This is getting me nowhere."

I slammed shut what I thought was going to be the last drawer when one more name came to mind. It was silly, but no more ridiculous than Roosevelt or Winters.

I opened the drawer labeled *D-Dill* and flipped through the folders. I kept flipping until I saw the name I was looking for but not expecting:

"Denbrough"

⁓⁓

By the time I got back to the Lafayette the late-winter weather had whittled the number of protestors to a scanty few. It was almost one o'clock and, the heck with chilly, it was down right cold outside. Most of the survivors were shivering too hard to bother glaring at me as I walked past them.

"Semper-fi, cats," I said as I went inside. "Everyone in here is pulling for you."

In the auditorium the goat blood had been mopped off the stage and rehearsals were under way. Orson was sitting in the balcony, keeping an eagle eye on his production while frantically scribbling sheet after sheet of notes. I made my way upstairs to talk with him, and was more than a little irritated to find Welles sitting alone, Chinaman nowhere in sight.

Orson was in his usual spot, a center aisle seat six rows from the front of the balcony. I took the chair across the aisle from him. He noticed me and forgot about the rehearsals, leveling me with that eighth grader's gleam, lips pursed as if to sing, "I know something you don't know. Nah, nah, na, nah, nah."

"What?" I whispered.

"Pardon me?" Caught in the act, Welles feigned innocence.

"What is it? I know that look. Cats get it when they play handball with mice."

"You are becoming paranoid in your middle age, Sassafras. Can I help it if I'm anxious to hear how your expedition to Ben's attorneys panned out?"

Oh, please. I was in no mood to banter, so I ignored the obvious and instead recapped everything as quickly and quietly as I could. Welles was intrigued when I told him about the Denbroughs' file. "This is getting quite delicious. Like something from a Mr. Moto novel."

"It might be a coincidence, though my women's intuition begs to differ. But that's all I've got. Suspicions."

"What was in their file?"

"Most of it was in legalese and I can't make heads or tails out of that gobbledygook. Except Leonard Denbrough's death certificate. That was plain enough. De Shields was right on the money about Norton's papa's suicide."

Angry furrows corrugated Orson's brow. "Tragic. Stupid and tragic.

The report confirmed he shot himself?"

"Yep. With a Webley on Black Wednesday. That was a bad day for a lot of folks."

Orson shook himself, as if a chill had skittered up his spine.

"I wish I could tell you more," I said, trying to get the kid's mind off of Leonard Denbrough. "At least we don't have to wonder if the Andersons are really Ben's lawyers. All we have to figure out is why they're representing him."

It worked. The immediate mystery monopolized Welles' thoughts again.

"Amazing," he said. "How can he afford them? Manhattan attorneys charge at least one hundred dollars a day. We're only paying him $23.86 a week."

"That's what we're going to find out. By the by, I had a talk with Andre De Shields earlier. We agreed to try to share what we each dig up with the other. Maybe that way we can get this mess cleared up before things get out of hand."

"When did you have an opportunity to see him?" Welles asked, startled.

"At Rose's apartment. He was coming out while I was going in."

His face went sour.

"Hey, I would have told you in the cab, but I couldn't get a word in edgeways between here and CBS." I considered telling Orson what De Shields had said about Rose and Jack Carter, but opted to keep my trap shut. He had enough problems directing *Macbeth* without me adding to them. Nobody could prove anything anyway. If, or when, I uncovered something concrete, then I would tell Welles, but not before. "Has Rose ever showed up?"

"No." Orson shifted from agitation into irritation. "No, she never has."

"Do me a favor? Don't get on her case about it. Okay? She's had a tough go of it the last couple of days, especially with me and De Shields snooping around her place one after the other."

He mulled this over and finally nodded. "The absence of a Lady-in-waiting is the least of my concerns. As long as her absenteeism doesn't turn into a habit."

I couldn't think of any further business, so I settled into my seat and let Welles get back on the job.

Maybe I don't know art, but I could practically quote *Macbeth* chapter and verse by this time, and I knew the actors were beginning act two, scene three. The set was the courtyard of the Citadel. A persistent rapping began off scene, the cue for the Porter to make his entrance.

A stately Negro stepped out on the boards wearing the servant's costume. He had jet-black hair, dark skin, and the largest nose I ever saw on a colored man.

"Who's this guy?" I asked Orson, expecting Ben's understudy. I didn't recognize this actor.

"I decided to heed your advice about Ben," Welles said, leaning forward, concentrating on the stage. "I won't replace him, but we're experimenting with the concept of an understudy's understudy for the Porter. Just in case."

"Here's a knocking indeed!" the actor on stage recited. "If a man were porter of hell-gate, he should have old turning the key. Knock, knock, knock! Who's there, i'th' name of Beelzebub?"

It was Shakespeare played on a jew's harp.

The theater became deadly quiet, then erupted as Orson started laughing so hard he almost fell into the aisle, tossing Big Chief notebook paper into the air. Beneath us the cast and crew joined in, while Chinaman turned to look up from center stage and waved, face flushed with pride.

"Hello, Mr. Winters," he said. The illusion was shattered. Chinaman was no longer a Negro. He was Al Jolson signing "Mammy."

"What did you do to him?" I asked as I stood up, dumb-founded.

"We thought he made-down rather well," Orson said.

Made-down was how colored performers described darkening their natural complexion with makeup for the stage, as actors like Kanter, Carter, and Miss Thompson had to do.

The director hauled himself up out of his chair and clapped me hard on one shoulder. Tears ran down his cheeks, and his face was bright with blood. Orson was having a wonderful, marvelous, Welles of a time.

"I'm sorry, Sassafras. At least, I think I am." This started a second brief round of hysteria. I kept my cool and rode it out. "I should have told you. I know. And I tried. Sort of."

"Orson." I drug his name out. "My patience isn't infinite."

"Well, you see, Chinaman and I were discussing the witches' scenes while Abdul slaughtered our goat herd. And he told me how the witches' incantations reminded him of Medea's in Greek mythology."

"Of course he did." In my mind I was estimating how far I could throw Orson from the balcony. My arm felt good. The stage might be stretching it, but the orchestra pit was a safe bet.

"It didn't take long to realize your valet knows all thirty-six plays in Shakespeare's canon by heart, not to mention Jonson. So I asked him to stand in for Ben tonight. It was so much more fun than just using the understudy. Forgive us? I can't tell you how happy I am you introduced me to Chinaman!"

Maybe in the morning this nonsense would be funny. Maybe not. Right now I had had my fill of *Macbeth*, African drummers, goats, Communists, valets, and Broadway prodigies.

"I'm going back to my hotel," I said, trying hard to maintain my concentration. "I can use some sleep. Besides, there's a few errands I want to attend to tomorrow. I'm sure you know what I mean. Canada and Chinaman can watch over you here tonight and tomorrow. And, believe me, Welles, somebody should be watching over you. If you catch my drift?"

Orson caught it, all right. So did the rest of the Unit. And they all started laughing again. Except for Chinaman. Chinaman never laughs. He just smiles politely, which can be really infuriating sometimes.

I turned and walked away. "Hard-working tax-payers, like my grandfather, are forking over their dough so you can watch my butler prance around in blackface and pantaloons," I said as I walked. "You are a sick tuna, Welles. A sick tuna."

If anything, this only made cast and crew laugh harder. Except Chinaman, of course.

Chapter Seven

The telephone rang with the clash of cymbals. All in the same instant I recalled having trouble falling asleep, realized I must have finally dozed off, and mourned that I was awake again. The last time I looked at my watch it was nearly three o'clock. Now, a few seconds and three hours later, it was just after six in the morning.

I answered the telephone.

It was the desk clerk. "There's a Virginia Welles to see you, Mr. Winters. She says she's brought your car around."

"My...'car'?" *What car?* "Tell her to wait in the lobby. I'll be right down."

Downstairs, sure enough, Welles' wife was waiting for me. Virginia wore a simple cloth coat over a black morning dress with a white collar. She was no stunner, but she did exhibit a kind of quality that magnified her gentle prettiness into the type of beauty seen too rarely anymore.

"I hope I didn't wake you up," she greeted me. Her smile was so pleasantly insincere I couldn't be mad at her.

"What's this about a car?" I tried to sound cross. I failed.

Virginia opened her purse and rummaged about until she hooked a set of keys. She held them up and rattled them. They sounded like the jingle bobs on a pair of cowboy spurs.

"It's a present. From the Welleses to you. Orson's feeling generous."

"I haven't exactly woke up all the way yet. Could you be more specific?"

"What's the problem, Sassafras? Orson telephoned me this morning to say you had business around town today. He suggested we help you out by giving you our car."

She dropped the keys back into her purse and clapped the thing shut.

"I hope you're in the mood for a walk," she said.

Despite my common sense, this was getting interesting. "Lead the way."

Virginia took me by the hand, as if we were the dearest friends, and we left the Cosmopolitan. Outside we strolled side-by-side. I was surprised I hadn't noticed before how tall she was. Her brunette hair was in a coiffure.

"How far away is it?" I asked.

"Not far. Have you ever been inside the Waldorf before?"

"Me? Give me a break."

"Good. Because you won't be going inside today, either."

We strolled the couple of blocks to the famous hotel under a morning sky that had blossomed into a rosy dawn. True to her word, Virginia veered us away from the famous hotel proper and led the way into its garage. "The last time I saw our car," she said, "it was parked in the basement."

"And how long is that?"

"Quite some time."

"You really use it, eh?" I was being sarcastic.

"Me? Never. I'm addicted to Checker Cabs." She was serious.

"Orson doesn't ever drive it?"

"Hardly. Orson can't drive."

Down in the depths of the basement, Virginia hunted patiently through the shadows until she triumphantly yawped, "Here's Big Bertha!"

"Big Bertha?"

She was pointing at the dusty remains of an Essex. Its body was dented and its wheel wells rusted, the concrete under its axles tattooed with grease and oil. Inside, behind the windshield, a generation of spiders had made a comfortable connection of cobwebs, which gave the glass the appearance of having been kissed by a brick.

"This is your car?" This had to be a joke.

"Oh, yes."

I looked at the Essex again. "This is a joke, right?"

"This is our car."

"This car is a joke."

"Her name is Big Bertha. We drove her here from Lake Geneva last fall, before Orson secured work with either CBS or the WPA. We had high hopes, you see. Skipper gave her to us. She cost him thirty-five dollars when he purchased her."

"Who's Skipper?"

"Skipper is Roger Hill. Orson's mentor."

"Orson has a mentor?"

"Naturally. You know about Dadda?"

"Orson's guardian."

"Yes. Skipper really should have been Orson's guardian. Orson loves him so. More than he loved his own father I sometimes think, not that I can blame him. Skipper was the physical education instructor at the Todd School, but he was also in command of dramatics. He let Orson get away with murder. I don't believe Orson would have the success he does today without Skipper."

In its way Virginia's story was a sad one. But nowhere near as sad as the Essex. "Does this thing even run?"

"We drove her here under her own power. That's all I can tell you. I sort of thought I'd never see Big Bertha again. It's actually kind of nice. She brings back good memories. Orson and I weren't married very long when we came here from Wisconsin."

Virginia was suffering from a bad case of nostalgia. That was fine. I ailed from the same disease time and again myself. All honest people do. Her face was cool but her eyes were sad as she opened her purse and pulled out the keys again. "Here."

I took them from her. "Thanks. I appreciate it." It was a lie, but I was trying to make her feel better.

I opened the driver's side door to climb in. I expected the billow of dust that rose from the seat when I sat down, so I wasn't surprised by the musty smell. I even anticipated the repulsion I felt when I swiped away at the cobwebs, the architects scurrying for safety to the various nooks and crannies of the Essex. The only thing that could have caught me off guard was if the car started. But miracles do happen. With a cough, a wheeze, a backfire, and a chug the engine turned over.

"Shazam."

I was quick to release the choke. The car's idle ran a bit rough but she seemed seaworthy. I looked at Virginia, a stupid smile of triumph smeared across my face. She smiled back, but it seemed as if she had patted a sad shade of blue makeup on her cheeks while my attention had been on the car.

"Can I give you a lift somewhere?" I asked after I rolled down the window.

Mrs. Welles shook her head and waved me bon voyage.

I took the hint, shifted into first gear, released the clutch, and prayed. The old boat threatened to move, then rolled ahead under its own power. Its bald tires somehow supported Bertha's weight, and most of the oil managed to flow where it should flow instead of out on the street.

Wonder if this thing needs any gas? Wonder if the gauge even works?

As I steered out of the garage I caught a glimpse of Virginia in my rearview mirror. The woman watched Bertha leave the way most people looked back on their childhood.

At the first stop sign I came to I reached into my coat pocket and pulled out a page I had ripped from my phone book the night before. Circled in bright green was the listing for ANDRE DE SHIELDS, EXAMINER OF QUESTIONABLE DOCUMENTS, PRIVATE INVESTIGATIONS, with separate addresses for his office and residence. The time was a quarter to seven, so odds were De Shields was home in bed. I coaxed Bertha to the 140s, where I drove around like an idiot for ten minutes until I finally found the dick's crib. It was a none-too-shabby residence renovated into a duplex. I had imagined De Shields living in some second-floor flat, his overcoat thrown over the bed and an easy chair situated near the phone. This place was nice.

Wonder how much he charges his clients per day?

Without a little apprehension I turned off the engine. At first the spark didn't want to die, but with a few gentle words, followed up with a swift but loving kick to the firewall, Bertha finally shut down. I settled back with the web spinners while late morning frost hazed the glass.

Putting a tail on De Shields was a long shot. I knew that. The smart money would have me concentrate on Ben or Rose. But De Shields worked for Claudette Denbrough, and the Andersons had been her lawyers long before Ben became one of their clients. De Shields was my only link to the Denbroughs, so for one day at least I decided to play a hunch and discreetly tag along with him.

An hour later the inside of the car was so warm I had to wiggle out of my coat. I folded it beside me and kept waiting. Three and a half hours after that a taxi rolled up to the curb, honked, and De Shields finally came out.

"About freakin' time."

De Shields climbed into the passenger side as the cabbie flipped up the flag on the meter. I crossed my fingers and turned the key to start Bertha as the cab pulled back out into the street. The Essex obliged me, and we trailed the hack.

At first things seemed to be going my way. Bertha had to work two years worth of kinks out of her system, but before too long she was performing like a pure-breed bloodhound. Meanwhile the cab had pulled onto Seventh Avenue and stayed on the thoroughfare past 135th Street into Harlem.

Oh, yeah, I thought. *Here we go.*

A cloud passed over the sun a few minutes later when De Shields' cab parked and let the peeper off in front of a large brownstone. A congregation of scruffy locals were milling in front of the building, slowly but surely making their way inside.

I had never seen this brownstone before, but I had heard members of Orson's WPA troupe talk about it often enough to recognize it. De Shields had come to pay a call on Heaven, headquarters for the ministry of Father Divine, Harlem's most popular evangelist and self-proclaimed Living Word returned to earth.

Divine was the director of a handful of other brownstone and storefront Heavens, scattered throughout the borough as well as in cities as far away as Pittsburgh and Philadelphia. Every Heaven catered to the public's spiritual needs and offered free meals to the destitute. Today was business as usual, as unemployed and homeless people milled outside Heaven's door, waiting for the noon whistle to blow.

I couldn't help wondering if De Shields wasn't so cheap he didn't come here to cop a free meal. More than likely he was following up some kind of a lead. The third possibility was that he was working on a case for Divine. Whichever the truth turned out to be, all Bertha and I could do was camp along the thoroughfare to wait for De Shields to reappear.

Traffic never stopped sweeping past us during our vigil, its direction regulated by a narrow strip of park that bisected the boulevard. Glancing up and down the street it was hard to believe that, come Saturday, Seventh Avenue would once again turn into the Great Black Way, glorified as New York's premiere promenade in *The New Yorker* and *Age*.

Every weekend, like clockwork, gussied men could be seen strolling the avenue wearing silk toppers and velvet-colored Chesterfields, walking with women in high-cuffed peek-a-toe slippers and dresses trimmed with kolinsky fur. Big name pimps and racketeers would cruise Seventh Avenue in Phantoms and Rolls Royces, while prostitutes in expensive-looking cut-rate duds from Delancy Street patrolled the sidewalks.

During the week, however, all those silk lead sheets were neatly folded in their boxes. From Monday through Friday the gangsters and whores disappeared, and Seventh Avenue once more belonged to the laborers who earned their living along the Great Black Way.

Harlem's working stiffs maybe had two nickels left over to rub together after they scraped up enough ready each month to pay their landlord and the corner grocer. Many were too proud to accept Divine's charity, however, even for a free lunch. They managed each day with a butter sandwich packed in brown paper, or a pear stuffed into one of their coat pockets. If any of these Joes ever did find themselves with a spare dime for lunch, they instinctively avoided the smaller restaurants and cafes lining the boulevard. They knew ten cents at the right Seventh Avenue bar would buy a couple of beers where a guy could discretely wolf his fill of free cheese, salami, and crackers.

The sun came back out from behind its cloud just before one o'clock. About the same time I spotted a couple of boys as they ambled down the thoroughfare along its parkline, tossing a bruised and battered brown baseball back and forth. Cars skimmed by heedlessly on either side of the kids, while the workers hurried back to their jobs. Very few people bothered to notice, much less appreciate, the children as they played their game of catch. I watched them until they were out of sight, and for a few minutes I felt a lot like I had imagined Virginia Welles must have that morning, when she watched me drive out of the Waldorf's garage with Big Bertha.

De Shields strolled out from Heaven a few minutes later. He looked satisfied as he picked his teeth with a fingernail, a ketchup stain on one of his lapels.

You grifter! You did steal a meal!

The detective flagged down a passing cab and climbed in.

Gee. Maybe he's actually going to get around to doing some work today.

I figured we would stay inside the borough, or maybe stop off at De Shield's office, but I was wrong. It didn't take long to realize his cab was headed uptown.

Okay. So where are we going now? Ben's lawyers?

Strike two. At West 55th the hack turned into the driveway of The Tamara, a *tr'es chic* apartment building. The cabbie waited long enough for De Shields to pay him, then sped away while his passenger walked across the forecourt. I hid back at the mouth of the driveway, long enough for De Shields to pass through an arched frame in dishpan mosaic and up a small flight of marble stairs. The entrance was at the inside of an L, where a Negro porter opened the door for De Shields. Once the detective was inside the lobby, I steered Bertha up the drive and past a pale blue neon light that pointed the way into the basement garage. No attendants were in sight, so I parked Bertha in the first available stall.

"I'll be right back," I assured the car as I patted its dashboard. "I promise."

Back upstairs and outside, I strolled to the forecourt to wait for De Shields. The doorman immediately gave me the once-over, so I started to march to an impatient tune and occasionally glared at my watch. He had no reason to doubt I was anything more than a guy who was here to wait on a gal or a pal inside the apartments, which wasn't all that far from the truth.

Fifteen minutes later De Shields stepped out of an elevator and into the lobby, his face cast down and his shoulders tucked in close. He looked disappointed.

I glanced at my watch one more time, tossed my hands into the air, and said, "Hey, to hell with her!" just loud enough for the porter to hear me before I tramped back into the garage. Once I was beside the stairwell I stopped, turned around, and watched as De Shields asked the doorman to flag down a taxi. In a rush I went back to Bertha, cranked her up, and drove out of the garage in time to see the detective leave the Tamara inside his third cab of the day.

Our next call was over in Gramercy Park West. The cab pulled up alongside a squat curb that ran parallel to a high brick wall speckled with hail chips and veined with bare ivy vines. The wall circled around a languid antebellum mansion, interrupted only by an iron arch in whose decorative rusting curlicues could be read the name "Denbrough."

Unlike our last two stops, De Shields told this cabbie to wait as he moseyed through the arch and up the main drive. He stepped under the portico and knocked on the recessed front door, ignoring the lion's head knocker and careful to avoid metal filigree that resembled a portcullis. A starched butler with a face fresh from the embalmer's dutifully answered, and the detective was ushered inside.

It took a lot of willpower to keep myself from running up the Denbroughs' drive to introduce myself to Miss Claudette. Fortunately I didn't have to restrain myself too long. I hardly had time to shift

Bertha into neutral and turn off the engine before De Shields stomped back out of the mansion. He was obviously outraged, his scowl uglier than the wrath of God. De Shields jumped back into his cab, slammed shut the passenger side door so hard the vehicle actually rocked, and barked, "The Astoria! Now!"

The cabbie was a wise man and did as he was told with as little fuss and delay as possible. Once De Shields was safely inside the salon, I parked my own car up the street and made my way back to the Astoria's picture window. As casually as I could I peeked inside between the hand-painted "I" and "A." De Shields was hunkered down in a rear booth, two bottles of Knickerbockers in front of him, one beer having already given up its life for the cause. The detective was sulking and steaming, not at all in a good mood.

My first reaction was to go inside and buy him a few rounds. Do my best to buck up his sagging spirits. That's what you did for a friend, and while the detective and I were hardly pals, I couldn't help but feel kindly towards a colleague. He could have zipped his lip about the Denbroughs, Rose, Ben, and Jack Carter, but hadn't, which I figured was worth something.

On the other hand, it didn't take an Einstein to figure out how De Shields would respond if I sauntered into the Astoria and confessed I had followed him from one cab to another all afternoon. A better idea seemed to be to backtrack and question the people De Shields had paid a call on at Heaven and the Tamara. But even there I had a problem. Who exactly had he talked to? And what would I ask them?

My best bet seemed to be to pay a call on the Denbroughs. Something had definitely happened at their place. Something I doubted De Shields was going to feel like telling me about anytime soon.

But there, again, was a problem. How did I approach Norton's grieving mother without offending her? One wrong word and Miss Claudette would probably never tell me what had set De Shields off.

You could always take Chinaman with you.

That was true. He was an expert in etiquette and fluent in hoity-toity.

Better yet, why not break the ice with a celebrity?

"Orson." Now there was an idea. The brat spoke hoity-toity as well as Chinaman, and scarcely a day had gone by since rehearsals for *Macbeth* had begun that some Knickerbocker newspaper hadn't exploited his mug or his name.

So which is it going to be? I asked myself. *Your big-nosed penguin of a valet or the Wisconsin Wunderkind with the untamed mouth?*

There was only one intelligent way to decide. I pulled a silver dollar from one of my pants pocket and got ready to fillip it above my head. "Heads, it's Orson. Tails, it's the penguin."

The coin shot into the air.

It came down, I caught it, then slapped it on my wrist.

I pulled back my hand to see who had won.

Chapter Eight

In spite of his *Black Mask* bravado, Welles wasn't very keen about lending me a hand with Claudette Denbrough.

"What good could I possibly be when it comes to interrogating some stuffy old matriarch?"

To be fair he was already committed to his "long rehearsal," which for all intents and purposes was turning into a marathon. Since I had seen him Orson had telephoned CBS to beg a few days off from work, time he desperately wanted to dedicate to *Macbeth*. Technical details, like lighting and voodoo drummers, were beginning to jell, but his actors remained a stubborn problem that sorely tested Orson's capabilities.

Except for professionals like Ellis, Young, and Burroughs, no member of Welles' troupe had read much less performed Shakespeare before being hired by the WPA. Fortunately for Orson his actors "exhibited a propensity for the Bard of Avon," what he called the "Negroes' innate sensitivity to iambic pentameter."

Propensity aside, the actors had a lot to learn before they were going to be proficient, and with opening night a month away, Welles didn't have time to waste if he was going to whip his cast into shape for a Broadway performance.

"Fine," I said. We were in the balcony again, me in my seat across the aisle from Orson's perch. "You're the one who offered to help if I needed you."

"I offered my advice." Orson never diverted his eyes from a path between his legal pad and the stage. The rehearsal had come to *Macbeth*'s fifth act, where the thane is told about his wife's suicide, her guilt finally getting the better of her conscience.

"Whatever. Looks like I'll have to take Chinaman. Where is he?"

Welles didn't say a word. He didn't have to. His eyes shifted twice, back and forth inside their sockets, a guaranteed tip-off he was going to fib. I glanced at the stage and the actors, Chinaman's cameo as the Porter on my mind.

"What is it? You don't have him playing Rose's part now, do you?"

"No! Don't be ridiculous."

"So where is he? And no lies."

"Why should you want to take Chinaman with you?" he stalled.

"Because I do."

"But..."

"Orson." I drained my voice of patience.

"He's in Ben's dressing room. Rose is with them."

"Ben's back? Why didn't you say something? I want to talk with him. Ask him how he can afford his lawyers, stuff like that."

"That's the thing, Sassafras. The police were very rough with Ben. You know that, of course. As it turns out, he was with Rose all last night. That's why she was absent. She was tending to his bruises."

"Peachy. So why don't you want me talking to him?"

"Because he is still very rattled from his arrest. Chinaman suggested Ben take his mind off the whole ordeal and concentrate on the play for a while. They're talking about the Porter's role right now."

I couldn't believe what I was hearing. "You're taking orders from my valet?"

"His recommendations." Welles looked at me as if this was the most logical thing in the world for him to do. "Actually, Chinaman has some interesting observations about the Porter. Rather insightful stuff really. He compares the character to that of the Fool in *King Lear*."

"I don't care if Chinaman wants to compare the Porter to Mortimer Snerd! Orson, I know better than anyone how charming and persuasive Chinaman can be, but Ben has been accused of manslaughter."

"It also occurred to me," Welles continued without missing a beat, "that, given enough time, Chinaman might win over Ben and Rose's trust. If so, it is possible he might learn more from them than you could asking a few questions."

I zipped my lip and bit my tongue until I could swallow my words. It hurt like hell, but it felt better than making an ass of myself.

"Okay," I finally said. "I guess that makes sense. Good thinking, Orson."

"Well..." he paused, then, "actually it wasn't my idea. Chinaman suggested that, too."

Catching a glimpse of the eighth grader behind Welles' eyes, I counted to ten before saying anything.

"Okay, smarty-pants, that brings me back to you. I've gotta have help. I can't afford to muck up this interview. And, remember, the sooner the mystery of Norton Denbrough is cleared up, the sooner you'll know if Ben is even going to be available to play the Porter, the Fool, Romeo, Juliet, or whoever."

I had a good argument, and Orson knew it. He just didn't like it. Welles stared at me for what could have been a moment or an hour, then, "Perry!"

Welles' associate supervisor came when called, and the director instructed Perry to keep the rehearsal rolling until he returned. "When you reach the end of this act, just start the play over again. Don't stop. You're trapped on a merry-go-round. Understand?"

"Yes."

Orson shoved his legal pad and pen into Perry's hands then pointed at his seat. "Don't forget to take notes."

"I won't. But where are you going?"

This time Welles was prepared. He lied instantly and easily.

"We're going to the Port Authority. It's time to arrange the release of that shrunken head the bureaucrats have tangled up in red tape."

It was a wonderful performance. A thing of beauty.

Orson led the way out of the balcony and I followed. Just as we reached the top of the stairs leading to the mezzanine, he paused to listen to Jack Carter from the stage:

To-morrow, and to-morrow, and to-morrow,
Creeps in this petty pace from day to day,
To the last syllable of recorded time;
And all our yesterdays have lighted fool
The way to dusty death. Out, out, brief candle!
Life's but a walking shadow, a poor player
That struts and frets his hour upon the stage,
And then is heard no more: it is a tale
Told by an idiot, full of sound and fury,
Signifying nothing.

Welles urged Carter on throughout the speech, reminding me of Governor whenever he listened to a Green Bay Packers game on the radio. You could tell by the way my grandfather rocked in his chair that in his mind he was running with the players on every down. Orson was doing the same thing with Carter, but judging by Welles' expression the actor must have pulled up lame on the ten-yard line.

"He sounded okay to me," I said.

Wrong thing to say. Welles frowned before he could stop himself, and then just as quickly shook his head to disguise his frustration.

"I'm sorry, Sassafras. No need to take things out on you. Jack's elocution was perfect, but there's no enthusiasm, and I am stymied as to how to get him to put more passion into his performance."

"Maybe you should ask Chinaman." It was a cheap shot, but I couldn't resist.

Welles frowned again before we went downstairs. "Touché, Winters. Touché."

∽∾

Except for an abrupt chuckle when he first saw Big Bertha, Orson didn't make a pleasant noise during the whole drive to Gramercy Park West. Most of the time he mumbled to himself as he slouched in the passenger seat and stared out his window. There was very little I could decipher, but from what I did it was obvious Welles was still fussing over *Macbeth*. The pressure he was putting on himself and his cast and crew were beginning to get the better of him.

When I pointed out the Denbroughs' estate, Orson told me to follow the drive and park in front of the house. I did like he said, we got out, and I motioned for him to take the lead. He gaveled the front door with the lion's head knocker, then asked me, "What lie have you concocted to explain our visit?"

"No lie. We're here to ask Norton's mommy some questions. That's all."

"Good God, Sassafras! It is a good thing you insisted I accompany you."

The dour butler answered the door before I could say anything, the servant's appearance unimproved from my first glimpse of him three hours earlier. The guy could still double for Boris Karloff in *The Mummy*.

"Yes?" he asked.

"How do you do? I am Orson Welles, and this is my associate, Mr. Sassafras Winters. We were present the morning Mrs. Denbrough's son met with his unfortunate accident, and we have come to pay our condolences, if this is agreeable to your mistress."

Rather his mistress minded or not, Im-ho-tep had no problems with us dropping by unannounced. He ushered us in, I removed my hat, and the manservant told us to wait in the foyer while he relayed Orson's message to Miss Claudette.

Welles seemed right at home in our new surroundings. Not me. I felt uneasy, the same discombobulated feeling I got whenever Governor shamed me into visiting a museum with him. Every footstep on the checkered marble floor, laid with onyx and ebony squares, echoed in the ludicrously tall hall. A stairway banked in a heady curve up to the second floor then came around again up to the third. The foyer was sparsely decorated with glass...cut, crystal, and colored...and lousy with antiques. All the Denbroughs had to do was prop their butler up in one corner inside a sarcophagus and they could start charging admission.

"Do you think they'll buy it?" Welles asked me as soon as he was sure we couldn't be overheard.

"Why not? It makes perfect sense."

"It would make more sense if they were mourning."

I didn't understand, so Orson pointed to the front door.

"There is no black wreath," he said, and he was right.

"Well, the police haven't drug up Norton's body yet. I don't suppose you can blame them for wishing for the best. Doesn't mean a person can't stop by for a neighborly visit."

Orson mulled over my suggestion. "Perhaps you're right."

We heard footsteps. Orson gestured for me to stand next to him. I stepped over and we painted concern on our faces.

Tutankhamen conducted a man and two women into the foyer. The younger of the two women was holding hands with the fellow, so I assumed if she were Beatrice Denbrough he had to be her intended.

Joyce-Armstrong, if that's who he was, was approximately Orson's age and handsome like Leslie Howard, with the lithe and sinewy physique of a serpent. He had wavy sun-bleached hair, gray-blue eyes, and unseasonably reddish brown skin, the deep kind of tan I used to get when I played Class D ball down in Florida. This guy either didn't live in New York or had been visiting abroad in sunnier climes recently.

A second glance at the young woman affirmed her identity. The resemblance between her and De Shields' photograph of Norton Denbrough was striking. Beatrice was a bright and bubbly personality, with cornstalk hair and a face and figure that brought Mae Clarke to mind. Next to Carole Lombard, Mae Clarke was my favorite actress to dream about.

Beatrice's mother caught me appreciating her daughter and shooed me off with a frosty glare. Miss Claudette appeared to be in her late 50s, and exhibited the fostered class and gothic grace common to folks who had seen the sun set on the Victorian era. And, where the resemblance between Norton and Beatrice was strong, the one between Beatrice and her mother was uncanny.

The butler introduced the elder lady to us, then announced us as "Mr. Orson Welles and Mr. Sassafras Winters." Beatrice giggled when she heard my name. She meant no malice, but that didn't keep her mother from shifting that icy stare from me to her. Beatrice apologized, and I accepted. Miss Claudette then excused the butler and approached Orson, leaving her daughter and the young man behind.

"Have you come with news about my son?" she asked, the personification of serenity. The only hint that she was camouflaging any type of apprehension was a razor's edge of anxiousness cutting through her voice.

"I'm sorry, no we haven't, Mrs. Denbrough," Orson said, startled by her question. "I told your man that we've come to pay our respects. That's all. I'm sorry if Mr. Winters and I have come at a bad time."

"Not at all," she said, a bit relieved but more disappointed. "My daughter was visiting with her fiancé, and I was in the kitchen tending to trifling matters." Miss Claudette beckoned the couple forward, and they obeyed. "This is my daughter, Beatrice, and her husband-to-be, Dell Joyce-Armstrong."

I traded nods with Beatrice while Joyce-Armstrong reached out and pumped Orson's hand.

"I've read about you," the chestnut man told the director.

"So have I," Beatrice chirped in. "You're directing that play that has Harlem in an uproar."

"I don't know about that, but I am directing *Macbeth* for the WPA at the Lafayette Theater."

"They're calling it *Voodoo Macbeth*, aren't they?" Joyce-Armstrong asked. "I mean, isn't that what the niggers are calling it?"

"Dell." Miss Claudette's voice, though restrained, resounded with the awful snap of a hickory switch whisked across someone's butt.

"I was only asking a question. From what I understand, quite a few of them are unhappy with the play and Mr. Welles."

"You are being impolite. I won't tolerate bad manners in my house, and that includes vulgarity. Do you understand?"

I would have bet a week's pay Joyce-Armstrong sure as hell did understand. He bowed his head like a smart-aleck schoolboy scolded by his second grade teacher.

"Please accept my apologies, Mr. Welles. I meant no offense."

"None taken."

Both men were lying through their teeth, but Orson was the only one who acted believable.

"At the risk of being impertinent myself, Mr. Welles," Miss Claudette said, "your name sounds very familiar to me. Would you tell me if you spell your last name W-E-L-L-S, like the author, or W-E-L-L-E-S?"

"The latter. Have we met before?"

"No. My paternal lineage is traceable to the *Mayflower*, you see, and the genealogy of any of the Pilgrims' descendants fascinates me. And, if I'm not mistaken, the Welles family has three different bloodlines that can be traced back to Plymouth Rock."

Orson's face lit up like the St. Louis World's Fair, the little boy from Wisconsin overwhelmed his father's name had been recognized by an Eastern aristocrat.

"Actually," he said, "there are four bloodlines. Cooke, Warren, Alden, and Mullens. John Alden married Priscilla Mullens after the voyage to America."

"Imagine that?" Unless she was as accomplished in acting as Orson, Miss Claudette was authentically delighted. "I never would have realized. Perhaps, if you can spare a few minutes, you will allow me to accept your respects in our library. Beatrice and Dell can entertain your associate. It would help take my mind off Norton to investigate your heritage further."

Orson agreed, which was fine by me. With them out of the foyer, I might be able to weasel some information out of Beatrice and her dimwit boyfriend.

"You'll have to excuse mama," Beatrice said when we were alone. "She just can't resist gossiping with blue bloods."

"Orson ain't exactly a blue blood."

"He is to mama. It doesn't matter if you're rich or poor, so long as your ancestors were Protestant and came to America in 1620."

"It's the most exclusive of exclusive clubs," Joyce-Armstrong added. "The closest thing this country will ever have to royalty."

"Now look who's being a snob," Beatrice scolded her fiancé. "Dell's always bragging about how his family is related in one way or another to the Bourbon King Philip V of Spain, three or four hundred times removed."

"I never brag about that! And it's only three times removed. You'll have to excuse Beatrice, Mr. Winters. She has inherited her mother's beauty, but none of that excellent lady's breeding."

Beatrice blew Joyce-Armstrong a Bronx Cheer.

"See what I mean?"

"My faults must not bother you too much if you've agreed to marry poor little me."

"My dear, your comeliness more than compensates for any embarrassment your ill manners may afford me." Joyce-Armstrong took Beatrice's fingertips and barely kissed the knuckles of her right hand. "Now, if you'll excuse me, my father is waiting for me at our club. A pleasure, Mr. Winters."

I shook his hand and said, "See ya'." I hadn't found Joyce-Armstrong to be that big a pleasure.

Beatrice escorted her fiancé to the door, kissed him on the cheek, then came back to me.

"Would you like to wait for your friend in the sitting room? There's fresh fruit on the epergne, and I can ring for some sweet cider."

Just the sound of the menu made my lips pucker, so I shook my head. "If you don't mind me saying, that tit for tat between Dell and you didn't all play like romantic banter."

"I don't mind." And that's all she said.

"I'm sorry if I offended you."

She giggled. Even though it was aimed at me again, I was beginning to like the sound of her laugh.

"If I had to guess," she said, "I'd say you don't like Dell Joyce-Armstrong very much."

"It shows?"

"Uh-huh. You didn't like what he said about 'niggers'. Neither do I. And he knows full well that mama's granddaddy was an abolitionist during the Civil War."

"So why did he say it?"

"Because Dell doesn't like Negroes. More than a few work on his family's rubber plantations in Amazonas. I haven't visited yet, but from what I hear the calendar is stuck on 1760 down there. Woven straw hats and bullwhips are all the rage."

"That's it?"

"No. Mr. Orson Welles was stealing the spotlight. Dell Joyce-Armstrong simply must be the center of attention, except whenever his papa, the Colonel, is in the same room. My fiancé might have an inferiority complex, but he'd never dream of upstaging his daddy."

"Well, nothing personal, Miss Denbrough, but Dell sounds like a dope."

"He can be a real douche bag, that's for sure."

I coughed up a laugh before I could clap a hand over my mouth.

Beatrice was pleased with herself and giggled again. It sounded better each time.

"Don't tell me I shocked you, Mr. Winters?"

"I'm not complaining."

"No. You don't look like a complainer. Dell can be a complainer when he wants to be, so I should know. You look more like a doer."

"If Dell is all you say, why marry him?"

"For his money."

Okay. De Shields had already told me this. True. But that didn't dull the impact. This was one blunt lady.

"Shock you again, Mr. Winters?"

"I'd be lying if I said 'no'."

"Are you disappointed?"

"I don't know you well enough to be disappointed, Miss Denbrough."

"Well, if you are, don't be. The idle rich arrange this sort of thing all the time. That is, some do if they want to stay rich."

"I wouldn't know. I'm poor."

"Well, we're not as rich as we look. And I have every intention of earning the money, just like my mother did before me. It was my father who couldn't hold up his part of the bargain. Instead of adhering to the stipulations of their marriage contract, he cheated and cut out on mama."

"'Cut out'?" I figured it was best if I played dumb.

"Suicide. Something a lot of supposedly honorable men resorted to on Black Wednesday, instead of facing up to the challenges of the Depression."

"From what I hear about your brother, you both must have taken after your mother. It sounds like Norton was putting in a lot of overtime at work."

"Did you know my brother?" she asked. I could tell she knew I hadn't.

"No. Like we told your butler, Orson and I were in Harlem when your brother disappeared Sunday. I did talk with the private dick who crashed the party."

"What did he tell you?" Her wariness increased. Beatrice was nobody's fool.

"He told me about your brother and that your mother had hired him to keep an eye on her son. That's about it. I hope you don't mind me talking with De Shields. I was just doing my job."

Beatrice cocked her head and smirked. "And what is your job,

Sassafras Winters?"

"I'm Orson's bodyguard."

"Really?" Her eyes kindled and her eager smile returned. "Is it getting that dangerous in Harlem? Norton used to take me there all the time before mama forbade it after the riots last fall."

"I don't know if it's as bad as that, but the Workers' Party in Harlem is making a mountain out of a mole hill about the play. They claim *Macbeth* is going to be some kind of minstrel show, and we have picketers marching in front of the Lafayette around the clock."

Beatrice tilted her head, and for a second I thought she was doubting me again, but that wasn't it. More familiar with the noises in her house, she recognized Miss Claudette's and Welles' footsteps approaching from the library a few seconds before I could. She closed the distance between us, so quickly I wasn't sure what to expect, but it certainly wasn't what she whispered in my ear: "We really must continue this conversation later. Call me." After that she winked and stepped back so there was some daylight visible between us. "Did you two have a nice chat?" she asked when her mother entered the foyer.

Miss Claudette appeared to be enchanted with Orson, but when she looked at her daughter and me and noticed Joyce-Armstrong was gone, she returned to character, as stern as nails. "Where is Dell?"

"He had to go. And so do I. Nice to meet you, Mr. Welles. Mr. Winters."

Miss Claudette fixed her gaze on me again while her daughter took flight up the stairs. I outweighed Beatrice's mother by at least eight stones and she had nearly twenty years on me, but I didn't have the guts to peak at her daughter once while Miss Claudette stared at me.

"Nice daughter you have there," Orson said, free to ogle Beatrice to his heart's content.

"Yes. As you know, she's getting married."

"To a very nice fellow, I'm sure," I said.

"I like to think he is."

Orson and I kept our opinions to ourselves.

"It was so good talking to you, Mr. Welles," Miss Claudette said as she offered her hand. "Your consideration is most appreciated."

"My privilege," he said as he took her hand and lightly bowed. "If any of us at the Lafayette Theater can be of further help, please don't hesitate to let us know."

"Thank you. Please come back again." She didn't bother to look at me when she said this.

ಆ⁓

If nothing else Orson was a lot better company going back to the Lafayette. His chat with Miss Claudette had been as much a tonic for him as it had been for her.

"I don't suppose you managed to bring up the subject of Andre De Shields with Mrs. Denbrough?" I asked as I drove us out of the estate, steering Bertha back to Harlem.

"As a matter of fact, yes, I did. Mrs. Denbrough was naturally curious to know what I had seen during the course of Rose's party. I told her as much as I could, piecing together what you and Canada told me, then gracefully directed the conversation towards De Shields. She was graciously accommodating."

"Did she happen to tell you why De Shields left her house in a huff this afternoon?"

"Yes. He was fired."

Fired?! "No fooling?"

"No fooling."

"Why?"

"He fell victim to the laws of the economic jungle. Nothing personal."

"I don't follow."

"The police are investigating Norton's disappearance free of charge, so De Shields' services have become an unnecessary luxury."

"That's sort of cold, ain't it?"

"The family is up against it, Sassafras. Of course, Mrs. Denbrough didn't let on to that in front of me."

"She ought to talk to her daughter. Beatrice sure as hell didn't mind telling me."

Orson leered like Lugosi. "Yes. You two looked rather chummy. I can believe Beatrice Denbrough would be unable to keep any secrets from you."

"Jealous?"

"She is an attractive young woman."

"She told me to call her."

Welles' eyes exploded in their sockets. "No! No, it's too cruel!"

"Yes."

"And the papers claim the flapper era is over. What are you going to do?"

"I don't know. I'd be lying if I said I wasn't tempted. But she's engaged, for God's sake!"

"To a smarmy cosmopolitan who deserves to be a two-timed, if you ask me my opinion."

Orson hadn't found out anything else from Mrs. Denbrough, so we spent the rest of the ride agreeing about Beatrice's good points and Joyce-Armstrong's bad ones. By the time we got back to the Lafayette it was nearly five o'clock. The number of picketers was somewhere around forty, everyone behaving themselves as we ignored them and entered the lobby.

"Well, that wasn't so bad," Welles said as he hurried towards the stairs leading up to the balcony. "Coming?"

"I think I'll hunt up Chinaman first. See what he learned talking to Ben and Rose."

"Fine. You'll know where to find me."

I began to turn away when something dark dashed out from one of the lobby's early evening shadows and charged Orson. Before I could react, Orson was lifting his arms over his face to protect himself from the sinister thing that was tackling him. Both figures fell to the stairs, the thick carpet cushioning their impact.

I yelled for help as I ran to Orson. Closer, I could make out Welles' attacker was a Negro man, wiry and swift, the assailant flaying his right arm up and down in front of Orson's petrified eyes.

I hauled the stranger off Welles, but he yanked free and swiped at me with his right arm. I dodged by stepping back, in time to notice a glint from some kind of metal taped underneath his wrist.

Razor! The crazy had taped a razor to his arm!

That did it. I lost it. I punched the stranger, a right across the chin, before he could swipe again. That made him woozy but, not taking chances, I hammered his kidneys with an illegal rabbit punch and, when he bent over, clobbered him with a barroom roundhouse. Cartilage broke, blood squirted out both nostrils, and the loony sailed off his feet, landing next to Orson, who was picking himself up off the stairs. I stood ready, just in case, but it was over. Our new friend wasn't going to wake up any time soon.

The Lafayette's cast and crew stampeded into the lobby a few seconds later, Canada Lee leading the charge with Chinaman right behind him. Meanwhile the picketers had overheard the fight outside, and now a handful were stepping into the theater to check out what had happened.

"Are you hurt, Sassafras?" Canada asked me. I shook my head, too keyed up to talk.

As soon as Chinaman knew I was all right he moved over to Orson, who was rattled but otherwise undamaged.

Jack Carter, dressed in Macbeth's uniform pants, boots, and shirt, stepped up next to give the unconscious attacker a good once-over. He shivered when he examined the maniac's right arm.

"Holy sweet Jesus," Carter groaned.

At first he just stared at the razor. Then, slowly, he stood and glowered at the picketers, his face twisting like John Barrymore's Mr. Hyde. The fingers of his hands stretched and crooked like the talons of a hawk.

A moment before the lobby had been buzzing with crowd noise, but things got awfully quiet as the actor advanced on the intruders, one deliberate step after another.

"Get out of here," Carter muttered.

"We doan haf anythin' to do wit' dat man," one of the protestors argued, his voice quivering. "Yo' can't blame us fo' what dat idiot did."

"I said, *'GET OUT OF HERE!'*"

The picketers didn't have to be told a third time. None of them wanted to tangle with the big man, even though they meandered back out slow enough to be disrespectful.

"There it is," Orson whispered, so quietly I could barely hear him, even though I was standing almost right next to him.

"What's wrong?" I asked.

"Nothing's wrong. There's the passion, Sassafras." He was still whispering, absolutely delighted about something that he didn't want anyone else to hear. "What we talked about before." He couldn't take his eyes off Carter.

"Orson," I said, "Carter is furious. He's only a whisker away from cutting loose and dismembering those people!"

"I know, Sassafras. I know. All I have to do is figure out a way to get him to draw upon this fury while he is performing."

This was madness. I didn't want to hear any more. Didn't he realize he had almost been killed? I did! My legs were shaking, my skin was sweaty, and I didn't know how much longer I could keep choking down my lunch. But all Welles could think about was his play.

I asked Chinaman to go phone the police while I went into the auditorium. If I hurried I might be able to throw up into an empty fire bucket before the Unit returned from the lobby. Canada stopped me before I got too far to tell me he was sorry.

"Sorry? For what? That you thought I could be a decent bodyguard?"

"Certainly not. Because you could have been killed. Because it would have been our fault. We were sincere when we said we believed no one would attack Orson if they saw he was under constant watch."

I patted Canada's shoulder. "I knew better than that when I took the job. And everything worked out for the best. So don't get bent out of shape."

Canada seemed to buy what I said, as I was sure I would later. Right at the moment, leaving my old buddy behind to be alone with my bucket, all I could think about was what might have happened if my reflexes had been a fraction slower, or if the stranger had known the first thing about fighting dirty.

Chapter Nine

The cops barely had time to drag Orson's mugger out of the Lafayette before Welles darted up to his balcony, bellowing, "Everyone! Back to your places!"

He was charged. Orson couldn't have been more electrified if Dr. Frankenstein had zapped him with 10,000 volts. Welles wasn't distressed in the least by the attack. If anything, he was grateful.

"After all, Sassafras," he explained as cast and crew resumed their normal posts, "we're both unharmed. No sense bemoaning a fate that didn't befall us. Try looking at the bright side."

"There's a bright side?"

"Certainly! Look how agitated and inflamed the troupe is! I doubt they'll get themselves worked up into such a lather again before opening night. All I have to do is help them funnel their energy towards the rehearsal. This is a wonderful opportunity! I predict all the actors will make great strides."

"Wonderful, but aren't you ignoring that you came this close to getting killed? Even closer to being mutilated." I couldn't stop my voice from warbling. My imagination was constantly replaying scenes of the attacker's razor slicing vertical grooves into Welles' forehead and through his eyes.

"Your brush with either fate was just as close as mine. Which reminds me, thank you again for your intervention. I don't know how I'll ever repay you."

"You could start by fainting. Aren't you even going to call Virginia and tell her what happened?"

"Why? Nothing happened. Not really. Anyway, it's best if I wait to tell her in person. Quite likely she'll be upset, and I should be there to comfort her."

"Mighty thoughtful of you."

There was no getting through to him, and I was fed up with trying. I left the balcony and went downstairs to the lobby. Chinaman was standing at the bottom of the steps, patiently waiting for me. "I attended to your bucket, Mr. Winters."

"Thank you, Chinaman."

"Are you feeling yourself again?"

"Getting there."

"And Mr. Welles?"

I sat down on the next to last step. My legs were still rubbery and I needed the rest. "He's on top of the world. Couldn't be happier."

"I hope he isn't experiencing denial. It's best to confront your emotions directly after a near tragedy."

I shrugged then glanced down the lobby to the front doors. Outside two plainclothes detectives were questioning the protestors about the attack.

"Tell me something," I said. "When you were talking to Ben and Rose in the dressing rooms earlier, did you find out anything I should know?"

Chinaman hesitated. "Well, Miss Ramsey doesn't like you very much, sir."

Really? "Anything else?"

"Mr. Kanter was disquiet about his experience with the police. Their degradation and humiliation unsettled him greatly, and their brutality did take a toll on his health."

"How bad are his wounds? Did you see them?"

"No. I did offer my services, but he declined. He assured me Miss Ramsey had satisfactorily tended to his cuts and bruises."

"Did he say anything about his lawyer?"

"Mr. Kanter is being represented by Herman Bogart. From what I was told, Mr. Bogart was a distinguished corporate attorney until the stock market crash."

"So how did Ben get hooked up with him?"

"Mr. Bogart approached Mr. Kanter. They had never met before Mr. Kanter's arraignment, and he is grateful for Mr. Bogart's legal assistance."

"That's just spiffy, Chinaman, but that doesn't answer my question."

"Apparently Mr. Bogart read about the circumstances leading up to Mr. Kanter's arraignment in Monday morning's *Times*. The publicity that this trial could potentially attract in turn attracted Mr. Bogart to Mr. Kanter's plight. By successfully representing Mr. Kanter, Mr. Bogart hopes to reinvigorate his career, this time as a litigator. Because of that, he is donating his legal services."

"Makes sense," I said, and it did. "Except for one thing."

"Mr. Winters?"

"Did Ben say anything about Bogart working for the firm of Anderson, Anderson, Myers, and Watson?"

"Mr. Bogart was the only attorney we discussed. As far as I know, Mr. Bogart is not associated with any legal firms."

I shook my head and blew out my cheeks, mannerisms I once reserved for those soul-strengthening occasions when one of my sliders got belted over the ivy and out of the park at Wrigley Field. "Christ, this is turning into one fat mess."

"Sir?"

I told Chinaman about following Ben and Bogart to the Andersons' office after the arraignment, then about the Denbrough file.

"It is quite a coincidence," he admitted, "if it is a coincidence."

"Well, now, that's the question, ain't it? I mean, I still can't figure out why Bogart didn't take Ben straight to a doctor or a hospital after the arraignment. I'm not kidding, Ben was in crummy shape."

For one of the few times in our relationship Chinaman couldn't think of a thing to say. *Swell timing, pal.*

"Well," I sighed, struggling to my feet, "I'm not doing anybody any good hanging around here. Nobody's going to try pulling anything funny inside the Lafayette again. Not with Jack Carter's blood on the boil. I think I'll hunt down De Shields."

"Are you sure you are all right, Mr. Winters? You're most unsteady."

"Just getting my sea legs. They'll work themselves out by the time I get to the car."

Chinaman was mortified. "You're in no condition to drive, sir. I doubt you will be for several minutes. The body needs time to readjust its metabolic balance after an epinephrine rush."

"I appreciate you talking to me like I knew what you just said, but, whatever it was, I am fine. I'm just a little shaky. Some fresh air will do me good."

"Yes, it will, but no, you are not fine. If you insist on leaving right away, then I will have to go along. It is a small leap from being a valet to becoming a chauffeur, and I would be remiss in my duties if I did not insist on driving you."

It was obvious he wasn't going to take no for an answer either, so I tried to stare him down. Give him the evil eye. Let him think a bean ball was coming if he didn't back off from the plate. In short, do my best to resemble something that crawled out of an unused corner of hell. I've been told it's a talent I have a knack for, but even my best efforts were wasted on Chinaman. He just looked at me, calmly and patiently, as if he had nothing else in the world better to do. The guy didn't even blink. It was kind of spooky. Like trying to out stare a cat.

"I am not sitting in the back seat," I said.

"That's up to you, sir."

"And I don't want you wearing one of those silly gray caps."

"No, sir. It would clash with my uniform."

I started to leave and he dutifully followed. "And another thing."

"Yes, sir?"

"Don't make fun of my car when you see it. It's a gift from Orson and Virginia."

"I wouldn't dream of it, sir."

"Good. Her name's Bertha, and she's sensitive, so no wisecracks."

He paused, then, "Are you sure you're all right, Mr. Winters?"

❧❧

I had Chinaman sit with Bertha while I peeked through the Astoria's picture window. De Shields wasn't in his booth, so I stepped inside the cafe and nosed around. No sign of him. I asked some of the help if they remembered seeing the peeper leave. De Shields was a semi-regular so I was in luck. It seemed he left not very long after I skedaddled to grab Orson and visit the Denbroughs.

"He phoned for a Checker," the bartender told me. "Didn't say anything about where he was heading. Wasn't in a very good mood, I can tell you that. He didn't leave a tip. That's not like Andre. He's usually a real Joe."

Back in the car I gave Chinaman directions to De Shields' apartment. He weaved through the borough as if he knew its roads like the back of his hand, taking advantage of side streets to get to the duplex in no time, but De Shields wasn't home.

I opened the glove compartment and pulled out the page I had ripped from the phone book the day before. "Here," I said, handing the paper to Chinaman and pointing out the address to De Shields' office. "I suppose you know the fastest way to get there."

"Of course, Mr. Winters."

Chinaman drove to a modern office building less than two miles from De Shields' residence. Not as pretentious as the Andersons' skyscraper, but it was amiable enough that De Shields had to be forking over at least half a C-note every month to keep his name painted on the pebbled glass in his door. The lights inside were off.

"It seems he isn't here, either," Chinaman said.

"So where the hell is he?"

Chinaman took his pocket watch from his vest pocket. "It's not quite eight o'clock, sir. Perhaps he is having a late dinner before taking in a play or movie?"

"Somehow, I don't think so." It was time to select a lock pick from my wallet. Bending down to one knee, I set to work.

"Mr. Winters? What are you doing?" I really don't think he knew.

"Picking the lock. Be quiet."

"Picking the...that's *illegal!*" His jew's harp was in fine tune tonight.

"Want to keep your voice under a dull roar? Janitors have been known to mop floors around this time of day."

I have no idea if De Shields or his landlord had installed the lock, but whoever it was had my respects. Unlike those cheapskate Andersons someone had invested some berries in this honey, a Rogers & Englehart precision lock set with eight tumblers and a stainless steel bolt.

"What if we are caught?" Chinaman asked, nervous as hell. "We'll be arrested! I don't want to be arrested, Mr. Winters. Not after what happened to Mr. Kanter."

"Might do you some good. A little time in stir can be a real character builder."

"Please, sir, there is no reason to invade this office!"

"Chinaman, no one is going to catch us if you'll just stay jake and put a sock in it."

He did shut his pie hole, which was good, but then he started bouncing on the balls of his feet, and every time he came down the hard rubber heels of his patent leather shoes whacked the polished floor of the vacant hallway, making more racket than a chorus line performing the cancan.

"Chinaman, stand still or go outside and wait with Bertha." It had taken nearly two minutes, but I finally had the first seven tumblers in their proper positions to release the bolt. That left tumbler number eight, the trickiest of the bunch. If I didn't readjust it correctly on my first try, springs attached to the other seven tumblers would automatically pop them out of position. I would have to begin all over, no closer then when I started.

"How can I wait 'with' Bertha, sir? Bertha is a car. An automobile, albeit a poor excuse for one. It is positively filthy. I can't believe Mr. Welles could ever allow his property to go to seed like that, if you'll excuse the regionalism."

The final tumbler snapped into place and the door opened with a twist of its knob. Before Chinaman could start jabbering about anything else, I yanked him into the office, shutting the door behind us.

Turning on the light I expected to find a small antechamber, not the comfortable front office that greeted us. There was even a desk for a receptionist, which, judging by the typewriter, telephone, and filing cabinet, was semi-regularly occupied by a girl Friday.

"Goddamnit. Nice digs."

"Must we have the light on?" Chinaman was still jumpy.

"You want to see where you're putting your feet, don't you?"

"Not as much as I would like to avoid someone seeing us."

"Relax, will you? Listen. Nobody outside is going to spot us. Okay? And anybody walking by in the hall will just figure De Shields is putting in a little overtime. Now stay cool."

Chinaman managed to nod without snapping his head off, and I opened the door into the back office. De Shields'. The first thing I noticed after switching on the light was the door leading in to a private bathroom with tiled floor and a cast-iron claw foot bathtub.

"Dear Lord! Chinaman, come in here and see how swell this slob lives!"

The valet poked his head through the threshold and took a peak. "Yes, sir. Very nice." Then he pulled his head back out.

By the looks of things De Shields hadn't been in his office all day.

His date book was laying on top of his desk, so I leafed through it to see what appointments he had scheduled for that day and night. Nothing. *Great. Still no idea where he's at or who he gabbed with at Heaven or the Tamara.*

Laying the date book back on De Shields' desk, I told Chinaman to scrounge around in the filing cabinet out in the antechamber.

"I don't believe I should do that, sir," he called back.

"Damn it, Chinaman, show some backbone and dig into that cabinet! Tell me if you find anything relating to the Denbroughs or Ben Kanter. Hurry up!"

It wasn't long before he struck pay dirt. De Shields had compiled reports on Beatrice, Claudette, and Norton Denbrough, as well as Jack Carter and Rose Ramsey. There was a file for Ben Kanter, but it wasn't any thicker than its counterpart at the Andersons' office. De Shields had also collected information about Orson, Edna Thompson, Canada Lee, and, believe it or not, even me.

"If nothing else Mr. De Shields is a very thorough investigator," Chinaman said after I had him tote the files into the back office.

I started with Ben's file, and was surprised to find a carbon copy of his arrest report. It was dated 2 PM Sunday afternoon, and there was a crease running down its middle. In my mind's eye I could imagine De Shields hiding the report in his coat pocket all the while he was guzzling free beers in the Astoria.

"That sneaky son of a dog."

De Shields had also scavenged carbons of Ben's WPA forms and pay vouchers, but scrounged up nothing about the actor before the Federal Theater Project hired Kanter.

"How queer," Chinaman said, looking across De Shields' desk at the file. "It's almost as if Mr. Kanter simply materialized out of thin air."

"That'd be a neat trick, now wouldn't it? Odds are Ben doesn't have enough paper work floating around with his name on it for De Shields to collect. From what Canada tells me, unless a Negro joins the army or ends up in the slammer, the only official documents our government ever requires from them are certificates at birth, marriage, and death. And sometimes not even then."

I closed the cover on Kanter and opened Rose Ramsey's file. "Born and raised in Harlem," I summarized out loud. "Fifth grade education. Single. Supports herself by harmonizing for local bands, more often than not during recording sessions. *Macbeth* is her first dramatic credit as an actress."

"All that is common knowledge, sir."

"Afraid so. As far as her private life is concerned, she's been seen frequenting Harlem water holes this winter with Norton Denbrough, Ben, and Jack Carter."

"Mr. *Carter?*"

Oh-oh. I forgot I hadn't hipped Chinaman to Rose and Jack Carter.

"Do you think Mr. Kanter is aware of this?"

Think fast, Sassafras.

"I don't know, Chinaman, but tell you what. How about if we keep this bombshell under our hats?"

"But, Mr. Winters...!"

"Trust me on this one. Don't tell anybody. And if someone happens to bring the subject up, even joking around, just play dumb, or as dumb as it's possible for you. That includes Orson."

"Surely Mr. Welles should know! Mr. Kanter is only the Porter, but Mr. Carter is the lead!"

"Please, Chinaman. No. Orson has got enough problems right now with the play. He doesn't need this on top of all that. When the proper time comes, I'll tell him. It's my job. Okay?"

He didn't like it, but he agreed.

Having read quite enough about Rose, I moved on to De Shields' report on Jack Carter.

His mother, a Negress, was a member of the original Floradora Sextet, and his father, an anonymous white, was an European aristocrat. Carter, born in a French chateau, for some reason was never told about his Negroid lineage until after he moved to America in his late teens.

"Judging by his rap sheet, Carter chocked on the news," I said, taking a seat in De Shields' swivel desk chair. Chinaman was sitting on the near end of a leather couch, royal blue with brass upholstery studs, running the length of one wall, studying the Edna Thompson file. "Before turning to acting in *Porgy* he worked as a pimp and served his ten years for murder. Word of mouth has it that his underworld friends have been supporting him since *Porgy*, since he's usually too drunk to do it himself."

"That is sad," Chinaman commented, his voice hushed. "I had no idea Mr. Carter was such a tragic figure."

"What 'tragic'? I can list a dozen people...Negroes, mulattoes, whites...who would trade places with Jack Carter in a red-hot second. The guy's handsome, athletic, smart, talented, and popular. He's even descended from royalty. This is a curse? I should have it so rough."

"You misunderstood me, Mr. Winters. Mr. Carter is tragic because he suffers from a tragic flaw, such as the character he plays in *Macbeth*. In most tragedies this flaw is a hubris, usually pride. In Mr. Carter's case he seems unable to reconcile himself with his two heritages."

"You're right. I don't understand you."

"Logic would suggest, judging by where he lives and the people he associates with, that Mr. Carter considers himself a Negro, and throughout American history whites have denigrated Negroes. Negroes were our slaves, and seventy years after the Emancipation Proclamation whites continue to restrict Negroes' social and economic opportunities. Mr. Carter abhors this history, but he cannot deny that he is and always shall be half white."

"Hold the phone a minute. You think Jack Carter hits the bottle because his colored half can't stand living next door to his white half?"

"That is my hypothesis. He is undeniably continental, and I find most aristocratic Europeans are typically passionate men. They feel things more deeply than the average American. Mr. Carter is the kind of man who rebels without hesitation against his enemies. We saw that for ourselves today in the Lafayette's lobby. But what do you do when your worst enemy is the man in the mirror? This psyche struggle is what I was thinking of when I referred to him as a tragic figure. And unless Mr. Carter can reconcile himself to his disparate ancestries, his tragic flaw will decimate him as surely as ambition destroys Macbeth."

Now there was a cheery thought. Happily Miss Thompson's file was as uplifting as Jack Carter's was depressing.

Edna Thompson, a native of Harlem, debuted in 1916 at the age of twenty-one with Charles Gilpin and the Lafayette Players. In 1920, after appearing in two original one-act plays by Eugene O'Neill, *The Emperor Jones* and *All God's Chillun Got Wings*, she became the queen of the Great Black Way, holding court at the Alhambra, the Harlem Opera House, Hurtiq & Seamon's Music Hall, and Proctor's on 125th Street.

"Her career was in full bloom in 1934 when she almost died in that auto accident," Chinaman reported. "It appears her spine was severely strained, plus she suffered some nerve and ligament damage. Astonishing she ever walked again, much less returned to the stage. And Mr. De Shields has a note here about..." Chinaman suddenly went pale. "Oh, my."

"What is it?" I stood up and moved beside him, looking down at the file. Chinaman handed me the note, a piece of De Shields' office stationary with the detective's precise handwriting scribbled across it.

"It would appear Miss Thompson's recovery was facilitated by her lover, who remained by her side throughout the ordeal."

"I didn't know she had a lover." I went on reading until I found this mysterious Casanova's name, which didn't take long. "Whoa! Get a load of that." Even better was the address Miss Thompson's lover occupied. "Penthouse, the Tamara, West 55th Street, Manhattan."

I gave Chinaman the note to replace in Miss Thompson's file, then jotted down the lover's name on a piece of De Shields' scratch paper.

Next we dug into the Denbroughs' folder. There was the pink carbon of Leonard Denbrough's death certificate, a family tree and social register, some financial history, and precious little gossip we didn't already know.

"As far as yourself, Mr. Lee and Mr. Welles are concerned, may I assume we needn't bother with those files?"

I figured, "What the hell," and took a gander, to Chinaman's sorrow. As far as Canada and I were concerned there was nothing new in either file, although I was ecstatic to find a press clipping about a game I had played in back in the early 1920s.

"Look at this, Big C! I haven't thought about this game in years! It was a 15-inning affair on a scorcher July 4th. I was at the hot corner for the Cedar Rapids Bunnies, and we were at home against the Omaha Oaks. In the top of the 15th, Omaha had one out with Motorboat McCauley on first and Barnstormer Warner at the plate. Suddenly Warner hits a smoker up the third base line and McCauley is off to the races. I make a diving catch, get to my knees, and throw across the dirt so fast even a guy named Motorboat can't get back in time before he's tagged out. A 5-3 double play that kept two men off the corners, and in the bottom of the inning Gimpy LeRoy's dinger wins the game for us. Pretty fantastic, eh?"

Chinaman just stared at me, smiling paternally.

"You have no idea what I just said. Do you?"

"But I appreciate you speaking to me as if I did, sir."

To quote Orson Welles, "Touché."

We had spent almost an hour rummaging in De Shields' office, and Chinaman was perilously close to jumping out of his skin. I promised him we would leave right after we skimmed through Orson's file. "If De Shields has been thorough, the least we can do is be thorough, too." But breezing through the file was easier said then done. It was as thick as my hometown's telephone directory. *Orson's had himself a busy little life.* There were dozens of snippets from old newspapers, magazine articles, clippings, obituaries, documents and certificates, a couple of photographs, and sundry odds and ends.

"Mr. Winters." Chinaman picked up one of the photographs. "This picture of Mr. Welles' mother. It's extraordinary."

It was an Aristotype print of a pensive, delicate young woman wearing a lace-collared Edwardian dress, her dark hair pinned up and crowned with baby's breaths. She was tilting her head so one side of her face was bathed in light while the other was cast in a gentle shade. Her haunting, perceptive eyes were so pale they looked like the glass eyes of a China doll. Mrs. Welles was a beautiful, captivating woman, but that wasn't what had attracted Chinaman's attention. It was the similarity between mother and son. Where the resemblance between Miss Claudette and Beatrice Denbrough was uncanny, the one between Orson and his late mother had been nothing less than eerie.

According to the information in Orson's file his mother died in 1924, two days after his ninth birthday, after suffering from yellow jaundice for two years. His vagabond father died six years later in a

Chicago hotel fire. Orson's only immediate relative, his brother Richard, a schizophrenic, had, at the advice of Dr. Bernstein, been institutionalized by Welles' father in 1925.

"Holy Moe, Chinaman. And you thought Carter had it bad."

Despite its promising bulk there was nothing in Orson's file that concerned our investigation, so I had Chinaman replace the stack back in the filing cabinet.

Alone in De Shields' office I got to pacing. We hadn't found anything new in all the information De Shields had gathered relating to Denbrough's disappearance, and my instincts kept telling me there should be more. But where?

"I'm almost finished," Chinaman called from the other room.

Glancing up, I looked above the blue leather couch, noticing the scenic painting hanging above it for the first time.

Forget it. De Shields is too smart for that old trick.

I decided to take a peak anyway. Sure enough, there was nothing, but my common sense, humming like a diving rod, insisted I was close.

Chinaman started shutting drawers in the filing cabinet. "I can't tell you how delighted I will be to leave here."

"Uh-huh." Since the only place left to look was under the couch, I grabbed one armrest and slid it away from the wall. The first thing I noticed was that the floor was too clean. No dust bunnies. No dust film. The second thing I noticed was the small safe inlaid flush with the floor. "Bingo!"

"What was that, Mr. Winters?"

"Nothing."

Stooping down I put my ear to the dial and started fiddling with the combination. Compared to juggling the tumblers in the lock on the office door, pinching this safe would be a cold cinch. I had the door opened in two shakes of a bobtail. "Beat me, daddy, eight to the bar!"

Chinaman came back right then. As soon as he saw what I was doing he clapped both hands over his mouth and started screaming bloody murder.

"If you keep that up," I said, "I'm never taking you anywhere again."

While he simmered down I extracted a frayed accordion folder from the safe.

"Now what have we here?"

De Shields was assembling a dossier on George Baker, better known as the Heavenly Father *a.k.a.* Father Divine. Although there was nothing in the report to connect Divine with Norton Denbrough or anyone associated with Orson's troupe, it was interesting to find out the evangelist was keeping Andre De Shields on permanent retainer.

"It does suggest how Mr. De Shields manages to afford his flat and these offices," Chinaman said, jittery but trying to pitch in.

"Yeah, it does, but look at this." There were a couple of items in the folder with the dossier, including a prescription for Edna Thompson, written in Latin on a psychiatrist's pad, dated the previous June. The paper was wrinkled, from being crumpled, and stained by something brown, probably coffee. "Looks like De Shields fished this out of some pharmacist's dumpster."

I gave the prescription to Chinaman so he could translate it for me. The closest thing to a classical language I know is pig Latin, but Chinaman had an M.A.M.D. and could speak in more tongues than a Hebrew prophet. "Can you make heads or tails out it?" I asked.

"Yes, sir." He said nothing more. He just stood there and quivered, expecting Elliot Ness to kick down De Shields' door at any moment.

"You know, the quicker you give me the low down on that prescription, the sooner you and I can scram."

"Oh." That got his attention. "It's for a narcotic: 6 dimethylamine-4-4-diphenyl-3-heptanone."

"Come again."

"Methadone."

"The pain killer?"

"Yes, sir. Very likely for her back injury."

"Why is Edna Thompson's headshrinker prescribing pain killers for her? Shouldn't her regular doctor do that?"

"Psychiatrists are doctors of medicine, Mr. Winters." Chinaman returned the prescription, his hand shaking. The poor slob was really scared. "Miss Thompson will possibly require a pain killer from time to time for the remainder of her life as a result of her accident. Since morphine is a narcotic, a psychiatrist is actually better qualified to prescribe it than a general practitioner."

When it came to medicine Chinaman knew more than I ever would, so I hesitated to question him. I trusted his advice was right on the money, but I couldn't help wondering if that was all there was to the prescription. If not, then why did De Shields bother hanging on to it?

Keeping my doubts to myself, I slipped the prescription back in the folder and pulled out the last content. De Shields had scribbled down and notarized a transcript to a conversation he had had the day before with a stoolie, the informant's name withheld. The whole transcript was strictly Q&A in format so reading it didn't take long. In spite of its slim size, its kicker still packed a king-size wallop.

"What is it?" Chinaman asked.

"De Shields' stool pigeon swears Norton Denbrough did a deal to borrow one hundred Gs from a Jungle Hill loan shark last week."

"Why?"

"Doesn't say. Probably to tie his family over until his sister's wedding. But get a load of this. Norton and the shylock never met. All the negotiations were handled on Norton's end by Jack Carter."

"That is hardly suspicious. It makes good sense considering Mr. Carter's popularity and reputation in the borough, as well as his relationship with the local underworld. With Mr. Carter's assistance Norton Denbrough surely received far more satisfactory terms than if he had negotiated with the lender himself."

"So tell me how this makes sense. There were three meetings between Carter and the loan shark to set up this loan over the last two weeks. Rose Ramsey went with Carter to each meeting."

"We already know Miss Ramsey and Mr. Carter were seen stepping out together. This loan is the reason why. She accompanied Mr. Carter because of her concern for Mr. Denbrough."

"I'll give you that, but according to De Shields' stoolie, Denbrough was supposed to get the hundred thousand last Sunday morning during Rose's party."

Chinaman had trouble believing me, so I held the transcript to let him read for himself. The more he read, the more disappointed he appeared to be. "Oh, my."

"You said a mouthful, brother. Oh, my."

Chapter Ten

There was nothing more to see in De Shields' office, and I had no idea where else to search for the peeper, so Chinaman and I tidied up after ourselves then went back to the Cosmopolitan for a late dinner and some sleep.

I forgot to tell Chinaman I wanted to wake up early the next morning. My plan was to check in at the Lafayette, see how everything was going, then scoot over to De Shields' apartment and hopefully corner him before he left for the day. As it turned out Chinaman let me sleep in.

The telephone woke me up. Chinaman answered it in the bedroom, where he had set up an ironing board so he could press some of my careworn clothes. "It's for you, sir," he called out. "It's Mr. Lee. He says it is urgent."

I jumped off the couch and picked up the extension. "Hey, Canada."

"Sassafras! Where are you?" He sounded upset. Not angry, but uneasy.

"Don't'cha know? You called me?"

"We mean, why aren't you at the Lafayette?"

It dawned on me what I had forgotten to do. "I must have overslept. I'm sorry. Is there some kind of trouble? Is Orson okay?"

"Orson is fine, but he is very unhappy. Everyone is. You have to hurry and come down here. We need you."

"Canada, what's wrong?"

"The police are here. They're looking for Ben."

That didn't sound right. "What do you mean, they're 'looking' for Ben? He's right there, isn't he?"

"No. Nobody knows where he is, not even Rose. The last time anyone saw him was early this morning at the Hotel Theresa."

"What was he doing there?"

"According to the police, he went there to meet Andre De Shields. Sassafras, De Shields is dead, and the cops suspect Ben killed him."

Chapter Eleven

We arrived at the Lafayette to find two uniform officers and the youngest plainclothes detective I ever saw questioning the Unit. The cast and most of the crew were split between the two beat cops. Orson, Canada, Jack Carter, and Rose were being interrogated by the dick, an austere man nearly ten years younger than me with a whetted face, black eyes, and a hawk-bill nose.

As soon as Canada spied Chinaman and me entering the auditorium he pointed us out to the copper, who motioned everyone in his party to follow him as he started up the center aisle to meet us half way.

The detective looked at me and asked, "You Winters?"

I confessed.

He pointed at Chinaman. "Who's this?"

"Edward Everett Horton. Who are you?"

"Detective Sergeant Stan Dancer. I'm with homicide. Can I assume you already know why I'm here?"

"Yes."

"Good. Word has it you bumped into the late Mr. Andre De Shields once or twice since Sunday morning. Did you happen to see him yesterday?"

I peeked at Orson, who was standing directly behind Dancer and beside Carter. Welles knew what I wanted to know and wagged his head no, something Dancer didn't notice but Carter did.

"Can't say I did," I lied.

"But you were both working on the Norton Denbrough murder."

Chinaman cleared his throat theatrically. "Excuse me, sir, but to be fair to Mr. Kanter, there is no conclusive evidence that Mr. Denbrough was murdered. To be frank, no one can absolutely prove he is even dead."

"If you mean we haven't found his body, you're right," Dancer said, taking Chinaman's objection in stride. "But as far as that conclusive evidence jazz goes, that's a different matter. We found Denbrough's coat last night in the sewer pipes a few blocks from Ramsey's brownstone."

There was a chorus of "What?"s, followed by an unintelligible ruckus of individual questions.

"Simmer down! Simmer down!" The detective's stern face flushed pink. "I'm not in the mood to answer any questions. I came here to get some answers."

"At least tell us how you found it," Carter insisted. "How do you know the coat belongs to Norton?"

"Because it has his name stitched into a tag under the collar. Is that good enough for you, Carter? As for how we found it, we sifted it out from the silt mucking up the sewers left over from last weekend's storms."

Orson asked, "How can you know rather or not Norton Denbrough was wearing the coat when...(Welles caught himself)...*if* he went into the sewer?"

"Maybe because its pockets were weighted down, which, by the by, is a damn fine way to make sure a body you're dumping into any quantity of water is going to stay drowned."

"Den maybe he ain' dead," Rose said, wild with hope. "Ef his coat pockets were weighted, den maybe he was alive ef he went into de sewer. He might haf lived."

Dancer shook his head. "I doubt it. Even if he was alive when he went in, that runoff was too violent. But I don't think he was alive at the time. Your friend Carter can tell you how we drag plenty of corpses out of Long Island Sound with bullets in their heads and their feet stuck in cement. If you're going to kill someone, better safe than sorry is the key to success. Victims can be uncooperative when it comes to giving up their lives."

Rose didn't like what she heard very much. She was going to cry, hiding her face in Jack Carter's shoulder before the first tear fell. Carter, straining to keep his composure even as the whites grew wider behind his irises, patted her head and asked Dancer, "Do you have any more questions for us?"

"No. You two are excused. But don't try leaving the Lafayette until I'm through here. Either of you so much as look at an exit door, I'll slap the nippers on you and throw you in the can for trying to aid a fugitive."

"We've told you, Dancer. Neither Rose or I know where Ben is."

"I heard you, brother. And you heard me."

Carter's right hand twitched. "Consider us on guard." The big man led Rose away towards the dressing rooms.

"I believe I'll assist Jack with Rose, if that's all right with you, sergeant," Orson said. Dancer replied he couldn't care less.

Canada asked Dancer, "Couldn't you have said all that to Rose with a bit more tact?"

"Why?" the cop asked. "She's a big girl."

"What kind of an excuse is that?"

"Ease off, Canada," I said, surprising my friend and Dancer. "He's only doing his job." I looked at the sleuth. "A jitney says you were interested in seeing how Rose and Carter behaved when you told them point blank about Denbrough's coat."

The copper was appreciative. "Good guess, but you'd still lose two and a half cents. You're only half right."

"Half?"

"Afraid so. I also wanted to see how they reacted to what I didn't tell them."

Chinaman interrupted. "I'm afraid I am confused."

"Buddy, I left out the best parts. For instance, Denbrough's coat pockets weren't just weighted down; they were weighed down with silver dollars. Dozens of them. Between all the water that wool soaked in and all of those coins, the damned coat weighed more than William Howard Taft in full dress."

"Who'd waste all that money to sink a corpse?" Canada asked.

"That's what I'd like to know, brother."

"But there was no body?" I asked, double-checking.

"We haven't found one yet. Like I said, that runoff was cruel. If Denbrough's stiff was wearing the coat when it went into the sewer, those currents were more than strong enough to tug his corpse out of the sleeves and carry it off to the Atlantic."

"Have you notified Mr. Denbrough's family?" Chinaman asked.

Dancer nodded yes. "Last night. An hour after we found the coat. That was two in the morning. The same time an eyewitness saw Ben Kanter at the Hotel Theresa."

"This is where I get confused," I said. "What the hell was De Shields doing at Harlem's swankiest hotel last night? And why was Ben there? How did he even know where De Shields was?"

The dick shrugged. "I was counting on you telling me."

"There's something Sassafras doesn't know," Canada said. "De Shields was here last night talking with Ben and Rose. They had an argument. Carter tried to mediate, but that started a second argument, between him and De Shields."

"What?" *De Shields came here?* "When was that?"

"About five thirty. Right after Chinaman and you left for the day."

Dancer said, "De Shields talked with Ramsey and Kanter out in the mezzanine. Nobody could make out what they were saying, but everybody heard them shouting at each other. Carter tried to pitch in and square things, like your friend said, but that only made matters worse."

"Why were they arguing?"

"According to Ramsey's statement, De Shields implied that he had evidence linking her to Denbrough's murder. Kanter got noisy when he tried to defend her. When Carter showed up De Shields implied he had evidence linking him as well. Finally De Shields decided he'd done enough damage and blow, but not before calling Kanter a 'patsy' and a 'sap.' These two words were spoken loud enough so everyone in the auditorium has attested to their accuracy."

Hearing De Shields was at the Lafayette right after I left made my back teeth itch. After tailing him all day Tuesday, I didn't like the idea he might have turned the tables and camped outside the Lafayette Tuesday night, waiting for me to leave before hassling with Rose and Carter.

"Who saw Kanter at the Theresa last night?" I asked.

"A bellman. He was on De Shields' floor at the time delivering ice. Some swell San Francisco couple was throwing a real shing-ding in their suite. On his way back to the elevator the bellman spied Kanter jawing with De Shields."

"When did De Shields register?"

"Right after the night manager came to work at eleven."

Canada asked if the bellman knew Ben.

"No, but the bellman's description matches Kanter note for note. Maybe he shaved off a few inches when it comes to height, but aside from that the bellman couldn't have described our man better if he gave me a photograph."

Chinaman wasn't satisfied. He had an idea he wanted to chase. "It's only natural Mr. Kanter would want to talk with Mr. De Shields. The detective made unsubstantiated accusations against the woman he loved. Mr. Kanter would want to learn if Mr. De Shields did in fact possess any evidence."

"I won't argue with you there, Mr. Horton." Dancer winked at me.

"His name is Chinaman," I said.

"No!" The copper made a face, mock surprise.

"It gets better. He's my valet."

The surprise turned genuine. "Go on!"

Unaffected by the banter, Chinaman continued the chase. "Taking a cue from Sergeant Dancer, I believe it's critical not to forget what we don't know. We don't know how Mr. Kanter located Mr. De Shields. We don't know why Mr. De Shields was at the Hotel Theresa. Most importantly, we don't know if Mr. Kanter murdered Mr. De Shields. Sergeant, you said the bellman saw Mr. Kanter knocking on the detective's door, but did he see Mr. De Shields answer?"

"Sure did, and let me save you some time. You want to know if anyone saw Kanter shoot De Shields. Nope. Did anyone see *anybody* shoot De Shields? Same answer. Oh, plenty of folks heard the shots, but by the time the guests screwed up the berries to investigate, the killer was long gone."

"This bellman eyeballed Ben around two?" I asked.

"That's what I said."

"When were the shots fired?"

"Approximately a quarter after six."

"That's four hours. How do you know Ben didn't leave between two and six?"

Chinaman agreed. "Someone else could have come along at six fifteen and killed Mr. De Shields. Perhaps the night manager would know if anyone else visited him this morning."

Dancer gave the Big C a weird look. "What are you talking about? He didn't even know about Kanter!"

Chinaman was lost until Canada explained, "Negroes are not allowed to register or visit guests in their rooms at the Hotel Theresa. The only Negroes allowed inside the hotel are employees. Ben must have sneaked in."

"Then why wasn't Mr. Kanter escorted out of the hotel last night?"

"Because the bellman never reported him to the front desk," Dancer answered. "De Shields saw the bellman as soon as he opened his door, pulled out some Crackerjack box badge, and said he was an on-duty police officer. Told the bellman it wasn't worth his job ratting on Kanter to the desk clerk. The poor guy zipped his lip until we started questioning the hotel staff after the shooting."

"That's a risky lie," I said. "De Shields must have wanted to talk with Ben as much as Ben wanted to talk with him."

"Sounds like. Anyway, the manager claims no one stopped at the front desk to see De Shields all night."

"So, even with four hours between being seen with De Shields and the shooting, Ben's your suspect."

"You bet, pal. Just like we suspect him of weighing down Denbrough because he was standing in front of an open manhole. Kanter was right where he shouldn't have been on both occasions."

Canada snorted, disgusted. "Being at the scene of a crime does not make a person a criminal."

"That's true, but it will make you a suspect every time." Dancer's voice was as agreeable as a sleeping basset hound.

"Pardon me, sergeant, but to us it sounds as if you're saying Ben is guilty until proven innocent."

"Well, excuse me, Lee, but you're starting to come off like one of those screwy Bolsheviks squatting on your front walk. They seem to think, just because your director is a white pup, your play is going to be a minstrel show. Now is that fair?"

Oh-oh. The hound was awake and beginning to growl, while Canada was an eyelash away from popping his cork. I spoke my friend's name. "You two going off at half cock isn't going to settle anything. Go get some air."

"Sassafras..."

"Do it. For me."

Canada didn't want to back down but he did, and I wouldn't forget that I owed him.

After he was gone, Dancer said, "Sorry about the Bolshevik crack.

Your buddy was pressing the wrong button is all."

"Have you been a sergeant long?" Chinaman suddenly asked.

Dancer didn't like the question until he caught Chinaman's drift. Then he grinned. "A few weeks. This is my first time in charge of an investigation."

"What a coincidence! This is the first time Mr. Winters and I have ever investigated anything!" My valet couldn't have been more delighted.

The copper looked at me as if to ask if he heard correctly, not sure rather he should laugh or sigh. He ended up doing some of both.

"I don't blame Lee for getting tough with me. In a way we are railroading Kanter. All we've got is circumstantial evidence. Sure, we've got more than enough to bury him, fine, but that doesn't reassure me. I prefer evidence I can put on my desk. I want a statement from a witness telling me he saw Denbrough being dumped into the sewer. I want the heater that killed De Shields, fingerprints on the butt."

"Any idea what kind of gun killed him?"

"Not for certain. It was large caliber. Fires seven slugs. Ballistics is working on the identification. The whole shooting was real sloppy. All seven bullets were fired, and three managed to hit De Shields. We had to dig the other four pills out of the wall he must have been standing in front of."

"Mr. De Shields stood in place while his killer shot at him?" Chinaman gasped.

"Can't say. For all we know the first three slugs hit him, then the killer went on firing after De Shields was knocked to the floor by their impact. Firing seven times in any case tells me the shooter was hot about something when he shot De Shields."

"And Ben was upset with De Shields when he left the Lafayette yesterday," I said, finishing Dancer's line of reasoning.

"That's what people tell me. Of course, Carter wasn't very happy with him, either. Neither was Ramsey, for that matter. And they both had better motives for killing him. They just didn't leave the theater last night, not like that would have stopped Carter. All he'd have to make is a phone call."

I nodded. "We know about his mob friends, although Jack Carter doesn't strike me as a guy to let other people settle his disagreements."

"Me, neither. But say he is mixed up with Denbrough's murder and De Shields did have something on him. It wouldn't be too bright, Carter putting the kibosh on De Shields himself."

"In which case," Chinaman said, "perhaps Mr. Kanter is being used as a patsy."

"That's what I'd like to know, brother."

Curious to find out as much about what the bulls knew as I could, I asked Dancer if he had sent any cops by De Shields' office to snoop around. He stared at me with the same weird look he gave Chinaman earlier. "Yeah. What's left of it."

"Say again?"

"You don't know?" By my blank expression he could tell I didn't have the foggiest idea what he meant. "De Shields' office was torched this morning. Fire department was called in around eight. Not much more than smoke damage to the adjoining offices, but his rooms were gutted."

"Christ. You're sure it's arson?"

"Positive. The firebug jimmied the door, then struck a match to a bunch of papers in a wastebasket and set it on a sofa. Place went up like kindling. By some strange coincidence De Shields had sunk a safe in the floor under the sofa. The cheap piece of garbage buckled under the heat. There were some papers inside, but there isn't anything left of them now but ashes."

That's two for two, Sassafras, I thought. *You, Chinaman, and Ben seem to have something in common. We're at the right place at the wrong time.*

"How about where De Shields lives?" I asked. "Did that go up in smoke, too?"

"No. As far as we can tell no one has stepped foot in there since De Shields left for work yesterday. For all the good it does us. We didn't find anything there worth a crap to this case."

"Terrific," I said. "De Shields is on ice. His office is scorched by someone out to destroy something in his safe. Both jobs are rinky-dink at best, which seems to rule out Jack Carter or anyone he can enlist. But Ben Kanter, not a professional criminal, was spotted with De Shields last night after having an argument with the shamus earlier in the evening over Rose."

"Kanter does have a motive for both crimes, as well as a motive for killing Norton Denbrough. It all makes for a pretty package."

Chinaman finished the round. "Except no one knows why Mr. De Shields was at the Hotel Theresa."

Dancer peeked around the amphitheater to be sure he wouldn't be overheard, then asked us in a low voice, "Do you know if De Shields was seeing anyone?"

I wasn't ready for the question. "You mean like a girl?"

"A dame. A mama. Whatever."

"Uhhh...I don't know. I told you, De Shields and I weren't exactly buddies. Why? You think he was making time with a broad at the Theresa?"

The detective sighed. Scratched his head. "Like I said before, I was hoping you might tell me. Nobody else seems to know." Dancer deliberated something then shook his head, so hard you could hear all the different clues rattle. He seemed to be trying to get his thoughts to fall into a sensible order, sort of like dropping wooden blocks on the floor and hoping they'll randomly spell a word.

"Want to tell us before you do yourself an injury?"

He looked at me, then Chinaman, then figured he had nothing to lose. "When we found De Shields this morning, he was wearing his undershirt and trousers. No dress shirt, no socks, no shoes. And his bed was a mess. Sheets yanked out from the corners, blankets on the floor, the works. Either he'd been having one hell of a nightmare or one hell of a good time."

Now that is interesting. "You see! There you go! Maybe Ben didn't hang around until six to shoot De Shields after all. Maybe De Shields got tangled up in his own lover's quarrel."

Dancer looked at me as he screwed his eyes into a very tight stare. "There are all kinds of possibilities. I can even think of some sick ones involving Kanter and De Shields."

Chinaman was shocked. I muttered, "Oh, come on!"

"Hey, as private dicks go, in my book De Shields was okay. But as far as any of us cops know the guy hasn't dated a skirt in the nine years since his wife died. Believe it or not he was a handsome bum before he put on some extra weight. Some of the older single gals working the clerical pool at the precinct weren't timid about dropping hints they were available, but he was too shy to ask any of them out. Now he turns up like he did this morning. You tell me what to think."

The eternal optimist, Chinaman suggested, "Perhaps he preferred women who were not associated with his work. If he was involved with a woman, it may turn out that his murder has nothing to do with either Mr. Kanter or Mr. Denbrough."

The copper smirked. "What are you trying to do? Give me a headache?"

I thought it was funny. Even Dancer laughed. Chinaman, as expected, just smiled.

I said, "Listen, I'm sorry I don't know more about how De Shields wound up at the Theresa. Can you give me a day or two to think over whatever we jawed about Sunday and Monday? Maybe I'll remember something you can use. I mean, the sooner this whole mess is mopped up, the better for Welles and his troupe."

"That's no lie. I heard about the waltz he took with that crackpot yesterday. Also heard how you were Johnny-on-the-spot. Nice going."

"Just doing my job."

"Yeah. I know how it is." And I believed him.

"Not to change the subject, but you mind if I ask a favor?" I told Dancer I wanted to take a look at De Shields' hotel room and wondered if he could finagle a police pass for me.

The copper looked at me from the corner of his eyes. "I don't suppose it would hurt none. I'll call the Theresa and tell them to expect you. If you want to see the night manager at the same time, I already told you when he comes to work."

"Eleven."

"Right. Naturally I can depend that you'll tip me to anything we might have overlooked."

I nodded. Chinaman did, too, don't ask me why.

The detective handed me his business card. "My home number is on there, too. Don't be slack getting on the horn if you do find something."

I told him I would and Dancer walked away. Chinaman was standing right beside me when he mumbled, "Why did you and Mr. Welles lie to Sergeant Dancer?"

"You think I know why Orson lied?"

"Do you know why you lied, Mr. Winters?"

"Sure I do. Because I haven't a clue about what's going on." I grabbed Chinaman by the arm and steered him into the lobby. When he asked if we shouldn't be joining Mr. Welles, I told him we would get to Orson in a minute. "We need to talk, and there aren't as many ears out here."

"I still can't understand why you lied."

"Don't think of it as lying. Think of it as postponing telling the truth."

"However you look at it, lying is lying."

"Fine. I lied. But I had to. Somebody torched De Shields' office so something in that floor safe would be destroyed. We've got to find out what the firebug was after. Baker's dossier, Thompson's prescription, or the transcript?"

"The transcript seems likeliest, sir. Unless, of course, the arsonist was after something he believed to be in the safe that actually wasn't."

There were times when Chinaman could throw a screwball that would turn Dizzy Dean green with envy. "Now you're giving me a headache."

"I'm sorry, Mr. Winters."

"Look, whoever made a cinder out of De Shields' office is probably the same joker who plugged De Shields. I say we give the hardworking bum the benefit of the doubt. He knew what he was after, he knew it was in the safe, but he didn't know how to get his hands on it so he took the next best option."

"You're assuming the felon is a man. There is no reason to suspect isn't a woman."

"All the better that I lied then, since we have to find out if De Shields was sleeping with someone last night. If he was, was it a steady girl, somebody's wife, or a whore? And, whoever it was, was she with De Shields at either two or six fifteen?"

"It seems a daunting task."

I winked and gave Chinaman a friendly punch on the shoulder. "Never fret, Big C. Don't forget, whoever killed De Shields doesn't know we read everything in the floor safe. So before I spill the beans to Dancer, I'm going to visit with Miss Thompson's lover and Father Divine. Think about it. They might be more willing to talk to a private dick than a cop. I'm also going to ring up Checker Cab to see if De Shields rode in any more hacks after he left here and before he checked in at the Theresa."

Chinaman mulled over my words and finally agreed. "It appears to be the most logical course, however it is extremely unethical."

"Logic?" I said, choking down a guffaw. "Did I hear you say 'logic'?"

"Yes, sir."

"Are you kidding? I'm a thirty-five year old ex-baseball player trying to solve not one but two murders now and a case of arson. We're up to our armpits in Shakespeare, boy wonders, Communists, voodoo witch doctors, and sacrificial goats. And you're talking to me about logic?"

He mulled over my words, then smiled a very wide smile, his face beaming. "When you put it that way, Mr. Winters, it does sound most engaging, doesn't it?"

I give up. I waved for him to follow me to the dressing rooms. "You're to die for, Chinaman. Come on."

Chapter Twelve

Orson was as angry as a wet hen. For the record, so were Rose and Jack Carter, although he hid it well, and I'm sure wherever Canada was he was unhappy, too. Dancer had put them all in a sour mood, but Orson was more upset that the cop's interruption had put the brakes on rehearsals just when the actors were making progress. "Now all that headway is lost," Welles moaned. "The bubble is burst. The game is up."

"That's nonsense," Jack Carter insisted. "Things were running a bit ragged, I'll give you that, but everything is coming together. I can feel it. Besides, there's still time to run through the play at least twice before it's time to quit today. You have to give your troupe a chance. Show some faith."

The pep talk had some affect. Welles perked up enough to ask Rose if she felt like joining rehearsals again or if she'd rather go home. A sensible lady, she said, "Might's well keep busy. Nothin' Ah can do fo' Ben."

"Fine," Orson agreed. "Let's give it a go and see what happens." And the three left to get back to business, something I was eager to do myself.

I told Chinaman I was going to scoot, and asked him to stay with Welles after I left. "Stick with him this time while I'm gone. If you run out of rehearsal before I get back, escort Orson home. Ask Canada to join you. The way things are going, the more the merrier, if you know what I mean."

He did and we split up, Chinaman heading for the amphitheater and me for the Lafayette's box office, where I could use the telephone in private.

I asked the operator to connect me with Checker Cab, and before the second ring a dispatcher with an inability to pronounce his Rs answered. Taking a couple of seconds to introduce myself, I asked him if his log showed a fare leaving the Astoria Tuesday night around the time De Shields would have called.

It did. What it didn't show was another fare for that driver until after nine thirty, which made me want to talk with the man even more than before. "Is there any way I can ask your driver some questions? I'll make it worth his while."

"Hey, no problems there. Only he don't come back on duty for a couple of days yet. He moonlights from his regular job whenever there's an open hack, and his turn don't come up again till then."

As far as giving out the driver's name, that was against company policy. "Hey, you'd be amazed how many bums get a grudge against a cabbie, and send their big brothers after 'em to take a poke at 'em for the bittiest little thing."

I asked if the dispatcher was allowed to call the driver and tell him I'd like to talk with him. "Hey, no problem. Except he ain't got a phone. Can't afford one. That's why he moonlights."

I was running out of options as well as patience. *This is worse than a marathon!* I tried asking if another cabbie could deliver my message to the driver's home. "Hey, no problem as far as I can see. Only you'll have to pay the fare for a standard delivery to the guy's home."

"Sure. Of course. Can you bill me?"

No. That would be against company policy. "You'll have to come to our office and pay in advance. Sorry. We get a lot of skips and deadbeats. You know? Nothing personal."

I asked for the address, which was clear across town. No way I could get there and meet all the people I wanted to see that afternoon both. "I can't drop by until later tonight or tomorrow."

"Hey, any time is fine. We never close. And if your driver drops in before then, I'll have him give you a jingle here from the office."

I thanked him and gave him the phone numbers to the Lafayette and the Cosmopolitan. Hanging up, I left the theater.

∽∾

To be honest, I was sort of nervous when I asked the desk clerk at the Tamara to ring the penthouse. Richy digs have always made me feel like the pauper visiting his look-alike at the castle. But, to make matters worse, I had no idea what I was going to say. This was not the sort of dance I attended every day.

"Who should I announce?" the clerk asked. He was the usual puny creep of a guy who landed these sorts of jobs, with a pencil-thin mustache only good-looking slobs like Fairbanks get away with wearing, and his hair slicked back like Duke Ellington. On first impression I liked him as much as I liked Dell Joyce-Armstrong.

"Tell the Countess a friend of Edna Thompson's is here."

He did, and I was invited up.

Stepping out of the elevator, I waded through the moss that substituted for carpet in the Tamara's halls and pressed the buzzer to the top floor's suite. The door opened and I caught my breath.

The woman standing in the threshold looked like Kay Francis in

Trouble in Paradise, maybe only prettier. She was a brunette, her hair curled elegantly above the neckline, had almond eyes, a tiny V of a nose, and replete lips. Her clingy black collarless silk gown, trimmed at the elbows with fur, covered but didn't dare hide her slender figure.

"You're Edna's friend?" the Countess asked, her voice gilded with an accent, don't ask me from where.

"Yes, ma'am. In a way. My name's Sassafras Winters, and I work for the Harlem Unit."

"You're the director's guardian." She was stating a fact.

"Bodyguard? Yes. Well, actually I'm a private investigator."

She frowned gracefully, not approving of my occupation. Instead of shutting her door, which was probably her preference, she maintained her manners and asked me inside.

Her living room was at the end of a short narrow foyer. For the second time in as many minutes I held my breath. This was a classy flat. One wall was made up out of nothing but windows, the drapes tied back to reveal a Grand Canyon view of Manhattan. Elsewhere a fire was popping away behind a screen, an oak log on top of a gas teaser. Positioned in front of the fire were a silk Oriental rug and a nice rose davenport, Scotch and swish on a tabouret and ice in a bucket within easy reach.

"Did I interrupt anything?" I asked.

"Only a quiet moment." The Countess sat down on the davenport and took her drink. "Would you care for some? You'll have to pour your own."

"No, thanks. I only drink carrot juice."

"Then what can I do for you, Mr. Winters?"

"Mind if I sit?" Before she could say yes I plopped down in a chair upholstered in a faded floral pattern next to the windows. "I wanted to ask you about a visitor you had yesterday, another private detective, Andre De Shields."

I thought she might spit on the rug. "Are you two associated?"

"The only folk De Shields is associating with right now are angels." She was confused. "Excuse me. De Shields is dead. He was murdered this morning." I explained why the police suspected Ben Kanter, and how Ben was already a suspect in Norton Denbrough's murder.

"Yes. Edna told me all about the late Mr. Denbrough earlier this week."

"I'm not convinced Ben killed Denbrough. De Shields was. Of course we were looking at things from different sides of the fence. He was working for Norton's family, and you already know what side I'm on."

"What I don't know is why you're bothering me." She sipped her drink.

"Okay. De Shields came here yesterday. I saw him here, so there's no denying that. What I don't know is why."

"Is that any of your concern?"

"It is now that he's dead. Especially since De Shields kept a copy of a filled methadone prescription for Miss Thompson in his office. He also knew about your affair with her."

The Countess' eyes narrowed into slits while her fingers tightened around her gold-edged tumbler. My bet was she was either going to shatter the glass or pitch it at my head, but breeding won out again and she restrained herself.

"Perhaps you should leave," she suggested, her voice suddenly husky.

"I can't do that. If I leave without getting some answers, there's a good chance Miss Thompson's career and your relationship are going to suffer. I'd just as soon avoid both unless there's call for it."

Maybe what I said caught her off guard, or maybe she believed in my sincerity. Whichever, she wanted to hear more.

"The police dropped by the Lafayette this morning asking about Ben. It's no secret De Shields and me jawed about the Denbrough case a couple of times, so they asked me if he ever said anything that might have something to do with his murder. I dummied up about anything they didn't know already, but pretty soon they're going wise up that De Shields told me more then I let on. Now I don't mind taking some brass from the cops when it's for a good cause, but I'd like to be sure this is a good cause."

The lady weighed my words, absently stroking her glass, then nodded.

"All right, Mr. Winters. You've been fair with me, so I'll try to return the favor. De Shields tried to blackmail me yesterday."

Huh? "Excuse me?"

"Are you shocked? Did you assume he was incapable of extortion?"

"Well...yeah."

Try as she might the Countess couldn't check her smile, which wasn't malicious, just mischievous.

"Sorry to disappoint you," she said, "although, when it came time to cut to the chase, he didn't have the stomach for it. He told me he wanted five hundred thousand dollars. If I didn't relinquish that amount to him, he would make sure evidence of my affair with Edna would become available to every society reporter in Manhattan."

Half a million bucks? "What did you do?"

"I made it clear to him that lesbians of our prominence have no need to hide our sexual inclinations. We can afford not to. Attend any Van Vecthen party on Central Park West and you'll find dozens of homosexuals mingling with the celebrities and Lorelei Lees. We all run together."

"That's fine, ma'am, but what about the general public? Whether they're colored or white, most people buying tickets to *Macbeth* won't approve of what you two women are doing. Miss Thompson's comeback might be washed up before it gets going again."

A brief but passionate despair flashed behind the Countess' eyes.

"You were trying to bluff him."

She nodded. "What I said about our Central Park West crowd is true, but you're right when it comes to the public."

"Did he buy it?"

She nodded again.

I couldn't believe it. De Shields wasn't dumb. He understood people better than to fall for a bluff like this. The Countess had said De Shields didn't have the stomach for blackmail, but maybe he lacked the heart to go through with it. "What about the methadone? Why was he hanging on to a copy of Miss Thompson's prescription?"

The sweetest snort this side of paradise piped from the lady's wee nose. Even when she made the effort it was impossible for her to be one hundred percent vulgar.

"He had jumped to the conclusion she was an addict, even though he knew full well Edna had been in a serious accident. Her doctor was prescribing methadone as an analgesic for her back until a few months ago. She no longer requires it."

"Okay." That made sense. But why would De Shields risk blackmailing the Countess, much less ask for so much jack? *This tête-à-tête was supposed to clear things up, not muddy the waters.*

"Will you tell the police?"

Why? I thought. *There's nothing to gain by telling them.* So I shook my head. "Not if you're playing straight with me."

"Thank you."

I got up and she stood to escort me out.

"Does Edna know you're here?"

"No, ma'am. And as long as you asked I'd rather she didn't, at least for now. The same for anyone else."

"Yes. I'd prefer that."

"I figured you might. Mind if I trouble you about one more thing? Is there anything you can tell me about the Denbroughs?"

The Countess was at the door when she stopped and turned, surprised.

I said, "I'm just thinking, since you both mingle in high society, you might know a thing or two about them."

"No more than they know about me, I'm sure." She seemed to appreciate my naivety. "The Denbroughs gravitate towards different circles than mine, Mr. Winters. They're old blood. I'm from older blood, but I don't let it get me tired."

"Have you heard any poop about Beatrice Denbrough getting hitched to Dell Joyce-Armstrong?"

"Just what I read between the lines in the newspapers. The Colonel wants his Dell wedded to a pretty girl of breeding, and the Denbroughs desperately need to replenish their bank accounts. Tell me, Mr. Winters, have you ever read Oscar Wilde?"

My turn to be surprised. "In college, I think. Maybe."

"Let me give you some advice. Wilde wrote, 'In matters of grave importance, style, not sincerity, is the vital thing.' Bare that in mind whenever you deal with the Joyce-Armstrongs or the Denbroughs."

Chapter Thirteen

After the Tamara I went straight to Heaven and found a Negro half a head taller and fifty pounds heavier than me guarding the door.

"May Ah help yo'?" he asked.

People waiting in line for their lunch told me I had to talk with the doorman if I wanted inside. They said lines tended to be long on Wednesdays for some reason, and when this happened the meals had to be served in shifts. The doorman's job was to make sure only a set number of people entered for each shift.

"I wonder if I might see Father Divine."

"Wha' would yo' care to see de Messenger 'bout?"

"'Messenger?'"

"De Living Word. Father Divine. De Messenger."

"They're one short for bridge, ain't they?"

The doorman's stare suggested that he had already heard any joke I could think up. I wasn't in the mood to challenge him, so I asked him to tell Divine, "Sassafras Winters has come to pay his respects. I knew Andre De Shields."

The peeper's name seemed to ring a bell with the big man, who told me to wait while he passed on my message to the Trinity. Two minutes later he poked his head out the front door and waved for me to enter.

Inside Heaven the doorman led the way up a flight of crotchety wooden stairs that opened into a dining hall.

"Yow!" I was impressed.

"Big, huh?" he said.

The brownstone's second floor had been completely razed for this one purpose. A grand head table had been placed at the far end of the hall, two more tables stretching from either end. Practically every seat was taken, the hall whirring with the sounds of conversation.

"How many people can you serve here?" I asked.

"Three hundred's de limit at one time, but we'll feed twice dat many again befo' de shifts are done." Pointing to a man sitting in the middle of the head table, the doorman said, "Dat's Father Divine," then left me to return to his post.

God turned out to be a thin bald Negro man. Maybe sixty. He was less than five feet tall wearing a gray pinstriped suit, a bright striped shirt with a Barrymore collar, and matching tie. I waited where I was and watched while Divine diligently blessed a procession of platters and bowls graced with vegetables, meats, bread and desserts. Many of the diners and all of the angels, as Divine's most devout followers liked to call themselves, started singing a hymn while they waited:

"I want to go through, Lord,
I want to go through.
Take me through, Lord,
Take me through.

"Have your way, Lord,
Have your way.
I'll obey, Lord.
I'll obey."

When the last dish left his hand Divine stood to speak to his eager congregation in a soft, high voice.

"For the first time we have the true gospel on earth. I have left the world of Imagination, I have entered the world of Recognition, I have come into the world of Realization."

The dining hall echoed with a jubilant "Amen" and then everyone dug in.

The service over, I walked over to Divine. The little man acted happy to meet me, and asked an angel sitting next to him to give up her seat so we could chat.

Divine said, "Andre told me something about you the last time we talked. He seemed impressed with you."

"Really?" I would have liked to believed him.

"Oh, I know Andre could be contrary, but he had to confess to me that you exhibit a dogged nature, and to him persistence was a quality. And I don't think it hurt that you were once a ballplayer. He loved the game. He used to go to Ebbets Field whenever possible."

"I didn't know that. We only met last Sunday."

"Yes. I know. Andre and I shared a confidence, Mr. Winters. He told me a good deal about many things, including Norton Denbrough. Poor man. And Ben Kanter has murdered again, this time my friend. I'll miss Andre here on earth, and rejoice when we meet again in Heaven."

I was half-tempted to tell Divine I envied De Shields his connections, but decided I would be better off not. Instead, I explained to Divine that I wasn't convinced Ben was guilty of any crime. "Not totally convinced, anyway. Especially when it comes to De Shields' murder."

What I said didn't make sense to Divine. "But the police have a witness."

"Who saw De Shields talking to Ben four hours before he was killed."

"But who else would want to kill him?"

"Private investigators are known to ruffle feathers now and then. Can't you think of anyone with a grudge against De Shields?"

Divine cocked an eyebrow, as if to ask, "How should I know?"

"You kept De Shields on retainer. He didn't tell me, but I found out, never mind how. Believe me no one else is going to find out the way I did."

The little man stared at me for quite a while. From his expression I couldn't tell if he was thinking about my question or trying to decide to throw me out, until he said, "No. I'm certain. Andre made enemies, but anyone not directly involved with this Denbrough affair that begrudged him is either dead or incarcerated. I am absolutely positive."

Cared to swear to that on the Bible? I thought it, but I didn't say it.

"Maybe someone had a bone to pick with him, and neither of you knew it. Things like that happen. It might help if you tell me about the kind of jobs De Shields did for you."

I figured Divine would balk, but he eagerly if indirectly answered. "Many things. He was an invaluable employee. You know, the Docetists may believe as they wish, but rather in the form of Divine or Jesus God is human. Apostle Paul was so right when he wrote, 'Have this mind among yourselves which you have in Christ Jesus, who, though he was in the form of God, did not count equality with God a thing to be grasped, but emptied himself, taking the form of a servant, being born in the likeness of men. And being found in human form he humbled himself and became obedient unto death, even death on a cross.'"

"Come again."

"In this day and age, if I want to walk freely among you, I am answerable to the Internal Revenue Service and therefore vulnerable to questionable documents."

"So De Shields was your examiner?"

"Yes. And, being human, I am as susceptible to a bullet or a shiv as anyone. I purposely assumed the appearance of a timid man in this life as I did nineteen hundred years ago, and while it serves its purposes, it also has its disadvantages."

"Someone threatened you?"

Divine leaned towards me in his chair, whispering beneath the hall's steady babel. "From my lips to your ears only, there are some unscrupulous evangelists such as Elder Lightfoot Michaux, Mother Horn, and Sweet Daddy Grace who would like to see me once more lead the Choir Invisible."

"Your competition wants you rubbed out? Like George Raft and Edward G. Robinson?"

"Precisely like Raft and Robinson! I hired Andre in 1933, soon after a gangster took the Reverend George W. Becton into a Philadelphia alley and shot him in the head. At the time it seemed wise to hire someone to look out for my interests."

"Was De Shields working on anything in particular for you when he died?"

Divine sat back. "Nothing. He hasn't since last summer. Of course he was a fixture on the payroll, although he never received a salary."

"Then how did you pay him?"

"In many ways. He ate here, for one thing, free of charge. Andre had few friends, so he came often for the company. The last time was yesterday afternoon for lunch. Also the church provided him with a place to live and to work."

"His office? You gave him his office? *And* his apartment?"

"Why not?" Divine seemed amused. "The church owns several buildings in New York. It was a mutually beneficial arrangement. More so, my flock infrequently was able to supply him with information that expedited his other investigations, like Norton Denbrough."

"How did they do that?"

"Look around you." Divine stretched out one arm, motioning to the people eating around us. "This is Harlem. Every facet of what makes up the district is represented by the people sitting at my table, in the queue downstairs, and in the dining halls of my other Heavens. With the help of my angels, little goes on in Harlem that I eventually do not hear about."

"So you helped De Shields with the Denbrough case?"

Divine started to speak, then shut his mouth. After that he grinned. "Mr. Winters, do you think you've uncovered providence?" The guy wasn't stupid.

"Right about now I'd settle for a couple revelations. Listen, two people are dead and, like a lot of folks, you think Ben Kanter killed them both. But, like I said, all the evidence against Ben is circumstantial. I never met Denbrough but I did know De Shields, and I would like to be sure that the guy who fries for killing him is the guy who killed him, not *might* have killed him."

The little man weighed his options as he rubbed his bald head once with his right hand then pursed his lips. Eventually he asked, "What is it you need to know?"

I asked Divine if he knew about Denbrough's loan.

"Andre told me about it. He uncovered that through his own sources, although my flock did confirm that one hundred thousand dollars was delivered on schedule, as promised, to Denbrough last Sunday at Miss Ramsey's apartment. Four AM precisely."

"Any idea where the money is now?"

"No."

"Know if anyone was with Denbrough when all that ready changed hands?"

"Yes. Jack Carter was there."

"Anybody else?"

"No."

"Can you tell me how Denbrough got into Rose's bedroom to begin with?"

"Afraid not. Is that important?"

"Maybe." Actually I thought it was damn important. It was a given Denbrough was already in Rose's bedroom by the time De Shields camped out in the alley. But did Rose lock him in before the party started, or did he climb up the fire escape soon after the parlor social was in swing? If the former, maybe Rose had done more with Denbrough than simply lock him in before the party, something that could have set Ben off Sunday morning if he got wind of it. If it was the latter, then where was Denbrough hiding himself before he stowed away in Rose's bedroom?

"How about Rose slipping out with Carter. Know how De Shields found out about that?"

"Miss Ramsey and Carter never tried to hide when they went out together in public. They only went out a few times, and then only to establishments Carter regularly frequents. Being who he is, folks in Harlem are reluctant to spread gossip about Jack Carter. Nevertheless a number of my angels saw them together, and I told De Shields."

"When d'ya tell him?"

"Sunday night."

It was tempting to ask Divine if he knew about De Shields' dossier on him, but my gut instinct warned me to wait, even though keeping secrets was becoming a habit I didn't enjoy. But as far as the dossier on George Baker was concerned, there hadn't been anything in it worth killing over, so I really had nothing to gain by asking.

"How about De Shields' murder?" I asked. "Have your angels heard anything about that?"

Divine looked very proud as he reached into his inside breast pocket and pulled out a carbon copy of the police report. "Pretty slick, eh?" he said as he handed it to me.

I couldn't believe my eyes. "How did you get this?"

"'Mysterious are His ways.' Or, if you don't like that, try, 'Ask me no questions, I'll tell you no lies.'"

"It's all apples and oranges to me."

Everything read the way Dancer had laid it out. De Shields checked into the Theresa soon after eleven Tuesday evening. The bellhop had seen the shamus talking with Ben Kanter outside his room three hours later. There was nothing else to report until shots were heard coming from De Shields' room Wednesday morning. Witnesses found the door opened and the dead man on the floor. There were no reports of anybody fleeing the scene, but the witnesses confessed it had taken the fastest of them several seconds to come out of their own rooms after the shots had been fired. Apparently De Shields had died instantly of bullet wounds to the chest. The precise caliber or model of the weapon hadn't been identified.

"It's a preliminary report," Divine said, reading the disappointment in my eyes. "Perhaps there will be more information in the final report."

"When can you get your hands on that?"

"I'm not at liberty to say, but you'll get a copy as soon as I do."

"Thanks." I offered Divine the report back, but he told me to keep it. "You need it more than I do," he said, and I thanked him again, putting the report in my own breast pocket.

"Is there anything else I might know that could help you?"

That was a good question. And I had a good question to ask him. I just didn't like thinking how the little man was going to react. "Did you know De Shields tried to blackmail someone yesterday?"

Divine didn't flinch. His expression didn't sag. I was going to ask if he had heard me until I realized he wasn't even blinking. The guy was in shock.

"Wh...?" He was going to ask 'who,' but caught himself. "Never mind."

"I can't tell you anyway."

"Never mind," he repeated, turning away to look at the people eating around us. Or "through them" might be a better description. His hands were shaking and his upper lip trembled. It was an impressive display of self-control, and I felt like a heel. It was bad enough the poor Joe had to lose a friend. How much harder was it to lose his respect for De Shields in the same day?

"Why?" Divine asked himself, alone in the hall. "He didn't need money. He had everything he needed. I made sure of that."

"I'm sorry," was the only thing I could think to say. "That was the only reason I asked, because I thought you might have some idea why he tried it." I was suddenly glad I hadn't said anything about the dossier. Maybe keeping quiet wasn't always a bad habit after all.

"We'll do our best to find out." Divine was still looking away from me. "If for no other reason, I'd like to find out for myself." He paused. Breathed deeply, then let it out. "Was there anything else?"

Even if there had been, I still would have said no.

"Fine, " he said. "If you'll excuse me, there are some church matters that need my attention."

He stood, looking tired, like an old dog on its last legs. Before he could walk away I reached out and touched one of his coat sleeves.

"Father Divine, I said he tried. He didn't go through with it. He could have, but he didn't."

The little man stared at me the same way four year olds do when they need to believe in their parents. He stared so long that some of the diners were beginning to take notice. Finally he said, "Then I'll keep the faith. Until we know more. We'll talk later, Mr. Winters. Good night."

Chapter Fourteen

I had a hard time deciding where to go next.

The Hotel Theresa was closest, a short walk down Seventh Avenue on 135th Street. But it wasn't even the shank of the evening, and the night manager wouldn't be on the job for over eight hours. I wasn't in the mood to make two trips, so that errand could wait.

If truth be told, I had an itch to get back to the Lafayette. It pestered me that I didn't know when Orson was going to quit rehearsals, and I had a nagging hunch I should be there when he did. Don't ask me why.

Inside the Lafayette, I peeked into the auditorium to see how far along the play was until the end. On stage the fifth and final act had almost run its course, with Malcome predicting the royal lineage of the realm to Ross, Siward, Thanes, and Macduff. A papier-mâché reproduction of Jack Carter's head, its mouth wide in a never-ending scream, was mounted on a pike in Macduff's hands.

Cool deal, I thought. *Just in the nick of time.*

Upstairs in the balcony Canada and Chinaman were sitting together a few rows behind Orson, the director standing at the foot of the balcony. Canada was half out of his costume, Banquo having given up the ghost in act four. At first glance both he and Chinaman looked like they were concentrating on the stage. After a second look I realized they were staring at Orson, whose concentration definitely was riveted on his actors. Welles was also clutching a ream of paper in his left hand, the precious notes he had been jotting down since early Tuesday morning.

"How's it going?" I whispered, squatting in the aisle beside the two men.

Chinaman didn't seem to hear me. Canada pointed at Orson. I followed with my eyes and spotted the husk of a whiskey bottle laying at the young man's feet.

"That bad, eh?"

"It hasn't gone badly at all," Chinaman said, likewise whispering. "But nothing seems to satisfy Mr. Welles."

"That's for sure," Canada seconded. "When it comes to

Shakespeare we are not an expert, but for what it's worth we agree with Chinaman."

Down on stage Malcome told his comrades, "So thanks to all at once, and to each one, whom we invite to see us crowned at Scone." Virgil Thomson waved his baton, his small orchestra blared the final fanfare, and the curtains came down.

The play was over, and so was the long rehearsal.

Instead of exploding with applause the Lafayette was practically noiseless. Cast and crew waited while the old theater's timbers settled. Everyone from Jack Carter to the third assistant stagehand was anxious to hear Orson's verdict, but the director didn't say a word. He just glared from his perch and weaved a bit from side to side.

Canada bent forward and prompted Welles to speak.

"Very good job, people," the director said, going through the motions, like a cuckoo clock signaling the hour. "Very good. Many thanks to one and all. Come back here Friday evening. Six o'clock. Dinner will be provided as usual. I'll have notes for each of you. That's all. Have a pleasant day off. Rehearsal is finished." He sat down.

And the Lafayette erupted.

Everyone beneath the balcony cheered and clapped, leaped and yelped. Not even Thomson could resist jumping in, rearing back with his right arm and chucking his baton into the air, while Asadata and his weird crew started dancing and whooping like it was Mardi gras.

High spirits are contagious, but can also be painful. The Unit reminded me of us Cubs in 1929 and 1931. Like those teams the troupe had been trying to accomplish something and, after a lot of hard work, had succeeded. But as infectious as the celebrating was, I couldn't forget for a moment that I wasn't one of the players. I was a bystander. All I could do was cheer on the Harlem Unit from the stands like any other spectator.

Orson was slumped in his chair all the while, his sheaf of scribbles clenched in both hands, each line of every page crammed with things to fine tune, rework, or scrap. His face was oily from sweat, his eyes roving and scared. No doubt he was drunk, but that wasn't his whole problem. Welles was acting like a claustrophobic locked inside a coffin. Suddenly, from below, the actors began chanting his name and Orson jumped, jolted out of his nightmare.

"Orson!...Orson!...Orson!...Stand up!...Can't you stand up?"

He could, but it was no small task. Climbing to his feet, Welles tried slipping into character, changing from frightened young man into brilliant director as he leered over the balcony's railing. The act wasn't convincing.

"You're coming with us!" someone yelled from the stage. The cast wanted to celebrate.

"You're coming with us!" a new voice echoed.

Orson didn't speak. Only glared down at the revelers with his crazy eyes. He was drunk. An umpire could see that, but it didn't excuse what he did next.

"I come with no man!" he proclaimed. "I am a free soul!"

All cheering stopped on the beat of a clap.

The Harlem Unit stared at Orson. No one moved. No one spoke.

Then abruptly one of Abe Feder's assistants charged up the center aisle, screaming "Get him out of here!" and pointing to Welles. "Get him out of here before they hit him!"

It was plain to see nobody was in the mood to hurt Orson. The blanket reaction in the house was stunned disappointment.

"Perhaps you ought to help him home, Sassafras." Canada was just as disappointed, but he was more concerned for his director. "He'll be himself once he gets some sleep."

"Mr. Lee and I can attend to matters here," Chinaman added. "We'll wait for you to come back."

There weren't any better ideas on the plate, so I grabbed Orson's arm, maybe a little harder than necessary, and walked him out of the balcony. "My coat," he mumbled.

"Forget your lousy coat. It'll be here when you get back."

Things were bad enough without having to bother with the picketers. I detoured them by taking Welles through a fire exit that emptied into the alley behind the theater, where I had parked Bertha earlier. Marching Welles to the car, I opened the passenger side door and threw him inside. Walking around the front, I slid in behind the wheel and closed the door. When I looked beside me, Orson's seat was empty.

"Where are you?"

I heard a groan. Orson was laying on the floorboard, his big frame wedged under the glove compartment, notes clutched against his chest like a kid holding a stuffed bear.

"I can't do it," he said.

"Do what?"

"Direct this play. I can't do it the way it should be done."

What did I look like all of a sudden? Some kind of dope? "You're not doing this play the way it should be done. That was the idea. Remember?"

"That isn't what I mean!" he wailed. "There's too much to do! I can't fix it all! Can't make it perfect!"

He started trembling, so violently his notes were in danger of being shredded. I reached over and yanked them out of his grasp. "You're drunk."

"Not drunk enough! Not enough to delude myself into believing I can pull this off."

"Damn it, Orson, the play ain't that bad!"

"Who says?"

"I say. Canada Lee says. Even your best buddy Chinaman says so."

Welles did his best to look smug as he tried to find enough room in the cramp space he had wriggled into to straighten up. When that failed he settled for straightening his shirt collar.

"Sassafras, with all due respect, I believe I am a better judge of theater than you, Canada, or even Chinaman."

"Well goody for you." *I need this?* "Let me tell you, buster, you are acting like a grade-A brat. It doesn't take genius to sit in an audience. Just because some bum sitting in the bleachers never played baseball doesn't mean he can't figure out what's going on if he watches enough games."

"Are you making a point? Because if you are, I would appreciate it if you skipped the analogies and say what you mean before I have to throw up."

"I'm telling you that I've seen *Macbeth* over a hundred times in the last month. All right, maybe I can only figure out every other word that's being said, but I can see the play is going to be a gasser. The actors are getting better, and you're doing a great job. I mean it. You've got the arm and you've got the eye. Do you know what I'm saying?"

His lips said, "Yes," but his eyes said, "Huh?"

"*Macbeth* is going to be a knockout. You're a good director. Even so, that doesn't give you the right to insult the Unit. I played for managers who got after their players to get 'em motivated, so that I can understand. But, Christ, Orson, I never figured you for a bigot."

"I am *not* a bigot!" He sneered at me, teeth gritted. "The Harlem Unit of the WPA is the finest collection of people I have ever worked with!"

"Well, right now, I don't think they know that."

"Don't you think I know that?" Orson bowed his head, his anger played out. He was trying to hide his face, but not before I saw one tear rolling down his cheek.

"I wanted complete control," he continued. "Instead I turned into an arrogant schoolboy. You're right. I am a brat. Always have been. Only whelps will call a man a nigger when they can't comprehend the meaning of either word."

I waited to see if he was going to break into a jag. When I was sure Welles had himself in check, I said, "I don't think you're that bad," I said. "Besides, most brats don't often admit their mistakes. There's hope for you."

I pointed out that everyone in the theater could tell he had been drinking and appreciate the pressure directing two straight days of rehearsals had been on him. "Apologize first thing Friday night. Chances are that will square things."

Nothing. Not a word.

"You awake?" I asked.

"Mm-hmm."

"Don't believe me?"

"Can't. I would like to. I sincerely would. But I doubt the Unit will forgive me with just a kind word."

"You're underestimating them."

"Am I? I don't mean to. Nevertheless, it's obvious they'll never trust me again."

"Trust is earned, and you've already earned theirs. Something like this isn't enough to make them doubt you."

He cackled, irritated and unhappy. "After what I've done? No. There's no excuse for what I said."

Orson was determined to feel sorry for himself, wallowing in his mistake with the same zeal he usually reserved for lauding his victories. Not sure what to say next, I started Bertha up and steered her out of the alley onto Seventh Avenue, honking once and waving to the disgruntled protestors.

"If you promise not to tell anyone else," I said, "I'll tell you a secret."

Orson lifted his head. "Will I get a sucker if I do?"

"Just promise and cut out the cute stuff."

"Fine," he sighed. "I promise. What's your secret?"

"The last time I got drunk, I did something ten times as stupid as you just did."

Misery loves company, and Orson never could resist gossip. "I didn't know you had a love child," he said, eyes suddenly bright.

"Not that kind of mistake, you jerk!"

"Oh." He readjusted himself so he could climb off the floor and sit in the passenger seat. "Fine, then. I'm all ears. What did you do that was so horrible?"

I told Orson about how the Cubs took the National League pennant in 1929, and about how I pitched in the last game of the season. "When the last man was out the team wanted to paint the town red. It was an away game, and I was three sheets to the wind before I even made it out of the locker room at Braves' Field. Not that any of my teammates were in much better shape." So off we all went, scouring Boston for tankards of ale and toothsome wenches, and, being champions, we found them.

Welles asked, "Are you absolutely certain you don't have a love child?"

"No! Now clam up." The last thing I remember about that night was gabbing with a bartender around three in the morning. "He was a nice enough guy, except for the way he talked. Had one of those god-awful twangy Massachusetts accents with the flat As."

"Delightful. When are you going to tell me what you did that was so stupid?"

"Is now soon enough for you?" The next morning when I woke up I was surprised to find me in my hotel room instead of on some park bench. "Couldn't work it out in my head how I got there. Not that my head was good for much. It felt like a bear with a bad tooth was rooting around my skull trying to claw his way out." I just wanted to crawl into a hot shower, but I was too far gone in my hangover to stand.

"Then it happened. Somebody lent me a hand and helped me to the shower." Things were looking pretty blurry to me. My best guess was that one of the Cubbies had dragged me back to my room then passed out. Now whoever it was was helping me to the bathroom. The warm water cleared my mind, and when I poked my head and arm out through the curtain to grab some soap from the sink I was feeling pretty good. "And there he was. Chinaman. Sitting on my toilet, polishing my shoes."

"So?"

"Don't you get it? It was the first time I ever clapped eyes on him! And there he was, in my bathroom!"

I finally won Welles' interest. "Where did he come from?"

"He said he was the bartender from the night before."

"Chinaman...*our* Chinaman...tended bar?"

"Hell, that ain't the half of it." When I asked Chinaman why he was in my hotel room, he told me I had hired him to be my valet.

"I did?" I asked.

"Yes," Chinaman said, "you did."

"But I don't need one. I can't afford one."

"That didn't seem to be a consideration last night. I was suggesting you had had quite enough to drink, and you told me I sounded like someone's lost butler. Apparently you felt sorry for me, what with my being misplaced and all, because you offered me this position so I would have a home."

There was only one logical conclusion I could reach. "You're making this up."

"I never lie, Mr. Winters. You may depend on that." He was very stern.

"But I don't want a valet."

"You should have thought of that before you hired me."

"I was drunk! You said so yourself. How could you think I was on the level?"

"At first I didn't." He spat on my shoe then started buffing. "I even explained to you that my accepting any permanent position is out of the question. For reasons I won't comment on, I frequently indulge in sabbaticals with no predetermined durations."

"So what did I say to that?"

I had told him that didn't matter, just so long as Chinaman knew he had a home waiting for him when his trips were over. "There was something touching about your offer," he said. "You were so persistent that I couldn't hurt your feelings by rejecting it. I suppose you sounded a little lost yourself."

My head started pounding again. "I think I'm gonna be sick."

"Shall I get the Rochelle salt?" He sounded sincere.

Orson was fascinated, staring at me like a child sitting on a department store Santa's lap.

"Chinaman's been with me ever since, on and off," I went on. "He'll be under foot, like he is now, for a couple of months, then disappear for six. Then he'll reappear and get in the way for maybe another three months."

"And you don't know where he goes when he's gone?"

"Some of the times. He likes to travel."

"How does he afford it? You can't be paying him much."

"I've never paid him one red cent, and he wouldn't take it if I tried. He's got too much pride, not to mention his own money stashed somewhere. How he comes by it, your guess is as good as mine."

By now Welles had forgotten all about feeling sorry for himself. "This is the best mystery we've had so far! But don't you worry when he's away so long?"

"Nope." Not really. Not a lot. "Well...there was this one time. He up and vanished for damn near a year, and my grandfather and me were convinced we'd seen the last of him. Then, one day, he waltzes through Governor's door, pretty as you please, face all weathered and tan, and crows, 'Thami el Glaoui, Pasha of Marakesh, leader of the Glawa tribe of the Western Atlas, says, 'Howdy, folks!'"

"Odzookens!" Orson was grinning, that interrogation mark of an eyebrow gleefully crooked. "How peculiar."

"Oh, you want peculiar?" *What the hey?* I thought. *I've told him this much.*

"There's more?"

"Haven't you noticed? Chinaman knows everything. I mean *everything*. Who do you think taught me what I know about legal procedures? And he always seems to have been about everywhere at just the right moment. Like how he was at your opening night in Dublin. *Dublin*, for Christ's sakes."

"Now you're exaggerating, Sassafras. That was just a coincidence. And nobody knows everything."

"Wanna bet? I've been trying to stump him for seven years. Can't be done. We'll be walking down the street and, BAM!, out of the blue I'll ask something like, 'What's the melting point of magnesium?'"

"Where did you dig up that question?"

"It was on one of my college exams."

"Did Chinaman know?"

"Uh-huh. 651 degrees Celsius. The boiling point is 1107 degrees Celsius."

Orson still wasn't convinced.

"Okay. Another time he was cleaning the bathroom at my grandfather's tenement. Nobody asked him to do it. He just started doing it. I came in, washed my hands, and asked him to recite the

Turkish alphabet."

"You speak Turkish?"

"No."

"Does Chinaman?

"Seems like. He shot back some gobbledygook that sounded Turkish to me." I didn't tell Welles about Governor stepping out of our apartment to say, "Yep. That sure as hell is right." *Like he knew.*

Orson asked, "How come he knows so much?"

"By going to school. He has about every college degree you can earn."

"Where did he study?"

"Who knows? He won't say, and he's never shown me any of his diplomas, but as far as I'm concerned he's got them. There's no denying he's smart, and he wasn't kidding about lying. Anything dishonest goes down his pipe the wrong way."

We had arrived at Welles' basement flat, 319 West 14th Street. I steered Bertha over to the curb and asked Orson if he needed any help.

He wagged his head and opened his door. "I'll be fine. Virginia should be home if I can't manage the keys."

"Okay."

I waited for him to step out, but he sat and stared at the windshield. After a few seconds passed I spoke his name.

He delicately moved his head up and down. "I just wanted to thank you. That's not always easy for me to say. Well, it is if you risk your life saving mine, but it's harder when it's tantamount to saying, 'I'm an idiot.'"

"You are an idiot." I winked. "We're all idiots now and again. So what? Don't worry about your troupe. They'll understand. Everything's going to be okay."

Orson shrugged. "Perhaps you're right. About everything." He rubbed his eyes with the heels of his palms before he clambered out. Before shutting his door Orson turned around and said, "Thank you for confiding in me about Chinaman. Nevertheless, I don't see why you were stupid. From what I've seen of you two together, it seems like the best thing that could have happened to either of you."

Before I could say anything he closed his door.

I waited to see if he had any problems getting inside before driving away. *He might be right,* I thought. *Maybe having Chinaman around isn't the worst thing in the world. Maybe we are good for each other.*

And maybe I could have swallowed all that hokum if the man with the sage advice hadn't decided to park it in the middle of the sidewalk, hunch over, and puke on his shoes.

Chapter Fifteen

Chinaman was waiting for me in the Lafayette's lobby. Instead of asking me about Orson, like I expected, he muttered that Dancer was back. "He would like to speak to you. I believe he knows you and Mr. Welles lied to him."

"About time he figured that out. Come on."

We went into the amphitheater, me leading the way. As far as I'm concerned, you're only being a hypocrite when you lie and fret after being caught. And it wasn't like I hadn't expected Dancer to figure out Orson and I had been holding back from him. Any cop worth his salt would have by now.

"There you are, you naughty boy," the detective said when he saw us walking down the aisle. Dancer was standing on the stage with Canada, Rose, Jack Carter, and Miss Thompson. The crew had apparently been too tired to strike the Glamis Castle set before excusing themselves, so these five were passing time in Macbeth's courtyard.

"Well, hello, sergeant. You're looking chipper."

And he did, too. So did everyone else. Considering the sour impression Dancer had made that morning, the group was being surprisingly chummy with him. Except Canada. He scowled at the policeman the way most folk look at something that needs scraping from their shoe.

"I've been waiting for you."

"Chinaman told me. What's up?" Chinaman and I stopped at the orchestra pit. Virgil Thomson and his musicians were long gone, along with most of the Unit.

"How's Orson?" Carter asked, but the cop interrupted before I could answer. Dancer said, "We've got to talk about something, pal. Right now."

"Yes, et's wonderful," Rose cheered, misinterpreting him. She was so happy she looked ready to try handsprings. "Ben didn' kill Norton. Ah was right. He didn' do et!"

I glanced at the Big C, who stared back. This was news to him.

"Then who killed him?" I asked.

"No one! Norton's alive!"

Dancer smirked like the cat that ate the canary. *Touché*, he winked. *I knew something you didn't know.*

"Alive?" Chinaman asked.

"Yep," the cop confirmed. "Denbrough dragged himself home a few hours ago. His family's doctor was giving him the once-over when I left."

I asked what was wrong with Denbrough.

"He's picked himself up one beaut of a cold. No surprise, really. Not when you remember he's been on the lam since Sunday. He's been hiding out in railroad yards, sleeping in boxcars, all in all enjoying the life of a hobo. The doc's worried that the poor boy could come down with bronchitis or pneumonia if precautions aren't taken. He's prescribing lots of bed rest and no visitors."

I glanced at Chinaman again, this time for advice. He sort of shrugged, his signal for "It ain't impossible."

"But that's neither here nor there," Dancer continued, coming off the stage to meet me. "Like I said, you and me have things to talk about."

"Excuse me, sergeant," Chinaman interrupted, the lawyer in him curious, "but how does all of this affect your charges against Mr. Kanter?"

"You're an inquisitive fellow, ain't you?" This sounded more like a compliment than a jab. "We've dropped the charges against him as far as Denbrough is concerned. Sure. But Kanter is still our number one suspect in the De Shields' murder. However, we're willing to release him without bail if he agrees to come in for questioning."

"That's mighty big of you," Canada said from the stage. "After the way you treated him when last in your custody, why should he trust you now?"

Dancer's face strained, and he whipped one finger at Canada. "I didn't have anything to do with that! You hear me! Kanter will know that. So one of you just make sure he gets my message." He lowered his finger.

"You really think we know where Ben is?" Carter asked, a question Dancer didn't dignify with an answer, the cop preferring to stress his point.

"When you see him, you tell him. And don't screw things up for him by suggesting he's better off staying in lavender. The longer he hides, the guiltier he's going to look, and the less inclined we'll be to extend this offer." That was all he wanted to say about that. Dancer jerked his head for me to follow him. "Leave Eddie Horton here."

We went into the lobby, where Dancer jammed his hands into his pants pockets, probably to stop himself from punching a wall. No doubt about it, Canada had lit the cop's pilot light, Dancer mumbling something about that "Smart-mouthed no good pip-squeak."

I tried to tell him that Canada hadn't meant anything personal.

"He's just worried about a guy he works with."

But the copper wasn't having any of it, and he wasn't in the mood to be put off about what Orson and I had done any longer. "Why didn't you two tell me you dropped by the Denbroughs' yesterday?"

"We didn't think it was important. I didn't anyway."

"Balls! You want to tell me you didn't think De Shields getting the sack was important either?"

No, I didn't, actually.

"You knew De Shields was fired, just like you knew about the loan."

"Loan?" Dancer caught me off-balanced. *You can't know I knew about that.* He had to be bluffing.

"Careful, Winters. Don't lie to my face. I've been willing to give you the benefit of the doubt up to now."

"How's that?"

"I've been figuring you haven't been lying so much as putting off telling me the truth. When anybody digs into an investigation, they're gonna dredge a lot of dirt on people. The hard part is figuring out what dirt is dirt and what dirt is pay dirt. Knowing the difference can save innocent people from getting hurt. I have no problem with that. But if what you're really doing is playing me for a chump, so help me God..." He let my imagination fill in the rest.

"I'm not playing you for a chump." I told him I had all the confidence in the world he'd find out about Orson and me. "I just never thought you'd get your dandruff up over it. And how come you were so sure I knew about the loan?"

He looked ready to say, "Trade secret," but instead said, "You ought to listen to Mr. Horton. He gives good advice."

"He ratted on me?"

Dancer had calmed down enough to take his hands out of his pockets. Now that it was time to turn the tables on me he was going to enjoy it. "No. What he said about 'remembering what we don't know.' That's handy advice."

"I'm still waiting."

"You asked me a lot of sharp questions this morning. I was impressed. Yes, sir. But when I told you about the silver dollars in Norton's coat, you never bothered to ask where they might have come from. And why would you, since you already knew, or had a fair idea."

Aww, jeez...! I struggled to hold on to my poker face as long as I could, which was a total of five seconds. Dancer couldn't help grinning himself.

"Bet you think you're pretty clever," I said.

He did.

"Did Norton Denbrough happen to tell you how his rather expensive coat ended up in a sewer?"

He had. When Denbrough spotted De Shields in the alley behind

Rose, he panicked. "That hand De Shields saw pulling Denbrough away from the window? That was Kanter. They had Ramsey stall the peeper while they rounded up all the clothes Denbrough had stashed at her place. Then they carried the pile down the fire escape and dumped it into the sewer." In all the rush to try and hide the fact Denbrough was living with Rose, the pair forgot they had stashed silver dollars from the loan into Norton's coat.

"The whole loan was in silver dollars?"

"Oh, no. Just three hundred bucks' worth." The duration between Jack Carter closing the deal on the loan for Denbrough and its delivery had been too brief for the loan shark to collect one hundred thousand all in paper currency. The shylock was forced to make up the difference in silver dollars, which he borrowed from the till of one of his speakeasies. "Anyway, right after they dumped the clothes Denbrough skedaddled, but De Shields found Kanter in the alley. The rest is history."

"So Ben kept quiet and took the heat for a guy who was after the woman he loved." It was hard to believe anyone could be that sweet.

"According to Denbrough, Kanter and Ramsey aren't in love. Never have been." I found that even harder to swallow, but Dancer said Denbrough insisted "He cooked the whole scheme up with Kanter after Carter got word De Shields was dogging him. The idea was, if De Shields did drag Denbrough home to mother, the peeper would report how Ramsey had been using the poor boy for a sugar daddy. His mother might be angry he'd gone loopy for a Negress and lost his job, but she'd also take pity that he'd been duped."

"Oh, come on!" This was getting ridiculous. "Denbrough can't believe he would have gotten away with that! I've met his mother. A sharp lady like her would smell that crock for bilge water straight off."

"Really?" Dancer smirked. "Well, I hate to break your bubble, brother, but she swallowed it all right. Hook, line, and sinker."

"Denbrough lied? He lied to his mother? You knew he lied and didn't say anything?"

"What's it got to do with me? Nothing. Denbrough's an okay Joe. He only told me about the scheme to take some heat off of Kanter. It's the least he owes the guy."

Things were way past ridiculous now. "You do know why Denbrough got that loan?"

"Sure. He needs the berries to carry his family until his sis gets hitched to some rich slob come June."

"Does he have the money? I mean minus the three hundred clams."

"Claims to. Why?"

"If he has the money, why bother lying?"

"Hey, I've met his mother, too. Proud woman like her wouldn't live off money from a loan shark. She'd starve first."

"What's that got to do with lying about Ben and Rose?"

"Nothing! That lie just puts him in a good light with his mother. Besides, as far as his love affair with Ramsey is concerned, it's over. He tried, he failed. Hell, who can say they're surprised? These couples that are black and white, they don't work out except in France."

"Did you ever stop to think that Denbrough's just buying time? As soon as Beatrice gets married and the family coffers are full again, he's going to pay off the loan and make tracks right back to Rose."

Dancer gave it some thought, and finally shrugged. "I guess he could at that. It doesn't sound bright, but so what? It's his life."

Throwing the words "so what" back into the cop's face was my first reaction, until I realized he was right. Getting carried away with the moment, I forgot that Denbrough didn't matter any more. Finding out if Ben shot De Shields was my problem now, although there was one more thing about Denbrough I did want to know first. "Who's been holding on to all that jack since Sunday?"

"According to him, he's been carrying it in a money belt all the time. Lucky for him someone didn't catch on and roll him. Plenty of folks around here will slit a guy's throat for less than a dime."

"So I hear. De Shields told me the other day how bad things have gotten in Harlem the past couple years, especially with all the riots."

Dancers' face got hard, like a statue. "Oh. Yeah. Yeah, I suppose. Except those haven't been about money. Well, not really. It's complicated."

"He said six cops wound up in the hospital after the last riot. He also suggested all the ruckus the Communists are making over this play doesn't help matters."

Dancer shrugged again, face still stern. "I suppose. But it's not just the Communists or your play. Times are tough in Harlem. The grocers are price gouging. Chicken's 26 cents a pound. Butter costs 28 cents. That's twice as much as you'd pay over in the Bronx. And rent keeps going up. But what it boils down to is color. Whites own most stores and they only want to hire whites, so Negroes can't get jobs.

"Not that it's easy for me to sympathize with them. At least not after our last riot. All over some hooligan trying to snitch a ten-cent pocketknife. A clerk catches him red-handed, and the little snot proceeds to sink his teeth into the guy's thumb and wrist. Clerk gets mad. Threatens to drag the kid down to the basement and beat the hell out of him, but winds up blistering the brat's ear instead and letting him go. But by that time word was spreading through the neighborhood that a white man was beating on a colored boy. An ugly crowd gets together in front of the store, and the owner calls us cops to scatter them. About the same time we get there an ambulance shows up for the clerk with the chewed thumb and wrist. The crowd figures it's for the kid, and the whole scene goes bananas."

Dancer paused to swallow, the only clue he was feeling anything behind his stony eyes.

"Four people killed. De Shields told you about my six colleagues. 125th Street was looted and there was about one hundred thousand bucks worth of property damage. You couldn't even walk on the sidewalk afterwards. Glass was all over the place, like sand on the beach."

I wasn't sure what to say. I settled for my old reliable, "I'm sorry."

"Why? It wasn't your fault."

"Well, yeah, but..." *"But" what?* "I just don't want the next riot to be my fault. Or our fault. The Harlem Unit. You know what I mean?"

He knew. "All the more reason I'm happy Norton Denbrough is safe at home with his mommy. And the sooner we find out if Kanter had anything to do with De Shields' murder, so much the better."

⁂

Dancer and I didn't have much more to say to each other. He had made his point, and now he had other things to do. We said goodnight, and I went back into the auditorium.

Chinaman and the actors, particularly Rose, were waiting to see if Dancer had told me anything else about Denbrough. I had no idea if Denbrough was telling Dancer the truth about splitting with Rose, so I said no.

Carter asked again if Orson was all right.

"He's okay. The last couple of days just caught up with him and he got drunk. He did sober up enough on the drive home to feel bad about hurting everyone's feelings. He's really sorry." I told them what I suggested about Orson apologizing Friday.

"Excellent," Miss Thompson said. "Jack and I already discussed this with the Unit, and I'm positive an apology will suffice. Orson's too sweat a boy for us to believe he was sincere." Carter agreed.

The actors got ready to close the theater and leave. I was hungry and tired of running all over town, so I gave Chinaman two sawbucks and asked him to scoot over to the Checker Cab office. "Give the dispatcher my name and half of this. He'll know what to do. Use the other ten for your own cab fare and dinner if you want."

"Yes, sir."

"I'm going to the Theresa tonight to look at De Shields' room and ask the night manager some questions, so the evening's yours. Do whatever you want."

"Yes, sir."

Chinaman left, and I found Canada to ask if he wanted to go grab some dinner. After the two-day marathon I wouldn't have blamed him saying no, but he didn't seem tired at all. "We would love to, Sassafras."

Parking in the alley had worked so well before, I had left Bertha there again. I led the way out through the backstage door, but as Canada and I started to climb into the car he pointed to the mouth of the alley.

Jack Carter was standing with his back to us, waving his hand, obviously flagging a taxi. I called out to see if the big actor needed a ride, but there was too much street noise for him to hear me. Besides, a cab had pulled up to him. I almost turned away before I noticed Rose getting into the hack with Carter.

"Canada." He had already seen her. We waited to see if Miss Thompson got into the cab with them, but the car drove away with only the two passengers. "Get in," I told Canada. "I want to see where they're going."

He did what I asked, but didn't know why I wanted to tail the couple. "They're probably sharing the cab fare, or have dinner plans together."

"Fine. I want to know what's going on for sure is all."

We drove past block after block, and before long escaped Harlem to head uptown. The further we drove, the more curious Canada grew. "Apparently your hunch was correct," he said.

"What hunch? I still don't know where they're going." Although by the time we came to Gramercy Park West I had a good idea. It just didn't make any sense that they would try to visit Norton Denbrough. "He's under doctor's care. And there ain't no way Claudette Denbrough is going to let Rose anywhere near her son." Nevertheless the taxi steered through the iron gate and up the drive to the estate.

I parked Bertha so we could watch from the street as Carter and Rose got out of the cab. The actor paid the driver, and the taxi pulled away while they went to the front door and knocked.

"Considering the circumstances," Canada asked, "doesn't that strike you as gross overconfidence?"

"And then some. If they need a ride back to Harlem, I guess we can always give them a lift."

Somehow we both knew better.

The Denbroughs' dour butler answered the door, and Carter and Rose were ushered in like old friends.

"You know what, Canada?" My voice sounded hollow.

"What is it, Sassafras?" So did his.

"I don't think I'm ever going to figure out what's going on around here."

Chapter Sixteen

Canada and I double-backed to Harlem, where we had dinner at the Clam House on Lenox Avenue. The food was good, but we left as soon as we finished eating, neither of us thrilled by the entertainers, Gladys Bently and Gloria Swanson. Bently was swell on the ivories, but her songs were either about ennui or laced with double-entendre, and we weren't in the mood. It didn't bother us too much that she cropped her hair short and liked to dress in men's clothing, but I can't say the same thing about Swanson, a transvestite torch singer.

"We get enough make-believe at the Lafayette," Canada cracked while I left the tip.

Bently's music did get Canada in a mind to hear a stride piano, so he led the way to Pod's and Jerry's, one of Willie The Lion Smith's favorite hang outs. It was the kind of spot where everyone from tush hogs to the biggest names on Broadway came to, and we spent a few hours rubbing shoulders, sipping drinks, and listening to the musicians. About the time Coleman Walker started blowing *In A Jam* on his horn, I glanced at my watch and saw that it was a quarter after eleven. I told Canada I had to get back to work and he followed me outside.

I asked him, "Going to bed?"

"No. We'd like to tag along with you, if you don't mind."

"Aren't you tired?" After two nights without sleep I know I would be ready to drop, but Canada was full of pep. He said, "It must be adrenaline. Our veins feel as if ants were racing with our blood. We haven't felt this excited since we won our last bout. But if you would rather we didn't come with you…"

I told him that wasn't it. That I was going to the Theresa and why. "I might try talking to some of the staff who worked last night. You'd be stuck waiting for me outside for who knows how long."

"Perhaps we can help."

"How?"

"While you are busy with the night manager, we can go around to the rear entrance and talk with the staff for you. We already know a person who works at the hotel, which couldn't hurt."

It sounded good to me. "You sure you want to bother with this?"

"We'd like to help Ben, Sassafras. Please."

He didn't have to twist my arm. We started walking, splitting up at the corner of 135th Street and Seventh Avenue. Canada headed for the alley while I went through the hotel's revolving front door.

The lobby wasn't as fancy as the Roxy, but it wasn't far off the mark. Except for a handful of people coming or going to the elevators I had the place to myself. I rang the bell at the reception desk and waited. Soon enough another one of those little clerks with the pencil-thin mustache came in answer. *Lord, Mr. Ford must mass-produce these weasels.*

"Yes?" he asked in a foghorn voice, drawing out the word until it became annoying.

"You the night manager?"

He said he was. "Barton Mudd's my name. How can I help you?"

I told him who I was. "Stan Dancer should have called to tell you I was coming."

"Dancer?" He rolled his eyes, pretending he had never heard the name before.

"*Detective* Dancer. Remember? He was here about your murder."

It wouldn't have surprised me if the sneak had said, "Which murder?" Instead, "Oh, yes. I do remember him. But no one from the police has contacted me since this morning." His fingers started in with a devil's tattoo as he feigned impatience.

"Look, I've the O.K. to take a peep at the room where Andre De Shields was shot this morning. Dancer also said I could ask you some questions. If you don't believe me, spend a nickel and check it out yourself."

"Oh, I'm afraid I'm too swamped right now to phone anyone. Perhaps you can come back later and I'll have had an opportunity to verify your story by then."

Yeah. Right. I made a production of looking around the lobby. "You're busy?"

"Paper work. Lots of paper work. Back in my office." He licked his lips. This twerp was some piece of work.

"Uh-huh." *For two cents I'd pick you off like a scab.* And enjoy it to boot, but it wouldn't get me any closer to home plate, so I pulled out my wallet and put two sawbucks on top the counter. "It looks like you've got some paper work to tend to here first."

"So it does." He snatched the money and handed me the key to room 316. "Just take the elevator to the third floor and turn right."

"Don't bother with the directions. You can show me the way."

"Oh, I'm afraid I'm much too busy..."

"What you're doing is pushing a good thing too far, Mudd. You might make me mad and I might leave. And if I walk, I'm taking my money with me."

Mudd said he would be only be too delighted to escort me to room 316.

Upstairs he unlocked the door and turned on the lights. What I had been told all day was a room turned out to be a suite that would have done an MGM set designer proud. Everything from the sofa to the fern-shaded wall lamps was expensive but damn depressing, thanks to the suite's achromatic color scheme.

The bedroom where De Shields died was waiting behind a pair of mirror-faced French doors. In here was a king-size bed, its silk sheets still unmade, a vacant wet bar, and two more sets of doors, one leading to a bathroom and the other to a balcony. The bulls had taped an outline on the floor where De Shields' body had been found. Blood had seeped into the ivory shag where his chest laid, the dried stains a crusty brown.

Nice digs, I thought, *but not nice enough where I'd want to cash in my chips here.* As far as giving up the ghost is concerned I'm with that Irishman. If I knew where I was going to die I'd never go to that place.

"I'm afraid you'll have to be quick," Mudd said, trying hard to act bored.

"Keep your pants on." He was starting to bug me. Giving him a dose was beginning to sound tempting, only it would have been too easy.

Figuring out where De Shields was standing when he was shot wasn't the hardest thing I've ever done. Five holes peppered the wall next to the bed. Since Dancer said the peeper had been shot three times I had to assume one bullet had managed to rip all the way through De Shields. A large crack busted the plaster where his body must have impacted. *Bad way to go.*

I glanced at the messy bed, recollected Dancer's confession about sick ideas starring Ben and De Shields, and then remembered Gloria Swanson. *Uh-uh. No way. Forget it.* There was no trace of mascara, lipstick, or long hairs anywhere on the bedclothes, which got me thinking about Gladys Bently. *Will you get your mind off that crap?!*

I studied the wall again. Something about the way those five holes were scattered pestered me. Two high, two low, and one way to the right, each hole with two or three feet between the other. Sure, the murder and the arson were sloppy, but this looked like the killer hardly had any control over their gun. *Big revolvers give one hell of a kick. Still, Ben's strong enough to manage. So if he's the killer, why the wide spread?*

"Something?" Mudd asked after I had stared at the wall for a minute.

"Just thinking. Whoever killed De Shields was a lousy marksman."

"Bad shot or no, the man is dead."

"That ain't the point." I stepped up and ran the tips of my fingers along the crack in the wall. It ran true and deep through the slats and plaster. *High caliber revolver all right. He must have really been airborne when he bashed into this.*

Examining the holes up close was pointless. The cops had taken their measurements that morning then pried out the bullets. All they had left behind were pits and craters. I decided to scope out the bathroom. The manager followed and asked if I could explain something to him.

"I'll try." The bathroom was as impressive and cheerless as the rest of the suite. The floor was laid with marble, and there was even a vanity with lighted mirror across from the raised claw-foot bathtub. Everything seemed shipshape and highfalutin after the first inspection, except that I could sense something was weird. Something I was only able to glimpse transiently out the corner of my eye. *Christ! This is getting aggravating.*

"I realize the police suspect this nigger actor, Kanter, but could the killer have been a gangster?"

"I don't know." Actually that wasn't a bad question, even if I didn't like the way he asked it. Not bad at all, considering what Divine told me about the late Reverend Becton. Maybe this dim bulb was on to something. "Why d'ya ask?"

"Because he reloaded his gun."

Did he? No. The police report Divine gave me confirmed the witnesses heard all seven shots fired one after the other. "But he didn't reload."

"Of course he did. There were seven bullets." By the tone of his voice Mudd could have been scolding a child.

"I'm telling you for a fact whoever shot De Shields didn't reload." As for the bathroom, after a second look everything still seemed in order, at the sink, in the tub, and on the vanity. Finally, on a third look, I found it.

"So the killer used two guns?"

"I don't think so." *Sas, you nitwit.* What was wrong were the towels. I had stayed at enough hotels in my day to know that even the swankiest ones stack towels the way Noah stocked animals. Two-by-two. "Did you know one of your hand towels is missing?"

The manager stepped beside me to count the carefully folded towels. When he saw I was right he winced then clicked his tongue. "Another one? Don't people realize how much good cotton towels cost? It's petty larceny like this that forces management to raise rates so often."

I hadn't read anything about anybody swiping a towel in the police report, so I asked if the cops had borrowed one.

"Not as I know. They said nothing if they did."

Whoo-ha, Dancer. I know something you don't know. If nothing was in the report and the police didn't take one, the killer must have nipped it. Now I just had to figure out why.

"Do you think it's important?"

Yes. I did. Not that I wanted the weasel to know that. So to get his mind off the towel I asked him why he thought the killer used two guns.

"You said he didn't reload. Obviously the killer must have used two guns if he fired seven bullets."

"What's with you? Have you seen too many westerns or something? There's no law that a gun can't shoot more than six bullets. The 1916 German Luger can hold eight bullets. Nine, if you want to load the chamber by hand."

Mudd looked insulted. "I never go to westerns. The only reason I asked is because I've read where gangsters have been known to empty their gun into a victim, then reload, and fire one last bullet. That's seven."

"Oh. Yeah. I read the pulps, too. They're great."

"I do not read pulp magazines!" I must have really wounded his pride this time. Or his self-importance. I couldn't tell which. Didn't much care, either.

I said, "Well, if you did, then you'd know the bad guys usually pump their signature shot into the victim's head or neck. Kind of like this." I curled up the bottom three fingers and thumb of one hand, extended the index finger, and poked Mudd hard in one temple.

"Ow! Hey, that hurt."

"Sorry."

He didn't believe me. "Are you quite finished?"

"After I ask you a couple more questions. Do you remember how De Shields was acting when he checked in last night?"

"'Acting'? What do you mean?"

"His mood. Was he mad, or in a rush, or laughing like a goony bird?"

"I really don't remember. I suppose if he had been behaving queerly I'd recall. My guess is he wasn't displaying any particular emotion. Few people do while registering. It makes my job a monotonous parade."

"How long was he planning to stay?"

"He registered for the one night."

"Did he have much luggage?"

"As far as I know he brought no luggage. He refused a bellhop, and the police found very few personal items here this morning."

"Did he make any phone calls?"

"Just one. To room service. According to the kitchen, Mr. De Shields inquired about our rates for champagne sometime around one o'clock. He said he would call back when he required a bottle, but he never did."

Having seen De Shields knock down Drerys at the Astoria, he didn't impress me as a guy who imbibed white wine. Neither did Ben Kanter, now that I thought about it. So why was the peeper going to order champagne? "Was De Shields alone when he registered?"

"As far as I know."

"Did he tell you he was expecting anyone?"

"No."

"Maybe a lady friend? Or a prostitute?"

One corner of his lip twitched. "I said no, sir."

"All right." This was something I might have to ask Divine about. "Now about Ben Kanter. Any ideas how he managed to sneak into your hotel?"

The manager sighed, trying to disguise embarrassment. "Well, to be frank, our night detective isn't the most observant or energetic man. All the nigger had to do to avoid him was come through the kitchen and up the back stairs."

"So why didn't the kitchen staff spot him?"

"They did, but they're predominantly colored. So are most of our menials. And their ranks change often if not regularly. They just assumed Kanter was a new employee coming to work."

"At *two* in the morning?"

He sighed again. "That means nothing to their kind."

"So nobody paid attention to Ben until the bellhop saw him?"

"That's right. The nigger was finally standing somewhere he did not belong, doing something he should not be doing if he worked for the Theresa. Even a darkie bellhop could figure that out."

From my point of view, it looked like the darkie bellhop was at least one up on the house dick. And if I could lay money on it, I'd bet a C-note against five to one that the "menials" weren't as stupid as this glorified desk clerk imagined. They were just minding their own business. "Yep," I said, "nothing calls attention to itself like the obvious."

"Pardon me?"

"Don't bother. You wouldn't get it. Maybe I'd better talk with your bellhop. Is he working tonight?"

"I'm afraid I can't help you there."

He was going to say more before I cut in. "Look, Mudd, I'm not gonna warn you again. You're getting on my bad side."

"That isn't what I mean." He gulped, suddenly nervous. "I can't help you because that bellhop has been discharged."

"You fired him?" My voice was loud.

"I had to. He disobeyed hotel policy when he failed to report the nig..."

"If you say 'nigger' one more time, I'm going to belt you. The man's name is Kanter. Ben Kanter."

Mudd bit his lip shutting up. He wasn't nervous anymore. He was scared. "As you say. Nevertheless, I had to fire him."

"He thought De Shields was a cop! He thought he'd get in trouble if he opened his mouth. If you're going to fire anybody, fire your house dick. He's the one sleeping on the job."

"That isn't how my supervisors or I see it. Yes, the house detective should have known Ben Kanter was inside the hotel, but he's not the one who saw Ben Kanter and he isn't the one who subsequently failed to report it to me."

"Not that the bellhop being colored and your house dick being white enters into your screwy logic."

"I never said our detective is white." He forgot about being scared. He thought he had caught me in some kind of slip up and smiled, like a spoiled kid who got his kicks insisting night was day. Before I knew what I was doing, I slapped him, once, then shoved him into the bedroom, where he tripped and fell on the unmade bed.

"What the hell do you think this is?" I barked, following. He tried getting up, but I pushed him back on the mattress. "You think this is some kind of game?"

Mudd started to screech about having me arrested for assault, and how he was going to sue me for every red cent in my nigger-loving bank account. I reminded him that *Detective* Dancer was my friend, not his, "So good luck trying to get the charges to stick." I don't normally bluff, but I was irritated enough to risk it, not to mention slapping Mudd for saying nigger again.

That shut his trap. He just laid there like a crumpled piece of paper, rubbing his cheek and staring at my feet.

"What's his name?" I asked.

"Whose name?" he mumbled.

"The bellhop's."

Mudd didn't answer right off. He had to think. He had sacked a man that morning and now he couldn't remember the poor Joe's name. And I thought I had seen red all during Rose's rent party.

"Banks! Roy Horton Banks."

"What's his address?"

"He lives in or near the Tenderloin. I'm not sure exactly."

"Figures." I reached down. Mudd tried scooting off the bed, afraid I was going to pop him another one. I had to latch on to his lapels and pin him down to dig my money out of his coat pocket.

All of a sudden he grew a backbone, chirping "Hey!" and making a grab for the dough. I wrapped my fingers around his face like Cagney grabbing a grapefruit, shoving him down again. "Stay there. Trust me. You're better off."

I was halfway across the living room when he decided it was safe to give me some lip. "Fine," he peeped, "keep your money! Who needs it? By the by, you were right, wise guy! I fired Banks because he's colored! Do you hear me?"

I heard him, and kept right on walking. Slapping him before didn't accomplish anything, so there wasn't much sense doing it again

I walked out of the suite, and nearly into a gray-haired Negro waiter wearing the customary white jacket. He motioned for me to keep quiet and follow him. We went down the hall, through a fire door, and into the back stairwell.

"T'anks for zippin' yo' lip," the old man said. "Et wouldn't haf done either of us any good fo' de manager to see me wit' yo'." He started downstairs.

"So where are we going?"

"To de kitchens. Yo'r buddy wants to talk wit' yo'."

∽∼

I would have thought the kitchen would be pretty quiet and vacant so close to midnight, but I was wrong. A crew of six men, four Negroes, one white, and an Asian, were busy filling orders for room service.

Canada was standing in one corner of the kitchen, keeping out of the way while jawing with two of the crew. He introduced me to Pete Elston, a white baker in his late 20s, Acie Armstrong, a middle-aged Negro chef, and finally the old gentleman who had escorted me downstairs, "Papa Ted Carfino, the best cutter to ever grace the fancy."

"Ah'm retired now, but let me tell yo', dis kid could fight." Papa Ted grinned as he put an arm around Canada's shoulder and hugged him. "Had some of de best moves Ah've ever seen. He could juke de opponent, de official, and half de audience out of deir socks wit' his best feint. An' his one-two combination!" The old man twirled his hands around each other and whistled. "Only de strongest and de quickest ever got past three rounds wit' dis mug."

"Seems to me his upper cut wasn't too shabby either," I said, shaking one fist at Canada, who was beaming like a pregnant woman.

"Papa Ted exaggerates." Canada was trying to stay humble. It wasn't working.

"Dat a fact? Yo' think yo' can win a title without talent like Ah'm talkin' 'bout? Ah'm tellin' yo' all, dis kid was one of de best!" Suddenly Papa Ted turned to me. "Not dat you were lookin' too shabby yourself jes' now, son. My boy here says yo' used to play ball for de Cubbies. Maybe yo' should haf tried out de square ring instead. Light heavyweight maybe."

Oh, swell. It was a nice thing for him to say, but now the cat was out of the bag. Canada wanted to know what the old man was talking about, and Papa Ted gave him a brief blow-by-blow of my slap fight with Mudd. In the few seconds it took to recount, the entire kitchen staff forgot what they were doing to stop and listen.

"Yo' stomped on Mudd?" Armstrong asked.

"Uh...just slapped him." The crew gawked at me. "Well, damn it, he had it coming! Didn't he?"

They thought so. Everyone in the kitchen except Canada and Armstrong started clapping or banging pots. The chef grabbed my hand and wrung it so hard I was scared he was going to dislocate my shoulder.

"Damn right he did!" Armstrong said. "Firin' Roy like dat. Roy's got a family to feed!"

"Roy always worked hard for his money," Papa Ted added. "He worked hard an' he got de good tips to prove it. Mos' de folks stayin' in de Theresa, havin' coloreds wait on 'em ain' no big deal. Dey got coloreds at home doin' de same thing. Yo' gotta be good at yo'r job to even scratch a nickel out of dem." The old man told me he knew Banks' address, and wrote it down on a loose napkin. "Here. Ef'n yo' need to talk wit' Roy, yo' jes' tells him my name. He'll know yo're legit den."

I thanked him and slipped the napkin in my pants pocket, while Elston, who was chewing on a carrot, cleared his throat and took center stage.

"I believe we might be able to assist yous in another way, Mr. Winters." Elston had a Brooklyn accent, so thick that he said "another" like it was two words.

"Call me Sas."

"Okay. Yous call me Pete. Anyways, me and Acie here, we overhears Mudd having a blow wit' some dude last night 'bout an hour before Roy spots your buddy Kanter wit' the late De Shields."

"Mind yo'," Armstrong interrupted, "we's helpin' yo' in difference to our better judgments. We are all Dodgers fans in dis kitchen. Especially Tsan Chen."

The Asian man somberly nodded once.

I told them I appreciated their willingness to overlook my shortcomings.

"Just so's you knows," Elston said. "What we heard was, me and Acie hears this loudmouth telling Mudd not to let slip that he was ever anywhere near room 316. He's shoutin' cause he don't see anyone in the lobby, but Acie and me are on break, usin' the head near the registration desk, so we hear everything just fine."

Armstrong laughed. "Dats no lie! De boy weren't too bright, barkin' out his secrets like dat."

"You sure this big mouth said '316'?" I asked.

"Positive," the chef said. "Dat De Shields cat, he calls down for prices on champagne same time de loudmouth is chewin' Mudd's rump raw. We all gets to figurin' 'bout den dat something' interestin' is goin' on in room 316. Not dat we guessed anybody was gonna git killed."

I asked why they didn't tell the police about the stranger.

"Cause we's don't needs to lose our jobs, dat's why," Papa Ted said.

"How could you lose your jobs?"

"Same way as Roy," Elston said. He explained that the loudmouth had threatened Mudd with his job. "Told Mudd if people found out he'd come to the Theresa, then the loudmouth was gonna buy this hotel just so he could fire the little jellyfish. And he looks like he has the cabbage where he could do it, too. We's figure, if he's willin' to go to extremes to fire a night manager, he'd be willin' to do likewise to give any of us the boot."

"Who the hell was this guy?"

"Afraid we's can't give you a name, friend, but Acie and me did poke our melons out of the head long enough to get a peak at him."

"He's a young archy," Armstrong said, "maybe Pete's age. Thin, though. And dark."

"Like a Cuban?"

"Dat ain' what Ah mean. He's jes' tan for a pink dis time of year. We figured he jes' came back from one of dem winter cruises rich folk like to go on so much."

The bells were going off in my mind. *Joyce-Armstrong?* "Did he have curly hair? And pale blue eyes?"

Elston's looked impressed, and Armstrong snapped his fingers. "Yeah," the chef said, "he did at dat! You knows dis joker?"

"Maybe. I'm going to have to find out."

"Well, perhaps we can help you there, too," Elston boasted, smugly rocking back and forth on his feet. "You go find your guy and see if he don't got himself a shiner over his right eye, compliments of the late Mr. De Shields."

"The peeper poked him?" Canada asked.

"Dat's where our hound is gonna sleep," Papa Ted said with a grin. "De way dese two chuckle-heads explained de shiner to me, Ah'd say et was real fresh, an' Ah ought to know."

"I'll be damned," I said. *This is great!* All of a sudden Ben wasn't the only suspect in De Shields' murder. Coming here was a long shot, but now I had the missing towel and Joyce-Armstrong, and I couldn't wait to talk with Beatrice Denbrough's fiancé.

"Have we helped?" Elston asked.

"Oh, yeah, I think you have." I reached into my pocket and pulled out the two bills I'd taken back from Mudd. "Here. Take this, go out, and buy a couple of rounds on me after work."

Armstrong started to refuse, but Elston grabbed the cash. "Thank you, Mr. Winters. We all might just have to drink a toast to the Cubbies for this. Except Tsan Chen, of course."

The Asian man started to nod, then stopped and said, "Aw, what the hell? As long as it ain't the Yankees!"

꿀꿀

Between talking with Papa Ted and the kitchen crew's chopping the Cubs, Canada and me were feeling nostalgic after we left the Theresa. In a mood to reminisce, we hopped over to Jungle Alley on

133rd Avenue and dropped in on Tillie's Chicken Shack.

Around a half past two a torch singer started crooning a suggestive rendition of *Stop It, Joe,* and Canada's stamina finally began to punk out on him. We decided to call it a night, and shared cab fare to our respective digs.

At the Cosmopolitan I started to use my key to unlock my room when, before I knew what was going on, the door opened from the inside. A handsome Negro man in his early 30s stood there with a drink in his left hand.

"Hello," he said. "You must be Winters. My name's Langston Hughes. Chinaman's told us so much about you."

Chapter Seventeen

There were ten more people in my room, not counting Hughes and Chinaman, my valet busy making the rounds with drinks and *hors d'oeuvres*. All of them except two were Negroes, a middle-aged white couple, and all of them looked a lot smarter than me. They all watched as I stepped inside and Hughes closed the door. There I stood, still holding my hotel key and feeling like I strolled into the woman's washroom.

"Good morning, Mr. Winters," Chinaman greeted, proud to see me. "I trust your evening was productive."

My mind went blank.

"We were hoping we'd meet you before we left," Hughes said, by my side, don't ask me how he got there. "None of us have ever met a private investigator before."

"That's nice," I heard myself say. "Who are you people and why are you in my living room?"

"Just some of the niggerati," the white man said. His impish smile and round face reminded me of Welles. *Oh, oh. Trouble.*

"The what?"

Chinaman put down his tray, came to fetch me, and led me into the bedroom. "Excuse us, please," he said as he closed the door. "I have some information for Mr. Winters regarding the case he is working on, and I'm afraid it's private."

I slipped off my jacket, threw it on the bed, then sat down and took off my shoes.

"There are people in my living room."

"I know, sir. I invited them. You did say I could do whatever I'd like tonight."

That was Chinaman for you. Always ready to throw your own words in your face. "But a party?"

"Perhaps I did overstep my bounds. If I did, I apologize. I meant no disrespect."

That was something else he was good at, making you feel lower than dirt.

"It's okay. They look pretty tame to me. No damage done, I'm sure."

"Oh, none. I assure you, Mr. Winters."

"Now who are they?"

"Friends of Mr. Van Vechten's. That is the white gentleman. The woman with him is his wife, Fania Marinoff."

Her name was familiar. "The actress?"

"The same, sir." If I had been talking to anybody but Chinaman, I would have been impressed. "Mr. Van Vechten is a celebrity himself. He is a writer, critic, and a photographer."

"A photographer? Really?"

"A very good one. And that isn't your only commonality. He is also a Midwesterner."

"Oh?" That was a good point. Could anybody from the Ohio River Valley who knew his way around a 4 x 5-inch Graflex camera be trouble, even if he did look like Orson? Not in my book. "And the others? What did Van Vechten call them?"

"'Niggerati,' sir. Harlem intellectuals. The man who answered the door, Mr. Hughes, is an accomplished poet. Some of the other guests are Countee Cullen and Claude McKay, likewise poets. Wallace Thurman, Rudolph Fisher, and Zora Hurston, all writers. And Aaron Douglas, a painter."

"Sounds like an interesting bunch."

"They are, sir. Extremely interesting. I can't remember when I have had such a stimulating evening!" He sounded enthusiastic, all right.

"Are you ever going to tell me how they managed to find their way into my living room?"

"That's very simple, sir." Chinaman had gone straight to Checker Cab early that evening, like I told him. "The dispatcher sent your message out directly."

"Great. Any calls?"

"No, sir. None all night." He went on, explaining how he left the cab company to go visit Van Vechten, an old friend. "His wife and he were entertaining a few friends, and they invited me to join the party."

"That was nice of them." I was sure he would get to the part I was interested in soon.

"Yes, it was. And as I began to mingle, I made mention of you, Mr. Welles, and *Macbeth*. As it turns out the guests are all anxious to see the play, and can't understand why the Communists are protesting it so vehemently. Anyway, it wasn't long before Miss Hurston recalled that the Nat Turner Center was holding a meeting that same night and suggested we all go and attend."

I held up my hand. "Who was having a meeting?"

"The Harlem Division of the Communist Party. They hold their meetings at the Nat Turner Center on 131st Street."

"YOU WENT TO ONE OF THEIR MEETINGS?" I was on my feet.

I was yelling. Judging by the look on his face, I was also scaring the bejeezus out of Chinaman.

"I didn't see anything wrong with listening to what they had to say."

There was a knock at the bedroom door, which opened wide enough for Hughes to stick his head through. "Is anything wrong?" he asked.

My gut reaction was to see if I could kick the door hard enough to decapitate Hughes, but I decided to count to ten instead. "Everything's fine. Chinaman will be out in a second."

Hughes nodded, pulled his head back, and closed the door.

Chinaman started to apologize again, but I cut in. "Look, I know you didn't mean any harm, but that doesn't mean you couldn't have caused any. Damn it, those people are protesting the Lafayette night and day. They've got this borough so stirred up that if the crazies aren't sending Orson death threats, they're coming out of the woodwork with razors."

I stopped to catch my breath. Chinaman didn't speak.

"I'll level with you, Big C. Ever since that nut went after Orson in the Lafayette...in the *lobby,* for God's sake...I've been scared. White-knuckled scared. And I think I've been kidding myself. I keep telling myself once I can prove if Ben killed De Shields or not, that will make things better somehow."

"I'm sure it will, sir." He spoke so quietly I couldn't help feeling bad. I never enjoy hurting anybody, especially family. "The Unit has so many problems with the play, the added stigma of one of their actors being a murderer is a terrible strain."

"I was talking about Harlem. All of it, not just the Unit."

Chinaman paused. "I'm afraid," he said, "that there is very little you can do for Harlem, Mr. Winters. Except do your job, and let everyone else do theirs."

He had a good point. It made a lot of sense. Didn't mean I had to like it.

"I think you'd better get back to your guests. I'll see you in the morning."

"Should I ask them to leave? I can have the couch ready for you in five minutes."

I shook my head. "No thanks. This bed's fine. Tell your guests it was nice meeting them."

"Yes, sir. Good night." And he left.

I didn't do anything for a few seconds. Just let myself feel numb. Eventually I took off my shirt and socks, turned off the light, and laid down on the bed with the too-soft mattress. I told myself I'd get up soon, take off the rest of my clothes, and climb under the covers.

Chapter Eighteen

Next thing I knew, the telephone was ringing.

I fumbled with the drawstrings on my eyelids, waiting to see if either Chinaman was home to answer the phone or the invader would hang up. I was so tired it never dawned on me the caller could have been De Shields' cab driver.

Finally the cymbals were cut off halfway through one ring, and I heard Chinaman ask, "Hello?" He paused. "Oh, yes, sir. He's home. I'll see if he's awake yet." Another pause. "Why, yes, I am aware it is after ten."

I made some kind of noise. A grunt maybe. I doubt I'll ever be sure.

"I believe I've just heard him. One moment, Mr. Welles."

Oh, not him! Not first thing in the morning!

I was trapped. My mind was wide awake and rooting for me to run for the hills, but my body was an uncooperative wet sand bag. Before I knew it, Chinaman was opening the bedroom door and asking me if I was up for the day.

Am I? Maybe this is just a bad dream.

"Mr. Winters? Are you all right?"

Chinaman wasn't going to go away until I said something. "Yes. I'm fine."

"Mr. Welles is on the telephone, sir."

"That must hurt."

Chinaman ignored it. "Shall I ask him to call back?"

My heart said, "Yes," but my smart mouth said, "No. No, that will only encourage him." I somehow managed to find my feet, and then almost tripped over a blanket Chinaman must have covered me with when I was asleep. Somewhere in the back of my mind I heard Governor yelling, "If they're callin' long distance, you tell 'em to go screw themselves."

In the living room, "What, Orson?"

"My, my. We sound perky. What's on the rail for the snail? Hot date last night?"

Go screw yourself...go screw yourself...go screw yourself...go..."I was putting in some overtime, boss. So was Canada, by the way."

"Really?" He sounded excited. "Well, well, well. Was it a profitable evening?"

"Fair to middling."

The sound of waves breaking against a reef snapped my concentration. I jerked my head to look at the wet bar, where Chinaman, coat off and sleeves rolled past his elbows, poured griddlecake batter on a hot plate burner.

"Sassafras? You still there?"

"Yeah. Just waking up, that's all." I talked Orson through the blueprint of last night's adventures as fast as I could and promised to fill in the particulars later. Chinaman was listening from his post, using a spatula to scrape the first batch of cakes off the hot plate. Tossing them away, he laid three strips of bacon on the burner, their grease hissing like rain.

"I've lost radio contact again, Sassafras."

"I'm here. What d'ya want?" The problem with bacon is, once it's cooking, it smells good in a hurry.

"Did I leave my coat in Bertha last night?"

"No, I don't think so." I stopped to remember where I had seen it last. It had stuck in my mind for some reason. "Oh. Yeah. It's up in the balcony at the Lafayette. Why?"

"Because it's March, it's chilly outside, and Virginia and I would like to go to Macy's, if that's quiet all right with you."

"Okay. Okay." *Jeez! What a grouch.* "I've got to go out soon. How about if I stop by the theater and pick it up for you. Can you give me an hour?"

He thought about it. "Fine. John's coming over for lunch anyway, so we can wait until after that before we go shopping. No later than two thirty, please."

"Got it. See you then." I hung up before Orson could say anything else. Sometimes it was safer that way.

Chinaman used tongs to pick the bacon off the hot plate, and then poured three dollar-sized pools of batter on the greasy burner. "Would you like some orange juice, sir?" I said sure. He took a pitcher out of the refrigerator and poured me a glass. I thanked him then downed the juice in two gulps. "More?" he asked, and I nodded. "You know, it isn't fair."

"What isn't?"

"Mr. Welles and his coat. You have to fetch it, which puts him and you both at an inconvenience. It isn't fair the protestors should be able to detour him from his own theater."

"After that screwball with the razor, Orson and I can live with a little inconvenience. Truth to tell, though, I'm not looking forward to going there alone. I've sort 'a been rousting the picketers the last couple of days."

Chinaman flipped over the griddlecakes.

"Listen, Big C, about last night, I'm sorry I got mad at you."

"No, sir, you were right to be upset. I had no business going to the Nat Turner Center."

"That ain't it. I trust your judgment. It's not like you went there picking a fight."

"Hardly my style." He scraped the three tiny flapjacks off the burner, put them on a plate with the bacon, and handed me breakfast. "Would you like an egg?"

"Please."

"Scrambled?"

"Like always."

I started eating while Chinaman rummaged an egg and a bottle of milk from the refrigerator.

"What it is, it's like I said. I'm scared. The Communists and their picketers make my skin crawl. Some of them, anyway. The weird ones."

"Is that why you provoke them?" he politely asked. I suppose I deserved it. He cracked the egg over a glass, poured in some milk, and stirred the mess together. I answered, "Probably. Suppose I'm whistling past the graveyard."

"Not all Communists are brutes or assassins, Mr. Winters."

"No, but you can't deny some are. And they can all be stubborn once they set their minds to a notion."

Chinaman poured the egg-and-milk concoction on the burner and used a fork to fluff the eggs as they cooked. I watched and caught him grinning. Not much. Just a little.

I asked, "What is it?"

He collected the eggs on a saucer and laid that on the bar next to the plate with the griddlecakes and bacon. "Catsup?"

"Yep. So what are you smirking about?"

"Last night's meeting. I have attended similar functions in Berlin, London, and Paris, naturally..."

"I would have been disappointed if you didn't."

"...but this charter is the most misguided collection of Communists. They organized a reception for the mothers of the Scottsboro Boys with the same conscientiousness as they deliberated a hunger march to Washington D.C. They behaved as if everything they did had the greatest of consequences attached to it, so I shouldn't be surprised that they also acted like spoiled children."

"Sounds fair to me."

"For instance, one man refused to work on the reception Committee on the grounds that that kind of thing is women's work. One woman in particular took him to task. She said what was good for one Communist is good for any Communist."

I could believe it. "Maybe some folks are taking themselves too seriously."

"You're probably right. More's the pity. Would you like more bacon? Pancakes?"

I would have loved it, but I had a hunch I had better not. "Think I'll pass. Might be best if I stay light on my feet today. Which reminds me." I stepped away from the bar and back to the telephone. I asked the operator to connect me with the Denbroughs in Gramercy Park West, and after the third ring the sour butler answered. "Hi. I'd like to talk with Beatrice Denbrough, please. Sassafras Winters calling."

The butler said, "I'll see if she's available."

Of course she ain't available, dummy. She's engaged. I thought it, but...

"Hello, Sassafras! What took you so long to call me? Are you trying to hurt my feelings?"

She had got on the blower a lot faster than I expected. "Now I ain't coming on that tab. You've been waiting since Tuesday for me to call you?"

"Can't blame a gal for flirting."

"I don't think I could blame you for anything. Listen, I need a favor. Can you tell me how to get in touch with your fiancé?"

"Dell? Now I am hurt. You'd rather talk to him than me? You don't even like him."

"I cannot tell a lie. I do not. But this is important. I've gotta talk at him as quick as I can. Won't you help a poor struggling private dick? Hmmmm?"

"Now don't go moaning like a lost puppy. I'll help you. A girl just likes to think she's appreciated for her beauty and charm, not because you want favors from her."

"Hey, I do appreciate your beauty and charms." I also wouldn't have minded some favors from her, but that was a different story. "I'll make it up to you. I promise." Not that I had any idea how.

"You'd better." She gave me the name and address of a private men's club in Manhattan that Dell frequented daily. "My darling always lunches there, right after an invigorating match of tennis. Then it's back again for dinner and a game of snooker with faw-ther. It's all so middlebrow and ever so dull."

I thanked her for the information and, just to be polite, asked how her brother was doing.

"Norton's fine, but I have to go. If you're ever in the mood to take me away from all this tragic boredom, be sure to call again. Bye-bye."

Beatrice had changed the subject and begged off the line so fast, I was left standing for a moment holding the receiver before I realized what had happened. *Wonder what came up?* I slipped the receiver back in its cradle, and then asked Chinaman to lay out some clothes for me while I got cleaned up.

Places to go. People to see. It was going to be a busy Thursday.

First stop was Roy Horton Banks' Tenderloin tenement on Sixty Second Street. His wife answered the door, and after I dropped Papa Ted's name and explained why I had come, she told me Banks had stepped down to the corner grocer for supplies. "Yo' welcome to come in an' wait. He shouldn't be gone long."

I thanked her and accepted her invitation.

Mrs. Banks closed the door, laughing as she did. "Dat old cutter Carfino, he's quite de character ain' he?"

"Yes, ma'am. The whole kitchen staff is a hoot."

"Doan I know et! Roy's only been gone a day, an' already he misses all dem boys bad."

She wanted to get back to some dishes she had soaking, and since the kitchen was hardly large enough for one person I waited in the living room, which was lousy with books. Books of all kinds, from Rafael Sabatini's romances to H.G. Wells' *Outline of History*. And magazines. Everything from *Harper's Weekly* to *Weird Tales* and W.E.B. Du Bois' *The Crisis*.

Banks came through the front door not long after. He was a big man, in his early forties, built like a heavyweight, complete with cauliflower ear and a messy left eyebrow that might have seen service from Papa Ted's razor. Banks didn't act as if he liked the looks of me. "Who are you?" he asked, ready to charge.

I let his wife talk for me as she came out of the kitchen to collect the groceries from him, but her husband wasn't convinced. He told me to "Say something."

"Huh?"

"Don't grunt, goddamnit. Any mick can grunt. Say something."

Mrs. Banks scolded her husband. "Now, Roy, dis poor man ain' Irish. Ah talked wit' him myself. Doan yo' think Ah can tell when an Irishman is talkin' to me? 'Sides, yo' gonna toss him out all by yo'self?"

"I certainly will if I have to."

He was serious. If I didn't start flapping my gums, he was going to start swinging his fists. But, like clockwork, my mind went blank from the stress.

"Honey," Banks asked his wife, "is this guy mute or just dumb?"

Some words finally came to mind. "'Fair is foul, and foul is fair. Hover through the fog and filthy air.'"

Banks leaned at me. "Pardon me?"

Christ! I'm spouting lines from the damned play! What the hell am I saying? But I couldn't stop. Not if I wanted to avoid a bruising. "'When shall we three meet again? In thunder, lightning, or in rain?'"

Banks cocked his scarred eyebrow, then smirked. "'When the hurly-burly's done, when the battle's lost and won. That will be ere the set of sun.' So you are working on that white boy's *Voodoo Macbeth* over in the old Lafayette."

"*For* the Harlem Unit. Like your wife said." *Thank God!* My mind was thawing and I could breath again. "Why did you think I was Irish?"

"Never said I did. I only wanted to be sure you weren't. White visitors to our home come as scarce as hen's teeth, and the mooks think they own the whole West Side. A day doesn't go by that some damn Hibernian isn't hassling a Negro here in San Juan or some immigrant down in the Fifties. I'm not a man who looks for trouble, but I won't run from it, so I'm not very popular with them. I don't like being wary of a man in my own home because of his skin, but I do a lot of things I don't like to survive."

What could I say? "I understand."

"I appreciate that. Please, sit down." Banks slipped off his wool jacket while I found a chair. Before he put the coat away Banks felt inside its pockets until he found a pipe and tobacco pouch. "Mind if I smoke?"

"It's your house. Speaking of which, I couldn't help noticing you like to read."

Banks chuckled as he struck a match against the sole of his shoe then lit his pipe. "I've always been a voracious reader. Now I've got my wife hooked, only she prefers magazines. She can't get enough of them."

"Well, I don't mean to be nosy, but when you first came in I would have bet even money you were a prizefighter, not a bookworm."

"Can't a man be both?" he asked, sitting down. "I still train at a gym to keep in shape. Good thing, too. I'll probably have to hire myself out as a sparing partner to some contender until I can land steady work." Banks bent towards me to whisper, "Don't tell my wife, but I'm looking forward to it. I'm anxious to see if I can still cut the mustard inside the ropes."

I wished him luck, and then asked if he minded me asking a few questions about the night he saw Kanter at the Theresa. He told me to fire away. "I was wondering why De Shields called about champagne. You know he rang room service about that?"

"Yes, I do."

"I bumped into De Shields a time or two right before he died. I didn't know him well, but I do know he drank beer like kids drink lemonade. Wine wasn't his poison. I think he was meeting somebody in his room that night. A woman. That would explain the champagne. He was trying to impress her."

Banks mulled over my words while he puffed on his pipe. "Interesting. Bubbly is certainly the soft drinks of lovers. But I'm afraid I didn't see anything that night that can help you."

"Are you sure?"

"Yes, sir. For one thing I was surprised to see a colored man on the third floor who didn't work for the hotel. I couldn't help staring at him, which is probably why the detective accosted me. For another, Kanter stood in the threshold of room 316, while De Shields stood just inside. My view inside the suite was effectively blocked. However, if it's any consolation, I doubt very much if there was ever a woman in 316 that night."

"How come?"

"Because De Shields never placed the order. I can believe he was expecting company. No, there is no evidence, but the champagne supports that hypothesis, just as De Shields' not ordering supports his lover never arrived."

It was a good point, and I said so. "My only problem is, I've got to find out if this hypothetical dame is real or not."

It was his turn to wish me luck.

"Thanks. Did you know a hand towel was swiped from 316's bathroom?"

"No. The police didn't say anything about it to me."

"They don't know it's gone yet. If it is gone. For all me, your pal Mudd, or God knows, the chambermaid could have left one hand towel instead of two by accident."

Banks said this was possible but unlikely. "If a maid forgets to leave a towel, a bar of soap, or an extra blanket just one time, she'll be working in the laundry room at ten cents less an hour before she can say Peter Cottontail. No, sir. Maids make mistakes like that about as often as I get white visitors. Of course, here you are, so it can happen."

"Which leaves me with another maybe. Maybe De Shields was meeting a lady at the Theresa. Maybe his killer swiped a hand towel."

"It's intriguing," he said, shifting himself in his chair and crossing his legs. All Banks was missing was the crushed velvet smoking jacket. "Why even take the towel? Was it splattered with incriminating bloodstains that linked him to the crime? Did he hide his gun under it just before he shot De Shields? Or perhaps the killer borrowed the towel to get rid of his weapon? Tie the gun and a few rocks or bearings up in the towel and then chuck it over the Brooklyn Bridge."

That last one was good. I hadn't thought of it. "I like that one," I told Banks. "No one recalls hearing De Shields shout anything before or after the shots were fired, so it might have been used to muzzle him. Of course, then why bother yanking the towel out of the peeper's mouth, but there's all kinds of possibilities."

"My point exactly. But maybes and possibilities will get you nowhere. You need something tangible. Mind if I make a suggestion?"

"Feel free. I'll take any advice I can get."

"Did Papa Ted and his boys tell you De Shields had another visitor about an hour before Kanter?"

I said, "Yes."

"This affluent stranger would be my primary concern. One thing I can tell you for certain is, when I saw Kanter talking to De Shields, their conversation was cordial. Judging by the black eye, it takes no leap of faith to believe the stranger's conversation with De Shields was more hostile. Murder is a blood crime. I'd seek the man who bares the sign of violence. Perhaps it is the mark of vengeance."

That was one piece of advice I had already taken to heart, although I didn't tell Banks. I just nodded and told him I appreciated his suggestion.

"Glad to help. I just wish I could do more. I've given that night outside 316 a lot of thought. After all, it cost me my job. Perhaps if I had been more observant."

"As far as the cops are concerned you were plenty observant. Your description of Ben Kanter is practically dead-center perfect. Sergeant Dancer told me you shaved a couple inches off Ben, but so what? Except for that you couldn't have described Ben better if you'd handed Dancer a photograph."

Banks cocked that messy eyebrow again, suddenly confused. "But I couldn't have been short."

"Not by much. No big deal. Ninety-nine out of a hundred is still an A-plus."

"You're misunderstanding. There is no way I can be wrong about Kanter's height."

Go ahead, Sas. Tell the heavyweight he's wrong. Go on. I dare you. "How come you're so sure?" I asked, quickly adding, "No offense."

"Remember when I said Kanter was standing in 316's threshold? The door opens to the inside, so he was standing quite close to the room number posted on De Shields' door. All room numbers in the Hotel Theresa are posted exactly five feet five and one half inches above the carpet. That's eye level for the average man. Kanter's head barely cleared the numbers three, one, and six."

It was a pretty nifty trick, but it didn't wash. "Look, you may end up slapping my jaw after all, and I hate to contradict a man in his own home, but..."

"But you're convinced I was short."

"Well, I've seen Ben Kanter nearly every day for the last six weeks, and I promise he stands five feet nine."

Banks chewed on his pipe some more, absently nodding again and again. Finally, "There can only be two conclusions."

"What?"

"Since the man I saw was between five feet five and five feet six inches tall, then either Kanter is not five feet nine..."

"He is."

"...or the man I saw wasn't Ben Kanter. Which brings me to mind of something I should have mentioned earlier. Rather the man I saw was or wasn't Kanter, I'm positive he didn't kill De Shields."

"You know this for a fact?"

"No, but think about it. Kanter, or whoever, managed to sneak into the Theresa, but couldn't go undetected for long. Do you honestly believe he could have actually escaped sight unseen after the hotel was in up arms after its guests heard seven shots fired?"

"So what are you saying? The guy you saw isn't Kanter?"

"I say it's possible."

"But it doesn't matter who it was anyway, 'cause there's no way your guy could have split the scene next morning without someone in the hotel spotting him?"

"It seems logical."

"Unless someone spied him and hasn't told anybody for some reason."

I caught him leaning towards second with that one. "Possibly. Nevertheless, I maintain it's unlikely any Negro could have escaped that morning without some person who was not an ally seeing him."

"Great. So I've got another maybe to go with the rest of my collection," I sighed.

Banks sighed, too. "I'm sorry. But you do have the man with the black eye. He might just have the answers to all your questions, or be able to lead you to them."

Next stop, the Lafayette.

By the time I parked Bertha across the street from the theater, Harlem was ready to go to lunch. Noon whistles were wailing all over the borough while I weaved my way across Seventh Avenue. Maybe thirty protestors were mixed in with the lunch crowd that clogged the Lafayette's sidewalk. Few of the picketers acted like they recognized me until I unlocked one of the theater's front doors.

"Hey, Mr. Eddie!" one demonstrator taunted me as I stepped inside. "What gives de likes of yo' de right to come here and shame us?"

I closed and locked the door behind me. *Sticks and stones, brickpresser.*

To turn on the lights in the lobby, mezzanine floor, and stairs I had to open the box office, where I grabbed one of two flashlights kept stored in an empty cashier's drawer. For reasons I never understood the house lights were controlled along with the stage lights from the big switchboard backstage. I opted not to bother with them. It was a lot faster to just run upstairs and use the flashlight once inside the balcony.

Orson's coat was right where we left it, draped over the back of the chair next to his customary roost. I flopped it over my right arm and started up the aisle when I stopped short. Before I knew what I was doing I switched off the flashlight. My heart was pounding, blood thumping over and over against my eardrums.

I was scared, but what the hell had me spooked?

Then I heard it. A sharp sound, like somebody cracking their knuckles down in the lobby, but I knew better. It was a lock. Somebody was coming into the Lafayette.

Orson? Naaah. A maintenance man? Janitor? Possible, if the

Unit had a maintenance man or janitor.

Intuition left me standing in the dark, waiting for a friendly voice. I could hear one of the front doors open then close, followed by two or three sets of footsteps. I wasn't alone, and my company was walking too deliberately, trying too hard to keep quiet, to be anyone but intruders.

Whoever it was, they had no idea how well sound travels inside an empty theater. Even from the balcony I could cleanly hear them tiptoe into the lobby and mezzanine, positioning themselves to wait for me.

No doubt about it, some of the protestors must have jimmied the lock and followed me. I was being stalked.

Awww, spit.

I had to breathe deep a time or two to keep from panicking. I needed a cool head. This was no time for me to go blank. And, besides, all the advantages were in my favor. Escaping was no trick. There were two fire exits in the balcony, one of which emptied on Seventh Avenue. Except escaping, the wisest option, didn't appeal to me. Avoiding hysteria had left me room for an even stronger emotion. Righteous indignation.

How could I leave the Lafayette after a couple of those scurvy, sign-totting swine had busted in? *It's like a captain abandoning his sinking ship! Stand and fight! Take no prisoners!*

This was war. No. It was better. This was hide-and-seek. A dangerous game of hide-and-seek, but I was good at playing games. It used to be my job. And, inside the Lafayette, I even had home field advantage.

I slipped off my shoes and sneaked to the east fire exit, where I could detour downstairs beneath the stage, to the wardrobe and property-rooms.

"Hey, kids," I whispered to myself as I assorted my arsenal, "let's put on a show."

~~

My opposition was made up of three men, two Negroes and a white, all of them bruisers.

The white man, Pizner, was a card-carrying Red. He had been protesting along with his two buddies when I happened along, and it had struck them as a good idea to get tough with the Harlem Unit's resident bodyguard. All the better to put the fear of God into the whole troupe. Opportunity only knocks once, don't you know.

They were waiting for the bodyguard to come back into the lobby from wherever he had gone into the theater. Pizner and one Negro, Gareth, were carrying knives. The last man, Anatole, liked to use a blackjack.

Five minutes turned into ten. There was no sign of the bodyguard.

Maybe the trio was getting nervous. Anxious. Perhaps having second thoughts. Perhaps not. They're the only ones who know, and they're not saying.

The first thing to catch their attention was the house lights coming up in the auditorium. They probably should have cut and run, but curiosity got the better of them and they decided to peak inside the amphitheater instead.

"See anything, 'Toly?" Gareth hissed to his friend with the blackjack.

"Nuthin'."

The den was empty. Nobody in sight. House lights were on halfway, but the stage lights were blazing down full on the courtyard to Glamis Castle.

All three made like moths, splitting up to come down separate aisles to check out the lights, alert with weapons ready. They weren't so stupid not to guess they had been found out, but were dumb enough to believe there was safety in numbers.

When they reached the front row, Pizner pointed to the orchestra pit and told Gareth to "Scrounge around there. See if that door's locked."

Gareth didn't find the bodyguard, and the tiny door used by the musicians to enter the pit from below stage was padlocked from the outside. "Ain' here." He looked up at the stage and the eerie citadel set. "Check up dere."

The trio raided Macbeth's tropical courtyard, Poe's House of Ushers in the tropics, the fortress ringed by oppressive vegetation.

"'Toly," Pizner ordered, "scope around backstage. Gareth, take those steps and look around up there." The white man pointed to stairs that led to the set's highest rampart, the scene for Macbeth's fatal duel with Macduff.

Both men did as directed, Anatole walking through a gothic arch to get behind the set. Gareth had almost reached the rampart when the voodoo drums began to chant.

Pizner: "What in hell is that noise?"

"Drums," Gareth said. "Voodoo drums."

"What?"

"Voodoo."

"Balls!"

"No." Gareth's voice quaked. "Dey got real witch doctors playin' deir drums. Dat screwball white boy even let 'em sacrifice goats fo' deir skins!" He started barking, "'Toly! Toly!"

Pizner told him to stop shouting. "'Toly's checkin' things out in back. He's okay."

"Den why ain' he answerin'?" Gareth raised his voice again. "'Toly!"

"Knock it off! For Christ-all-mighty's sakes, you're a Baptist! You gonna swallow this mumbo-jumbo?"

"Hey, screw you, meathead! Ah ain' messin' wit' no black magic." Gareth started back down the stairs. "Ah'm leavin' dis place 'fore Ah end up like 'Toly."

"He's in back, I tell you."

"Then how come he doan answer?"

Before Pizner could reply, the drumming quit. The Lafayette went dead quiet. Then both the house lights and stage lights dimmed until the auditorium was near to pitch black.

"Dat's it," Gareth said. "Ah am leavin'! Now!"

"Cut it out! It's that smartass bodyguard. He's tryin' to shake us up."

Judging by the quiver in Pizner's voice, the smartass bodyguard was doing a good job.

Before either Gareth or Pizner's eyes could adjust to the dark, a long, high scream pealed the air. The colored man shouted Anatole's name again, while the white man cried, "It's comin' from the balcony!"

There was a terrible laugh accompanied by a flashing green light that streamed down from the balcony to the stage. A light in the shape of a skull's face. And, on the stage inside the emerald pool, in front of the gothic archway, was Anatole, laying face down in a spreading puddle of blood.

"Sweet Jeeee-ZUS!" Gareth wailed.

Anatole's gory body was too much for Pizner. Things had gotten way out of hand too fast. Neither survivor was ready for the thunder that suddenly billowed throughout the theater, and even less prepared for the hag that vaulted out from the gothic arch to straddle the dead man in the eerie light. A Haitian witch with Medusa's face, draped in the furs and hides of sacrificed goats.

Gareth howled, "Baron Semadi! A hoodoo hand!"

The witch held up one hand, fingers clutching a shrunken human head, black as pitch and withered.

Pizner was still speechless. Gareth dropped to his knees and prayed for his soul.

The witch took advantage of their horror to wind up and hurl the head at Pizner. It beaned the white man, knocking Pizner dizzy long enough for the hag to rush forward and swat him senseless with Anatole's blackjack.

Gareth jumped to his feet. "Yo' lousy buck! Et's yo'!" He raised his snickersnee, crouched, and raced down the stairs. "Make a jackass outta me!"

The witch glared at him and reached under the furs to pull out a Wilkinson sword, worn by Macbeth's officers in the play. Yanking off its sheath and tossing it away, the witch leveled the sword at the astonished Gareth. Outclassed, the Negro dropped his knife.

I reached up and stripped off my witch mask. Sweaty, panting from running back and forth between the stage and balcony, my hair mussed up by the disguise, the pulsing green beacon glinting off the Wilkinson, I like to think I must have been quite a sight.

"Looking for me?" I asked.

Chapter Nineteen

I had to baby-sit my new buddies, so I couldn't poke my head outside the Lafayette when Dancer and the cavalry arrived.

I imagine the picketers weren't too happy to watch a squad car and paddy wagon come wailing up Seventh Avenue to park in front of the theater. Seeing Orson step out of the car with Dancer and two uniformed cops certainly didn't make their day. And I bet it was no fun watching two other cops throw open the rear of the patrol wagon to let out nine women and seven men. Two of these men were white, but all sixteen were Communists. Four more coppers jumped out of the back of the paddy wagon to take charge of the Bolsheviks, while the first four rushed into the ring of protestors to drag out two men and a dame, all Negroes and all Reds.

The whole thing was over in a flash. Orson led the cops and the Communists inside the Lafayette, leaving the remaining protestors and other spectators on a sidewalk getting more congested by the minute. Pizner, Anatole, and Gareth were waiting for them on center stage in the amphitheater, sitting back-to-back-to-back, trussed up with some hemp I borrowed from a free capstan. I was working in front of the gothic arch, my costume off and stripped above the waist to my undershirt, mopping up the phony blood.

Dancer and his associates sat the Communists together in the auditorium's front row. Orson came on stage to see what I was doing. He smirked at the frothy pink puddle. "Taking lessons from Abdul?"

"Yep," I played along, dunking my mop in its bucket. "I just graduated my class with goats, and he said I can start butchering theatrical prodigies on Monday."

Orson held his palms beside his cheeks, quivered them, and said, "Oooooh," sarcastic to the last. After a sincere chuckle Welles glanced at a small pile laying between my three playmates and us. It was my costume and mask, the Wilkinson, the shrunken head, and his coat. He peaked at the fake blood again. "I can't wait to hear this one."

"I can't wait to tell you."

Dancer joined us on stage. He stopped beside Anatole. "Hey, 'Toly," he said, recognizing the man with the crimson-stained face and clothes.

"What's an Eastman like you doing with these two naughty boys?"

"Yo' ain' gonna believe dis, sergeant, but we's innocent!"

Dancer told Anatole to bottle it. When Pizner asked if the three of them could please be untied, Dancer told him to bottle it, too. "I like you mugs fine the way you are."

One of the Communists in the front row, a woman, stood to bawl out the detective. "Why are we here? Wha' are yo's arrestin' us for? We ain' done nuthin'."

"I haven't arrested you, Anabelle. And we're here because you nitwits sure as hell have done something. You've carried this protesting way too far, and it's time to call it quits before someone gets hurt." Dancer pulled some bubble gum from out of his coat pocket, unwrapped the pink wad, popped it in his mouth, and started chewing. "Pizner broke in here so he could assault, maybe even kill, that defenseless pink over there." He pointed at me.

"Hold it!" Gareth said. "We wasn' gonna kill him! No way! Jes' rough him up some."

Pizner requested that Gareth kindly stuff a cork in it.

"Don't fuss with the barn door now," Dancer told Pizner. "The horse is long gone."

But Anabelle wasn't going to give up. "Ef dose three lunkheads broke de law, dat's deir problem. We got nuthin' to do wit' dat."

"Wrong again, darling," Dancer disagreed. "The only Communist on this stage is Pizner. 'Toly ain't no Red, and I bet this other dinge..." Dancer stopped to ask Gareth his name. "Are you a Communist, Gareth? Don't lie to me now."

"No, Ah ain'! Ah was jes' tryin' to help 'em!"

"That's right. You and 'Toly are volunteers, like most picketers outside."

Anabelle replied, "So?"

"So I know a Republican judge who likes Bolsheviks as much as he likes the Tammany tiger, and I'm not going to have any trouble convincing him this whole stupid stunt was Pizner's idea."

"Well, et *was* his stupid idea, sergeant," 'Toly offered. Gareth seconded. Pizner cursed a blue streak until Dancer reminded him to clam up.

The cop returned to Anabelle. "'Toly may be a creeper, but he's never been pinched for burglary or assault. How 'bout you, Gareth?"

"Not as Ah can recall."

"There you go. My judge can rule Pizner contributed to 'Toly's and Gareth's delinquency. And when he does, I'm going to turn around and ask my pal the judge to rule the Nat Turner Center is a hazard to public safety. And when he does that, I'm going lock your doors and shut you down."

"You *can't* do that!" the woman howled. Her comrades joined in, only to have their eight superintendents hush them up in a hurry.

"I *can* do it, Anabelle. You folks have set dozens of precedents for it, thanks to all those evictions we're always meeting at."

Orson and I had no idea where Dancer was coming from, but the Communists seemed to, judging by their hangdog expressions.

The policeman continued. "Okay. We know what I can do. Let me tell what I will do...if everybody's agreeable. You listening to this, Winters? Welles?"

"We're all ears," Orson assured Dancer.

"I'm going to take Pizner, 'Toly, and Gareth to the precinct. I'm going to hold them pending Winters filing assault and Welles illegal entry charges against them. If charges are filed, I'm calling my Republican judge. However, if by some inconceivable act of human generosity Winters and Welles don't press charges, then..." The cop let the obvious speak for itself.

"Excuse me, sergeant," I asked, "but what makes you think I'll let The Three Stooges cop a walk?"

"Because, if you do, Pizner's comrades will agree to call off the dogs and let the Harlem Unit rehearse in peace."

The Communists didn't believe that was such a hot idea.

Dancer nodded patiently, a family doctor prescribing placebos to hypochondriacs. "It's your decision, gang. Just consider the consequences."

That got the Communists to simmer down and discuss among themselves. They deliberated, debated, and argued. After all, this was a monumental decision. Then Anabelle, their foreman, presented the verdict. "Mah friends and Ah agree to git outta yo' hair."

"No picketing on the front walk?" Orson asked.

"No picketin'."

"No more whipping up racial tensions? No more accusations of white chauvinism?"

"Nope. No mo' 'til after openin' night, an' only den ef et's justified." She said the last word as "jest-ified."

Welles liked what he heard and said, "Deal." It was my turn to make a decision, but Dancer interrupted me. "I think Mr. Winters better cool off before he says anything he might regret later." The copper looked to his associates. "You guys take these nice people outside where they can tell the protestors their services are no longer necessary. When that's done, come back in here and escort 'Toly and his ugly stepsisters to their pumpkin."

The bulls herded the Communists out of the auditorium. Dancer stayed to wait for his men to come back. He stuffed his hands in his front pants pocket then strolled over to my three playmates. "What do you boys think?" he asked them. "Should Mr. Winters here forget all about you trying to stave in his head?"

I pointed out that only one of the three had brought a blackjack. "The other two carried knives."

"It wasn't like we was gonna hurt him," Pizner insisted. "Just rouse him. That's all. Honest."

"Yeah," 'Toly said, staring at me. "Wha's de matter wit' yo, man? Ain' yo' got no sensayuma?"

I said, "I'm laughing my head off. You stupids are the ones looking at a stretch up river."

Dancer asked me if that was what I really wanted. It was, but I also wanted the Communists to get off Welles' back.

"Ask me tomorrow," I said, then winked.

The cop winked back. "Be happy to." He eyed the red puddle and the pile. "You must have put on one heck of a show."

"You might say that. So what was all that about you and the Communists always meeting at evictions? You really took the wind out of their sails with that one."

Orson asked, too, but Dancer just waved it off as nothing. "It's not always me. Just cops in general. There must be something like a dozen evictions in Harlem every day. Sometimes twenty. It's like I told you, rent's skyrocketing in this borough."

"I remember."

"The Nat Turner Center will send a couple members to these evictions to make speeches and get everybody in the neighborhood worked up. You know firsthand that don't take much effort. Pretty soon the Reds have got neighbors helping the evicted folks move back into their old apartment. Landlord calls us up to move them out again. A few times things have got ugly and we had to send for the riot squad. That means bludgeons and tear bombs. People get arrested, people get hurt, and people get killed."

"And your Republican judge doesn't approve of such things?" Orson asked.

"Just like anybody else with common sense." The cop grinned at me. "Tell me, brother, did you glom anything interesting at the Hotel Theresa last night?"

I grinned back but said nothing.

"The night manager got me on the blower this morning. You made a real impression with him."

Now I was worried. "Is there a problem?"

"Not with me, and that's all that counts. I told Mudd if he had any complaints to tell 'em to your face. That didn't appeal to him. He's more of a letter-to-the-editor type."

"Thanks. And, yeah, I think I did find out something, but I've got to meet with a guy and double-check that I'm on the right track. Can I give you a ring tonight or early tomorrow?"

For a hot lead Dancer didn't care if I called him out of the sheets with Marlene Dietrich. "You still got my business card?"

"It's in my wallet."

"Great. Just do me one favor."

"Name it."

"Don't eat any bullets before you can call me. I've got one dead shamus on my hands now. I don't want another one."

Now that was a cheery thought.

※

Orson hung around after Dancer and his troop swept out the Unholy Three to keep me company until I finished mopping. At first I figured he just wanted to know more about what went on at the Theresa, but it turned out he was more interested in how I had bagged Pizner and company.

"The drums really spooked them?" he would ask, then, "Gareth *really* thought you were a voodoo hag?" The more he heard, the more his confidence in *Macbeth's* designs and effects grew, so I let him go on asking, even when he repeated questions two or three times.

When I was done cleaning the stage, I put my shirt and coat back on to leave. Orson took his coat out of the pile and we went to the lobby. Good to their word, Anabelle and the other Communists had disbanded the picketers. The front walk was empty.

Outside, a weight off both our shoulders, Orson looked at my watch. It was almost three. "Virginia will be shopping, but I can catch her at Macy's if I hurry. Will you and Chinaman still be picking me up tomorrow night?"

"Better safe then sorry. Five forty-five?"

"Fine. See you then." He stepped up to the street to hail a cab, while I forged across Seventh Avenue where Bertha waited, a note stuffed under the windshield wiper. Snatching the note, I climbed in behind the wheel and closed the door before I read it. It was from Dancer: *You think you can park your heap here all day without getting a ticket?! You owe me. Officer D*

"We'll see who's beholding to who, buster."

Cramming the note into my breast pocket, I cranked the ignition and pulled out into traffic. From Harlem I drove to Dell Joyce-Armstrong's club, the Athenaeum, a formidable two-story Romanesque building on Fifty-fifth Street. Parking Bertha again, I walked to the front door, pausing to read a plaque mounted beside the entrance:

> This is the Athenaeum Club; so wise
>   there's not a man of it
> That has not sense enough for six—in fact
>   that is the plan of it;
> The very waiters answer you with eloquence
> Socratical,
> And always place the knives and forks in
>   order mathematical.

Underneath this was the poet's name, "Theodore Hook," who had made the club sound more suitable for Chinaman and not a bum like Joyce-Armstrong.

Inside I had to piddle around with another desk clerk. He was spindly and uppity, which was common to the breed, but at least he didn't have one of those puny mustaches. The desk clerk told a page to track down Joyce-Armstrong. "Do try the tennis courts," he suggested.

I had to wait in the vestibule, where I passed time looking through a glass partition into a big indulgent room where men were sitting reading newspapers, each in his own tiny nook. It was weird.

Ten minutes later the page came back with not one but two men, Joyce-Armstrong and his father, the Colonel. Dell's dad was stockier then his boy, or Roy Banks for that matter. He was bald but compensated with a trimmed gray-metal beard and mustache. I could believe the Colonel was handsome in his day, and he still wasn't bad looking with his iron blue eyes, but the years and a strong will had chiseled hard lines into his face. Father and son were dressed in white tennis costumes and carried catgut tennis racquets, but only the boy had a left eye tattooed with a bruise.

"How do you do," the Colonel greeted me, gripping my hand to shake it. His skin was callous, and he talked with an abrasive Scottish brogue. "I'm Dell's father. He tells me you're a detective."

This guy didn't seem the sort to pussyfoot, which suited me fine, but instead of answering I urged we talk somewhere private. Dell seemed nervous, and the Colonel didn't look delighted by the suggestion, but he told the page to fetch a key from the desk clerk. After the page returned the Colonel led Dell and me down a corridor to a small apartment, where he locked the door behind us before tossing me the key.

"It's your play, Mr. Winters," he said. "What do you want?"

"I think you know."

He shook his head and sighed. "Buddy, if you've got something to say, say it, or I'll have you tossed out of here on your ass."

"A man after my own heart." I pointed at Dell's face. "Andre De Shields gave your son that black eye the night he died. I know it. You two know it. And, best yet, I can prove it. No problem."

"So what?"

Dell smiled.

"So, De Shields is dead, and your son's a suspect."

The Colonel's eyes lost all their blue, while his neck turned beat red. "That's preposterous. The police don't consider Dell a suspect."

"Sir, the police don't know Dell talked to De Shields that night, much less that De Shields poked him."

The old man didn't like that. He didn't like that at all. He snarled at his boy. "Is this true? You didn't talk to the Miltonians like you said?"

"The what?" I asked.

"The bulls! The bloody cops! My brave boy swore up and down that everything was square between him and the police!"

Dell said that he couldn't talk with the cops. "And I didn't kill De Shields."

"Then why don't you tell the police that?"

"I can't, father." He drew *father* out the way Beatrice had imitated him earlier, and I had to bite my lip to keep from laughing. Good thing, too. The Colonel wasn't in a jolly mood. If father and son had been alone I do believe the Colonel would have given Dell a matching tattoo. As it was the old man slapped his racquet hard against his leg before returning to me. "Now what is it you want then? Hush money? I don't cotton up to extortionists, sonny."

And up yours too, pal. "All the cabbage in the world couldn't stop me from spilling my guts to the cops. I just came to ask Dell what he was doing at De Shields' room. If he doesn't tell me, then he can tell the police, but I bet it might mean something if I could say to them that Dell cooperated with me."

Dell looked to his father for advice, but the Colonel turned to stare out a window. His son was going to have sink or swim on his own.

"As if it's any of your business," the boy started, "but De Shields was trying to blackmail the Denbroughs." He paused.

I waited.

"You're not surprised?" he asked.

You're too late for that, chump. "Get on with it."

"He came to the Denbroughs' home around seven Tuesday evening. He demanded half a million dollars. It's no secret that the Denbroughs no longer possess that kind of money, but De Shields didn't believe them when they told him. I went to the Theresa to try to talk some sense into him." His words had all the rhythm of a well-rehearsed song. It was sad he couldn't have come up with a better line.

"How d'ya know where to find De Shields?"

Dell hadn't thought about supporting his story. Thinking on his feet, he settled on, "He told Mrs. Denbrough where to bring the money that night. He was meeting someone at the Theresa. You're friend Kanter, I suppose."

I slid my eyes back to the Colonel. He was upset. I would be, too, if my kid couldn't lie any better than this.

"De Shields wanted the money that night?" I asked.

"Yes."

"And he demanded the money around seven o'clock?"

"Yes."

The Colonel turned on Dell, roaring like a lion. "Good Christ, boy! You've had two days and you can't make up a better load of dun than this? Whose son are you?"

"It's the truth!" His voice wavered.

"Are you a twit, then, or have you forgotten that there isn't a bank in Manhattan open on Tuesday after six o'clock?"

It was pathetic to watch Dell realize his error. I thought he was going to cry right there.

I said, "Look, junior, forget I even asked. I gave you a chance. The cops can worry about getting the truth out of you."

Colonel Joyce-Armstrong misunderstood my intentions and stepped between Dell and me before I could make a move. Brows knit and lips sneered, he looked very effective. "I'll be the one to handle this. You won't be dragging my boy to any precinct."

"Why the hell should I bother?"

The old man blinked.

"Like it or not, your boy's a suspect. That's what I'm telling the police. You can either haul his hams down to Harlem, or the bulls can come up here and get him. It makes me no never mind. And if Dell's dumb enough to run, that will just make him look a whole lot guiltier then Ben Kanter. Good day, gentlemen."

I went to the door and unlocked it. Before I could get away, Dell asked me, "How did you find out about my being at the Theresa?"

"How else do you think? The night manager told me."

~

I went back to the Cosmopolitan, feeling itchy and peppy, a lot like I used to in the bigs before I had to pitch. Inside the lobby I stopped at the front desk to see if I had any messages.

"Yes, sir, Mr. Winters," the clerk said. To my pleasure the Cosmopolitan snubbed the usual types for their desk help. This clerk was a pretty pixie girl, not even five feet tall, with cornstalk hair and violet eyes that could put lilacs to shame. *God, I love this hotel!*

I waited for her to take my message out of my key box, but instead she pointed back the way I had just come.

"The revolving door wants to see me?"

"No," she giggled. "There's a cabbie waiting for you.

Cabbie? "Oh! Great! Thanks!"

I stepped outside again and saw the hack I had ignored a half minute before. The Checker was parked maybe a half block away, its driver patiently leaning against a quarter panel reading a book.

"You waiting on me?" I called down.

The cabbie looked up. "Your name Winters?"

"Yep."

"Then I'm waiting on you."

I marched down to meet him. Far away he looked overweight, and the closer I got the wider he got. He was close to forty, a head shorter than me, and must have topped the scale at three hundred pounds. As big as he was his face, or what I could see of it under the heavy mustache and beard, was boyish.

"Name's Stick," he said, closing his book and tossing it on his hood. I glanced at the title. *The Mystery King,* by Gaston Leroux. "Dennis Stick."

"Glad to meet you. I was hoping you might remember a fare you had a couple of nights ago."

"Yeah. I know. Dispatcher told me what you were after already. I remember your guy. Andre De Shields, the dick what got himself popped over at the Theresa."

"That's him. Can you help me?"

"Don't know if I can or can't. I remember picking him up about seven that night. He was in a foul mood. Foul. I could smell he'd been into the suds, but he didn't act drunk. He struck me as a tough old bird."

I nodded. "I won't argue with that."

"I ain't complaining. He was a good fare."

"Where did you take him?"

"Over to the old Lafayette Theater. It's been closed for a couple of years, but they reopened it this year for one of them WPA deals."

"Really?"

"Yeah. He had me wait for him, and he's inside maybe ten minutes. After that he wanted me to run the meter to Gramercy Park West. Told me to keep it running while he goes into this fancy brick mansion."

That jived with Joyce-Armstrong's fairy tale, the part where De Shields came back to the Denbroughs', although I still didn't buy that blackmail nonsense. To double-check I gave Stick the Denbroughs' address.

"That's the house. De Shields goes in, then comes out all in a huff a few minutes later. Brother, he was steamed, ready to bite nails. No exaggeration. I wasn't looking forward to having this berserker sharing my hack with me. Only this dame comes out of the mansion and chases him. She talks to him, somehow gets him to get a grip on himself, then she pops back inside her palace like Tinker Bell. De Shields comes back to where I'm parked and he has me drive around awhile. No destination."

"Why?"

"Hell if I know. I do know I was racking up the dough, which is plenty hard to come by so I don't ask questions when it does. You know?"

I knew.

"I guess we got out of Gramercy Park West around seven thirty. That's a guess, okay. And probably an hour later he has me let him out on the Forties in the Tenderloin."

"Why there?"

Stick shrugged, giving me a queer look to say, "What am I? A mind-reader?" Then he said, "What am I? A mind-reader?"

Whoa. "I figured you might have a clue or a guess or something."

"Nuh-uh. All I can tell you is this De Shields guy climbed out of my hack and started walking back towards Harlem. He didn't look like he had any room in his head for a destination. The mug was real deep in thought. You know?"

I thought I was beginning to. "And that's the last you saw De Shields?"

"Last time ever."

"Okay." I took out a fiver and handed it to Stick for his trouble. "I appreciate it."

"Hey, no problem. Mid-afternoon's kind of slow anyway. I get a lot of reading done before the whistles start to blow." He grabbed his book, and I went back to the hotel.

Chinaman wasn't in our room when I got there, which was okay by me. I took Dancer's card out of my wallet, dialed his work number, and got him to answer on the second ring.

"Just the man I've been waiting for," he said, sounding happy. "I was afraid you might be dead by now."

"Hey, me and Philo Vance, we're like flivvers. We'll never die." I didn't give Dancer a chance to crack back, but dove in and told him everything I knew about Dell Joyce-Armstrong's visit to the Theresa, including his threat to Mudd. I also tossed in the champagne and missing towel at no extra charge. "Now here's the part I can't figure out when it comes to all this blackmail hooey, only you've got to promise me this stays between you and me."

"I can't withhold evidence."

"And I ain't asking you to. What I know isn't evidence. It's just...interesting."

Dancer thought about it. "All right. As long as it ain't evidence, this can stay on the Q.T. Spill."

I filled him in about what De Shields had tried to pull on the Countess. It must have been interesting, all right, because Dancer whistled loud enough on his end to pop my eardrum. "I never figured Andre to get into any kind of graft."

"As far as the Denbroughs are concerned, I don't think he was. If Joyce-Armstrong hadn't quoted that half-million price tag, I would have shrugged his fib off as a coincidence. What I'm thinking now is, Joyce-Armstrong knew De Shields had tried blackmailing someone. Maybe he even knows who and why. He just used what he knew to make up an excuse about why he went to the Theresa."

"So why did he go?"

"Damned if I know. Yet. But I've got a hunch. You willing to gamble on something with me?"

Dancer said he was willing to listen.

"If Joyce-Armstrong knows De Shields had turned extortionist, then it seems likely the Denbroughs do, too."

"I can buy that."

"And that puts me in mind of something I read awhile ago. Would you be a pal and dig up Leonard Denbrough's death certificate for me?"

Chapter Twenty

With the evening off I went to bed early to catch up on my shuteye. The next morning Chainman and I went into Manhattan, where we had lunch and split up. He took in the cultural high spots while I went to Radio City Music Hall to see the latest Chandu serial chapter and *The Invisible Ray*. By five thirty we were back in Greenwich Village to pick up Orson at his West 14th Street apartment, the young man as chipper as when we parted. His mood improved even more when we parked at the Lafayette and saw that the picketers were still making themselves scarce. Except for pedestrian traffic, the sidewalk was vacant.

"This is going to be a great night, Sassafras," Orson chirped as he hopped out of Bertha.

"I'd like nothing better."

Welles' caterers were putting the finishing touches on a dinner buffet in the lobby when we got there. Perry had unlocked the theater at four so the crew could come in and get things ready for rehearsals. Actors and musicians had started arriving an hour later. Everything was chugging smoothly along.

During supper Orson distributed his notes to the Unit, then made his expected apology, which was direct and sincere. The cast and crew appeared to accept it with no hard feelings, but as rehearsals got on track I started to have my doubts.

By seven o'clock a lot of the secondary actors were complaining that their costumes were too warm. By eight o'clock most of the crew was grousing about how hot the lights were. Before nine o'clock these two blocs united, threatening to walk out.

"We was jes' here!" one actor, a Citadel soldier, carped as he unbuckled his sword belt, letting Wilkinson and strap fall on the stage. "I ain' ready fo' mo'."

"Me, neither," another soldier joined in, taking off his sword and throwing it down. More soldiers enlisted in the strike, followed by a battalion of lords, gentlemen, officers, attendants, messengers, doctors, murderers, and apparitions. Crewmembers jumped on the bandwagon, and before he knew it Orson had a full-blown mutiny on his hands!

The director was about to bounce to his feet in the balcony, but I clapped a hand on his shoulder. "Don't," I advised. "You'll just make matters worse. Ball teams pull this kind of crap all the time. It's no big deal."

"Are you nuts? They're walking out!"

"They're frustrated and tired and blowing off steam. Let 'em. They'll be back."

I'm not sure he saw where I was coming from, but Orson did listen to Chinaman. "You have been working them awfully hard, sir. And there could be lingering resentments in spite of your apology. Mr. Winters is correct. The best course is to let them vent their emotions."

Give the kid credit. He only had an instant to decide and before time was up he nodded then stood so the troupe could get a better look at him. He said nothing, just let his detractors have at him. And they took advantage. Boy, did they take advantage. I had to admit to Chinaman, I was impressed with Orson's restraint.

Then, out of the blue, a giant figure in Napoleonic regalia bounded up Castle Glamis' parapet, shouting at the mutineers. It was Jack Carter.

"Had enough, have you? You're tired, is that it? Well, maybe you did just work for two days straight. So what? My part's bigger than any of yours so I've worked a lot harder at this gig than any of you! But what of it in either case? The fate of the Harlem Unit is at stake here. Oh, you do all remember the WPA's Negro Theater Unit, don't you? They're just the only people who bothered to hire any of you when nobody else would. This is an opportunity most of us never dared to hope for, and now here we are, living it.

"If men like Orson Welles, or John Houseman, or Harry Hopkins, or Franklin goddamn Delano Roosevelt are willing to risk their reputations on a project like the Federal Theater, then what are we complaining about? How can you even stand there bellyaching after the way Mr. Welles has worked, night and day, week after week, on our behalf, when he could just as easily have been earning a fortune on the radio, and you all know that's true. You don't seem to mind being here whenever he sets out the free food and drinks, paid for out of his own pocket, do you? If somebody's willing to go out on a limb to do so much for us, then there's only one thing we can do for that person in return: follow him, unquestionably, to the ends of the earth and stop screwing up this wonderful production with your stupid complaints. If you're so hot and tired, you can rest after the opening! Because you can sure believe me here and now, if our opening's a bust and *Macbeth* fails, through no one's fault but your own, we're all going to have the rest of our goddamn lives to rest in!"

Everyone in the Lafayette listened in silence. If anything could have snapped them out of their hostility, it was Carter's reprimand.

Quietly, deliberately, cast and crew returned to their places, the mutiny cut off at the roots.

Watching the Unit, Carter hollered, "That's it. Get yourselves back to work, you no-acting bums!"

And as quickly as the storm had passed, the heavens opened again.

When the brawl finally ended a fair part of Glamis Castle laid in pieces on the stage. More than a few folks suffered bumps and lacerations, but we were lucky. Rose was our worst casualty, bruising her back and butt after being accidentally pushed into the orchestra pit. We checked her out, and even though she was sore she didn't want to come out of the game.

All in all, the riot wasn't such a bad thing. Damage to the set could have been worse and was by no means critical, and the Unit seemed in better spirits. It had been a hell of a blow, but when it was over there were plenty of apologies followed by laughter, something even Orson could appreciate. "Just don't let John ever hear about this," he told the Unit before everyone started to pitch in to clean up the mess.

The amphitheater was pretty close to shipshape, the set as ready for rehearsals as it would be for a while, when Dancer came down the center aisle with two uniformed cops in tow. He sent his bulls on an errand elsewhere in the Lafayette, then tracked down Chinaman, Orson, and me on stage.

"You know," the copper said as he surveyed the damage, "this place looks different somehow."

Orson: "Yes, well, this is what happens when you try using Limburger for bait in your mouse traps."

"You'd think your rats could show a little more gratitude."

An abrupt commotion underneath our feet snuffed the jocularity. We looked down into the orchestra pit where Dancers' patrolmen were leading Rose and Jack Carter through the musicians' door, followed by Miss Thompson. One of the cops told the sergeant, "We found 'em."

Orson was flabbergasted. "What the hell are you doing, Dancer?" The scene immediately became the center of attention, the Unit gathering around behind us.

"You're not going to believe this, Orson!" Carter said. "This chump wants to arrest Rose and I!"

"I do not want to arrest you. Not right now anyway." Dancer looked at one of the patrolmen. "Did you knuckleheads tell Ramsey and Carter they were being pinched?"

"No, sir. We told them we had orders to place them into custody."

"There you go, Jack. I want to question you two, that's all."

"Then why don't you do it here instead of the precinct?"

"Who said anything about going to the precinct?"

That really confused everybody. Orson asked, "Where are you taking them?"

"Afraid I can't divulge such confidential information at this moment, Mr. Welles, but all shall be made abundantly clear at the appropriate time." Dancer motioned for his underlings to herd Rose and Carter out of the theater, then asked me, "You want to tag along? Bring your man Jeeves if you want."

This was just a formality. I was joining his party and he knew it. Chinaman was eager to get behind this mystery, so I let him come. Orson and Miss Thompson demanded they be allowed to follow, but Dancer told them to stay put. "You're practicing this play again? Just go on doing that."

"But you're taking away my star! How can I direct a play without a star?"

Dancer wasn't in a mind to sympathize. "You're the Great Black Way's whiz kid. Figure it out for yourself." He waved for Chinaman and me to follow him, leaving Orson, Miss Thompson, and the rest of the Unit to wonder what the hell could wrong next.

Outside the Lafayette we scrambled into the back of a patrol wagon with Rose and Carter, Dancers' cops bolting the door shut behind us.

"So where are you taking us, sergeant?" Carter asked.

"You're moving up in the world, Carter. We're going cross town."

Carter grimaced as if he swallowed his tongue. "Where, exactly?"

"Gramercy Park West."

"Why?"

"Got to make an arrest."

"Arrest who?" Rose asked.

"You're boyfriend, Norton Denbrough."

"Fo' wha'?"

"For killing Andre De Shields, that's what."

Chapter Twenty-One

"Norton didn' shoot De Shields."

Dancer asked Rose, "Can you prove it?"

"Doan have to. Norton can."

"S'that so? You know this for a fact?"

"Yo' jes' wait and see."

Carter wasn't as cocksure as Rose. "You haven't told us why you're dragging us to Norton's place."

"That's my fault," I said. My confession surprised Chinaman, who didn't know I was in cahoots with Dancer. "Wednesday night after rehearsals, Canada and me followed you two to Gramercy Park West. We watched you go inside the Denbroughs' house. You were expected."

"How can dat be?" Rose snorted. "We jes' found out Norton was alive."

I didn't bother debating. Neither did Dancer. Carter kept trying not to look too worried.

"I must not be acquainted with all the facts," Chinaman said, curious. "Why do you think Norton Denbrough is the guilty party? What is his motive?"

"Best damn motive you can have in a murder," Dancer said. "Revenge."

Chinaman waited for more.

"Look at all the nonsense Denbrough went through to keep his family liquid until his sister's wedding. And every step of the way, there's De Shields, tailing after him. Finally, just when Denbrough gets his loan and everything seems Jake, there's De Shields again. Man oh man, he must have royally been ticked off."

"But his mother retained Mr. De Shields' services. Mr. De Shields was only following her orders. If he had a gripe with anyone, wasn't it with her?"

"It wasn't his mother standing in that alley last Sunday," was all Dancer had to say about that.

"And don't forget," I added, "Denbrough just happened to return from the veil the same day De Shields crossed over to the other side."

"But where is the evidence?"

The copper grinned like a gambler turning over an ace kicker to complete a royal flush. "The murder weapon."

"You located the gun?"

"Don't have to, thanks to your boss."

Chainman glanced my way, followed by Rose and Carter. "I had a chat with Dell Joyce-Armstrong yesterday. He said something that got me to thinking. Told me De Shields tried to blackmail the Denbroughs the night before he died. That just didn't make sense. Oh, I know for a fact De Shields went back to the Denbroughs' after Claudette fired him, but whatever he had to say to them it wasn't about blackmail. My bet is Joyce-Armstrong was putting a spin on whatever De Shields really went there about to mislead me. But what was it? I tried recollecting everything De Shields had said about the Denbroughs, as well as what I had heard or read about them, and that's when I remembered Leonard Denbrough's death certificate. He had shot himself in the head with a Webley."

"A large caliber revolver that fires seven rounds," Dancer explained, "just like the gun that killed De Shields."

"That's preposterous," Carter said. "Norton's mother would have tossed that gun away years ago."

"Why?" I asked.

"Don't be dense, Sassafras."

"Speak for yourself. I had a chance to talk with Norton's sister about her father's suicide. She's far from sentimental about it, so is it farfetched that Norton and her mother might feel the same way? Why toss a perfectly good gun, not to mention an expensive one? They're hard up for cash."

Chinaman wasn't convinced. "I'm afraid I will need more evidence."

"Cool," Dancer obliged. "We compared the records of the bullet that killed Leonard Denbrough to the pills forensics dug out of De Shields. Guess what? They match."

It was sensational. Chinaman was floored, speechless. Rose and Jack Carter looked pretty impressed, too, for that matter.

"What do you say, wise guy?" Dancer asked my valet. "I've got motive, I've linked the weapon to Denbrough, and unless Claudette's boy can scrounge up one hell of an alibi, I can establish opportunity. Is that good enough for you?"

Chinaman had nothing constructive to say, so he didn't say anything at all.

"I'm glad you approve, because before I stopped by the Lafayette to invite you all along for this ride, I paid a call on a judge. Guess what he gave me?" The sergeant reached into his breast pocket and pulled out a writ. "And looky here. A warrant for the arrest of Norton Denbrough."

"Dear God, no," Rose groaned. "God, doan let dis happen."

"God had nothing to do with this, Miss Ramsey." Dancer put the writ away. "And for your sakes, you two had better not have anything to do with it either."

We rode without discussion the rest of the drive.

When the paddy wagon parked and Dancer's men unbolted the back door, we climbed out and discovered a patrol car was waiting for us. Waiting with the car were two detectives and Dell Joyce-Armstrong.

"Wha's he doin' here?" Rose asked.

Dancer asked back, "You've met Mr. Joyce-Armstrong before?"

"Sho' Ah have. He's Beatrice's fiancé. He brung her down to Harlem to see Norton a bunch of times."

I think Dancer suspected Norton had confided in his sister. I know I had thought about it once or twice. Whichever the case, neither of us were amazed by Rose's revelation.

Dancer left the uniformed cops with the vehicles while the rest of us hiked up the Denbroughs' drive. At the front door Dancer ignored the knocker and banged with the side of his fist, taking the writ out of his pocket while he waited. He was getting ready to pound on the door again when the dour butler opened it. I would have thought an entourage like ours would have been worth a gasp or a second take, but the butler didn't even blink. "Yes?" he inquired.

"I'm Detective Sergeant Stanley Dancer with the New York City Police Department. I need to see Norton Denbrough."

"Master Denbrough is under doctor's supervision and not allowed to receive visitors."

Dancer held the writ at eye-level. "Got any idea what this is?"

"I have, sir."

"You want to stand pat on that doctor's supervision excuse, or do you step aside?"

The butler opted for a strategic retreat, and we entered the checkerboard foyer. The sergeant surveyed the surroundings, then asked the butler where Denbrough could be found. The butler gave directions to Denbrough's bedroom, and Dancer told his detectives to go up and fetch the suspect.

"Excuse me, officer." Claudette Denbrough was strolling down the steps from the second floor. "I am not accustomed to policemen raiding my home as if it were some speakeasy."

"This isn't a raid, ma'am." Dancer met Miss Claudette at the bottom of the stairs, introduced himself, and presented her with the writ. She didn't bother to read it.

"I pride myself in knowing all the policemen in this precinct, sergeant. Aren't you overstepping your jurisdiction?"

"That warrant was issued by a federal judge, ma'am. That gives me and my men jurisdiction." The policeman looked at his detectives and jerked his head, motioning them to start upstairs again. "Be smart about it," he told them.

I'm sure they would have hopped to it if they had had the chance, but the detectives didn't move three feet before a familiar voice from the top of the stairs hollered, "You tell your cops to stay put, sergeant!"

It was Ben Kanter. That was the good news. The bad news was he had one arm wrapped around Beatrice Denbrough's neck, his free hand pressing a stiletto against her jugular.

"Mah God, Ben!" Rose was going to charge straight up the stairs, but Jack Carter restrained her. At the same time Dancer gripped Miss Claudette by the elbow and walked her a few feet to one side, while his detectives drew their revolvers and leveled the weapons at Kanter.

"Tell your flatfoots to holster their guns, sergeant," Ben said, voice trembling. He was scared, although probably not as scared as Beatrice, but his knife hand was steady.

"Please do what he says," Miss Claudette told Dancer, her manner unruffled. "Let him go, and he won't harm my daughter. Please."

"Listen to the lady, sergeant," Ben seconded.

From the moment Ben had made his entrance, Dancer hadn't been able to take his eyes off of him, and not for the obvious reason. The copper seemed fascinated by Kanter's face. Now, with Miss Claudette's request, he told his men to put away their guns.

"Sergeant..." one detective argued, but Dancer shouted him down. "I said put 'em away! Do it!" They did as ordered. "Fine. Either of you draws his gun without my say so, you both can kiss your pensions goodbye."

"That's smart, copper." Ben started down the steps, keeping Beatrice in front of him. "Just have your gang move away from the front door and everything will be silk."

"You can forget about going anywhere, pal." Dancer pulled out his own service pistol, cocked it, and walked up the stairs.

Carter cried, "What in the hell are you doing?"

"Sergeant Dancer," Miss Claudette said, "I asked you to leave him be."

"Listen to the lady!" Ben insisted, but Dancer wasn't buying. The cop said, "Mrs. Denbrough, if I didn't know better, I'd swear you were more concerned about Ben Kanter than your poor little girl."

Miss Claudette didn't like that crack. "This is my home, and I want you to leave that man alone before he kills Beatrice!"

"She's talking sense, sergeant." Ben had hit the brakes when Dancer took out the gun. The policeman had stopped just two steps below Kanter and his hostage. "I'll slit her throat!"

"Tell me another one while you're at it, brother." Dancer sounded sure of himself, more than anyone in his right mind should have in his situation. "Let's make this simple so there's no slip ups. You drop that knife by the time I count ten, or I'm going to blast your brains out. Here goes. One...eight..."

Pressed for time Ben reacted instinctively, whipping away the knife and shoving Beatrice at Dancer.

I broke for the steps like I was coming off third base during a suicide squeeze, the detectives at my heels, but all the action was over before I could cross the bottom stair.

The sergeant, ready for Ben's gambit, had taken one step up to brace himself, meet the girl, and grab her. At the same time he cuffed Ben in the forehead with his gun hand before the man could flee or attack.

Rose screamed. Carter kept a firm hold on her, outraged but helpless to do anything for Ben. Joyce-Armstrong just watched like a bystander at a train wreck. Miss Claudette stood her ground, not getting involved.

Chinaman and I followed the detectives to where Dancer was taking the stiletto out of Ben's hand. Ben was cockeyed, sitting on a step, his legs spread-eagle and limp. Beatrice, meanwhile, couldn't control her hysteria any longer and raced screeching upstairs to her bedroom.

"You think one of us should go after her?" I asked.

"Why?" Dancer said. "She ain't going anywhere, whether she wants to or not. I've got men waiting out front. Remember?"

"That's not what I meant."

"I know. Tell me something, Winters, you ever seen Norton Denbrough?"

"Pardon me?"

"You heard me." The gambler's smirk was back.

"No." Then I remembered the graduation picture De Shields showed me at the Astoria. "Yeah. Just a photograph. Why?"

"Well, let me introduce you." Quick like a rattlesnake Dancer reached for Ben's curly hair. His fingers bit in and the copper yanked. Instead of ripping Ben's head off, like I expected, Dancer jerked off a wig, revealing brunette hair underneath, short and straight.

Chinaman said, "Zounds."

I squatted and tried to peer through Ben's make-up. His cheeks were fuller and eyes more tired than in the gelatin-silver print, but sure enough behind the brown Pan-Cake it was "Denbrough."

"Hi, Sassafras," he said, grinning sheepishly.

For the life of me I don't know how to describe the sensation. I had worked with Ben Kanter for six weeks. I knew him as well as anyone in the Harlem Unit. He was an acquaintance, and he was sitting in front of me, but I was also looking at a stranger.

"Who are you?"

"Norton Denbrough, I'm afraid. At your service."

Dancer cut in, pointing the stiletto at the actor. "What the hell were you thinking, pulling a stunt like this? We could have killed you and your sister both. Killed you easy. You know that?"

"I'm sorry. We panicked. Our butler saw you coming up the driveway, and when we heard you wanted me I got corked up as Ben while Beatrice and I pieced together this plan."

"What plan?" I asked.

"Ben was going to confess to killing De Shields, make off with Beatrice, release her after we were a few blocks away, and then..." He held up one hand and whirled it like a stage magician waving away paper flowers into thin air.

"Vanish for good." Dancer sighed. "Aren't you forgetting we came here looking for you and not Kanter?"

"I was hoping you boys might forget about me after you started chasing after Ben. After all, Ben would have confessed."

"You hoped wrong." The sergeant was fit to be tied. This stunt hadn't impressed Dancer in the least. Chinaman, on the other hand, was nothing except curious. "Please," he asked, "Mr. Denbrough, why did you begin this masquerade?"

"It's a long story, and I'm too tired."

"What he doan want is his mama findin' out de whole story, Mr. Chinaman. But Ah've had enough of dese lies." Rose had composed herself so Carter could relax his hold on her. She walked at Norton's mother, Miss Claudette looking stiff and irritable. "Norton's a good man, but he doan always use his smarts properly, 'specially when et comes to dis family of his. But he loves yo' and he's worked so hard fo' yo' all."

"Of course." Miss Claudette said this as if it were a self-evident obligation and nothing to be admired.

"De bank fired him 'cause he loved me. Yo' know dat already."

"And I've told you, he doesn't love you. He's infatuated. You're a commoner. We're Denbroughs."

"Norton's a man. A fine, fine man. Even ef nobody would hire him 'cause of me, he kept on searchin', 'cause yo' and Beatrice needed de money, an' he took de only job he could git."

"Please, Rose," Norton said, "don't make me sound so noble."

The matriarch turned on her son, glaring at him. "There's nothing noble about shirking your obligations, Norton. You're worse than your father ever was. You deserted your blood kin for this woman."

Jack Carter couldn't stomach any more of Miss Claudette's venom. "Damn it, lady, you ain't being fair to either one of them. All Norton owed you was the money to pay your bills until Beatrice got married. His private life was his own."

"You hold your tongue," the lady said. "I won't be sassed in my own home. Not by my son, and especially not you."

"Jack didn't mean anything, mama." Denbrough was embarrassed.

"He is beneath our station, just like this woman. We are Denbroughs. Seventh-generation Mayflower Protestants. We are the nobility of America. That's why you can't be in love with her."

I glanced at Carter, the bastard son of European aristocracy, waiting for him to scold Miss Claudette. "What the hell makes you so noble because your great-great-great grandfather was a Puritan rebel?" I waited to hear. "My great-great-great grandfather was there to exile the Huguenots from France. I *am* nobility." But he didn't say a word. Rose kept mum as well. They were satisfied to let Denbrough speak for them.

"My God," the son said in a half-whisper. "Dear Lord, why did I do so much, sacrifice my all, for you?"

His mother was as compassionate and yielding as an oak tree. "You have no one to blame but yourself for your shame."

"I turned myself into a new person for you."

"You played make-believe for your own amusement, like a bored toddler."

"I hid myself away in a drawer to save you from ridicule."

"You ran away from reality directly into a minstrel show world. You abandoned me and your sister."

"I never abandoned either of you!"

"We were forsaken at the expense of your colored friends."

"You're *living* on colored money, mama! Don't you get it?"

No, she didn't, but judging from her expression she didn't like the sounds of it.

"I borrowed the money you're living on from a Harlem shylock. A loan shark. One hundred thousand dollars."

You could practically see the will to live shrivel inside Miss Claudette like a wilting tropical flower. "Oh, no." I could barely hear her futile protest. "Please. No."

"Yes! I did it for you and Beatrice. Borrowed the money so you could keep the estate and the servants and the cars and the pretenses. So you could go on being better than everyone else."

"You tainted our accounts with corrupted money?"

"Without hesitation. Without blinking an eye. And now we *owe* money to a commoner, mama. A criminal, no less."

She'd run out of words.

"Norton," Rose said. "No mo'. Yo' hurtin' her fo' spite. Dat ain' right."

Miss Claudette wasn't in the mood to accept Rose's sympathy. "Shut your filthy mouth!" she shouted. She was hurt and wanted to share her hurt. To Norton she said, "That money is coming out of our accounts first thing Monday. You withdraw it. All of it. Don't you leave one pagan cent. You hear me, boy?"

Dancer answered for Denbrough. "You'll have to attend to that yourself, ma'am. Come Monday morning, you're son is going to be in jail, waiting for another arraignment."

"Fine. Do what you will to him. He's nothing to me." And that's all she would say.

"Sergeant Dancer?" Chinaman asked, the argument having interrupted his questions. "May I inquire about one or two more inconsequential matters?"

The cop must have genuinely liked Big C. He wasn't trying to hide his impatience to move this investigation elsewhere, but he said, "Go ahead. Make it quick."

"Naturally." To Denbrough. "Mr. De Shields saw you tugged away from Miss Ramsey's bedroom window Sunday morning. We were led to believe the man pulling on you was Ben Kanter. Since that obviously isn't possible, who was it?"

Jack Carter coughed theatrically, tentatively raising his hand like a basketball player being sited for a silly foul.

"You, sir?"

"Afraid so. Norton and I were finishing up tucking away what we could of that loan into a money belt when he spotted De Shields."

"And, may I assume, you did your best to collect all of Mr. Denbrough's belongings while he made down into Mr. Kanter?"

Carter nodded while Rose said, "Ah tried to occupy De Shields at de front door until Norton could git away wi' de money."

"What about the blood?" I asked.

"Mine," Carter confessed again. "In all the hurly-burly I cut myself near the wrist but didn't realize it. Not a big gash, but it bled a lot for a while. Anyway, we thought it best to have Norton bolt the bedroom door before he ducked out of the window, so I had to slip my suit jacket back on and go back to the party. Good thing I wore navy, too. My sleeve sopped up what blood there was left until the wound closed."

"One last question, please," Chinaman said. "The money belt?"

Carter pretended he didn't understand. He was a better Macbeth than he was a liar.

"You are too wise a man to have allowed Mr. Denbrough to wander around with so much money. Did you keep it with you?"

The actor couldn't rein in a satisfied grin. "Oh, all right. It shouldn't matter anymore. I did hang on to the money belt, at least until De Shields kicked in the bedroom door. During all the ruckus that followed, I stole over to the neighbor's where Rose was storing her furniture for the party and stashed the belt in her couch."

"We kept hold of de money 'til Norton could be Norton again," Rose continued. "Dat's what Jack an' me were doin' when Sassafras and Canada followed us here t'other night. Bringin' him de money belt. Beatrice deposited et all de next day."

Reminded of the loan, Miss Claudette made a clucking noise, as if breadcrumbs were lodged deep in her throat.

Dancer, meanwhile, had used up his patience. "If that's everything, it's time to go, folks." He ordered Denbrough to his feet. "Carter, Miss Ramsey, and you, Joyce-Armstrong. We're all going to Harlem. I've got some questions of my own I want answered, and we can do that at the precinct."

"Me?" the Colonel's boy whined. "Why? I had nothing to do with any of this."

"You duked it out with De Shields the night he died, and until you can explain why to my satisfaction you're not leaving my sight."

"But, sergeant..."

"Let's go!"

Dancer's associates collected Rose, Jack Carter, and Joyce-Armstrong together, while the sergeant himself waited for Denbrough to climb to his feet, the young man still a bit unsteady from the cop's rap to his noggin.

I waited and watched. This was De Shields' killer. Denbrough had gone to the Hotel Theresa dressed as Ben Kanter, had it out with De Shields, and shot the peeper with the gun his father had used to take his own life. I was sure of it.

Even with four hours separating the time Roy Banks saw Kanter speaking with De Shields and when Denbrough finally pulled the trigger?

I was positive. The Webley proved that. It was Dancer's problem to figure out what had gone on between two and six fifteen. My bet was Denbrough had lost his nerve, left, then found it again and came back later that morning. One thing was certain, he spent part of the time taking off his disguise. That might explain the missing towel and certainly answered Banks' question about why no one saw Kanter darting out of the Theresa after the shots were fired.

Hey, De Shields was a sharp guy. Maybe he had already seen through Denbrough's masquerade.

And better, maybe the young man had come to ask the detective to keep his secret. More than likely the peeper would have told Denbrough to stick it. One look at Joyce-Armstrong's face told you De Shields hadn't been feeling agreeable that evening. On top of all the troubles De Shields' hounding him had put Denbrough through, Miss Claudette's baby boy finally blew his cork. People had killed for less.

So I waited and watched and chewed over the facts of the case and couldn't help marveling at, even with the wig gone, how much Denbrough seemed to be Ben Kanter to me. By some magic the make-up kept the illusion alive, and his expression didn't hurt the cause. Between being nabbed by the cops and his mother's uncharitable reprimands, he looked as defeated as he had in the jail cell when Orson and I came to call on him.

That's it!

"Oh...my...goodness." I didn't realize I spoke out loud.

"Mr. Winters?"

"What's up, guy?"

Chinaman and Dancer gazed at me as if I had clutched my chest with the first spasms of a heart attack.

I almost peaked around for Divine. *It's a revelation!* I thought. *Or like one.*

"Hey?" Dancer asked. "Cat got you tongue?"

Denbrough was on his feet, ignoring me. He had his own problems.

"I know who killed Andre De Shields," I mumbled, talking to myself more than anyone.

Now Denbrough was paying me attention.

"You're hiding the truth," I told him. "Just like at the jail. You knew you couldn't have killed Norton Denbrough. You are Norton Denbrough. But you couldn't tell anyone, not even Orson and me. Not while there was hope of sneaking the loan into your family's bank account."

"What are you gibbering about?" Denbrough was nervous, eyeballs wavering inside their sockets between Dancer and me. "I killed De Shields. Okay? You want a confession? I killed De Shields! Can we go now?"

Dancer told Denbrough, "No confessions until we get you to the precinct," and asked me, "What in the world are you blathering about?"

I looked through the cop at Denbrough. "You could have killed De Shields. There's proof enough for it. But it doesn't quite ring true. That bothers me."

"What is wrong with you?" Dancer was close to shouting. "You're the one who sold me on this evidence!"

"I was wrong. Okay? I made a mistake. Think about it. The blackmail. The towel. Joyce-Armstrong's black eye. Kanter talking to De Shields at two but De Shields getting shot after six. No witnesses seeing Kanter running away from the Theresa."

"I have thought about it, and I think Denbrough here offed De Shields. So did you when we came here."

"But he didn't." I turned back to Denbrough. "You're protecting her."

The young man couldn't return my stare. Instead he screwed his eyes into the tops of his shoes. "I don't know what you're going on about, Sassafras. I want to leave."

Dancer to me: "All right. I'll nibble. Who is he trying to protect?"

"Who else? His sister."

Denbrough laughed, too hard and too loud.

His mother stamped her foot and howled. "How dare you? You Midwestern plebeian. Don't try defiling my daughter's good name with such an accusation. I'll have you broken!"

"This is nonsense!" Denbrough shouted. "You've got your killer."

The sergeant told everyone to bottle it, then jammed a finger in my direction, his face a scowl. "Spill. What have you got? But, like I told your butler, make it quick."

"De Shields loved Beatrice."

This prompted another chorus of skepticism from Mrs. Denbrough and her son, with Joyce-Armstrong backing them up on harmony, but the copper waved them silent.

"Hey, he loved her," I said, "or was infatuated with her. One of the two. It doesn't matter. What does is that De Shields didn't want Beatrice marrying Dell Joyce-Armstrong. And since it was a marriage of convenience, he tried to turn himself into an acceptable replacement by scrounging together a lot of dough."

"Have you completely lost your pea-sized mind?" Joyce-Armstrong's face was flushed with blood, his lips tight against his teeth. "The idea of it! That shamus? Supplanting me?"

Dancer started down the stairs a couple of steps at Joyce-Armstrong before he caught himself, his self-restraint yanking hard on his leash. "I'm not going to say it again. Shut your trap!" Having said his peace, the sergeant turned back to me and snarled, "Hurry it up."

"Beatrice likes to flirt. I can testify to that. Nothing bad. School-girl stuff. She's young. She didn't mean anything by it."

"I get the point already. She teased you, so odds are she teased De Shields."

"Who was a lonely guy who was shy around women. You and Father Divine have told me as much. Ten years with his wife dead and gone..."

"I remember. Get to the good stuff. Your meter's running."

A voice suddenly whispered inside my ear, *The pressure's on, Sassafras. Don't blank out.* But I wasn't going to. I felt like I was in my natural element, in a comfortable zone where I couldn't do anything wrong. If I had been pitching then and there the strike zone would have looked as big as a roadster.

"De Shields can't scrounge up the kind of dough he needs, so he tries the direct approach. He comes here Wednesday afternoon and tells Mrs. Denbrough exactly how he feels about Beatrice. She gives him his walking papers."

Miss Claudette couldn't stop herself. "This is lunacy. De Shields' fee was a strain on our budget, and his services were no longer necessary."

Dancer snapped his face at her. He frowned without blinking and succeeded in intimidating her, something I hadn't thought possible.

"What can De Shields do now?" I asked, sidestepping the interruption. "Well, he knew about Norton's loan. I found out about it from him, in a roundabout sort of way. And it's possible he even knew Ben Kanter and Norton Denbrough were one and the same person. I think he did."

Dancer turned his gaze on the man in question. "We're gonna find out."

"De Shields went to sulk at the Astoria Cafe after he got the sack, but later he decides to hightail it back here. This time he only talks to Beatrice and lays it on the line. Either she dumps Joyce-Armstrong and walks the aisle with him, or he goes to the newshounds and tells them all about her brother's recent adventures."

"This is a fantasy," Joyce-Armstrong said. "Anyone can concoct a yarn out of whole cloth. Where's your proof?"

The sergeant agreed. "Got any evidence?"

"Not a lot, but it's the only scheme that makes sense," I said.

"Why?"

"I talked to the cabbie who drove De Shields here the second time Tuesday night. He said when De Shields was leaving Beatrice followed him outside. They talked and then she came back in the house. That has to be when they made their assignation."

"What assignation?" Miss Claudette demanded.

"To get together that night at the Hotel Theresa. That's why De Shields rented the fancy suite and called the kitchen to ask about the price of champagne. He was trying to impress her."

I guess Dancer liked what he heard, because he bothered to ask, "So then what? Joyce-Armstrong shows up to drag Beatrice out of there?"

"No. She hadn't arrived yet. See, Norton couldn't leave the house. What if his mother found him missing, gone and off to Harlem? It was too risky, so they called Dell-boy to go to the hotel and talk sense into De Shields. Thanks to Rose we know Joyce-Armstrong knew Ben Kanter's secret identity."

"The shiner suggests he crapped out."

"Uh-huh."

"That's when Norton decided to talk to De Shields."

"Uh-uh. I said it was too risky for him to leave the house."

Denbrough: "Enough, sergeant. You know I went to the Theresa that night. You have a witness."

"He's got you there," Dancer said. "And nobody saw his sister."

I shook my head, borrowing the copper's ace-in-the-hole smirk. "Wrong."

"How 'wrong'?"

"Nobody saw Norton, but someone did see Beatrice."

He ignored the first part. "Who saw her?"

"Roy Horton Banks."

"Banks saw Ben Kanter, and Ben Kanter is Norton Denbrough."

"Banks saw someone who looked like Ben Kanter but was three or four inches shorter. He can prove it. Beatrice is shorter, and there is a strong family resemblance."

I had hoped that would persuade Dancer, but all he said was, "Keep going."

"There's the towel. She cleaned off her brown Pan-Cake with it, so she couldn't leave it."

The brother urged that was what he had done.

"And the bed was messed up. That explains what was going on between two and six fifteen."

"My sister isn't a slut," Denbrough warned.

"No, she isn't," I said. "She's a practical woman. A lot like her mother in a lot of ways. That's why, when Joyce-Armstrong couldn't get De Shields to change his mind by force, she tried a more subtle maneuver. But come dawn and De Shields hadn't changed his mind..."

"I killed him."

A voice from above interrupted me. For one stupid second I thought I had thrown my voice like Edgar Bergen. Then, along with everybody else in the foyer, I craned my neck to see Beatrice standing at the top of the second-level steps, hands patiently clasped behind her back, gutters staining her cheeks from crying.

Denbrough shouted his sister's name. "Stop it! You don't have to protect me!"

"It's been the other way around, and enough's enough." Her voice was as calm as the eye of a tornado. "Remember what papa used to say? 'You dig your own grave in this world.'" She shined her sights on me. "You're right. I shot De Shields. Everything you said is correct. He'd have ruined my happiness, mama's, Norton's, Rose's, anyone's to get what he wanted. To have me."

"The strain's been too much on her," Denbrough insisted to Dancer. "Take me into custody and let my mother call our physician."

"You mean the one who swore you were as sick as a dog? I don't think so, pal. I'll see to it she's taken care of." Dancer called to Beatrice, "Better come down, miss."

But she never took her eyes off me, deaf to her brother or the cop. "I went to his suite prepared. He didn't act surprised to see the gun, and he didn't seem to care when I started firing. He made me so furious, staring at me as if I was betraying him, so I squeezed the trigger. Over and over. I finally hit him on the fourth try. That did surprise him." One last tear trickled down her face and fell off her chin, splashing near my feet.

"That's when I ran," she continued. "Straight to his office, to destroy his evidence. When I found his safe and couldn't open it, I did the only thing I could. And it worked. The fire destroyed everything. I was home free."

She took a deep breath. It was a brave front, but it was plain to see she was on the verge of cracking.

"Come down," I said. "Let's get this squared away." I was trying to play to her practical side.

"You're an intuitive man," she said, not budging. "Papa was intuitive. Norton takes after him." Then she brought her right hand from around her back and pointed the Webley at me.

I heard Dancer order "Everyone get out of the way!" as he was shoving Denbrough behind him, him and his officers training their revolvers on the girl. "Put that down now!" he commanded. Dancer didn't sound as confident as he had earlier.

"Bea," the brother pleaded, "stop this. It's all my fault. Please don't pay for my mistakes."

Miss Claudette was of like mind. "Beatrice. Listen to me. Norton's right. None of this would have happened if he had behaved properly.

Don't throw away your life because of his immorality."

"Poor mama," the young woman said, a clothesline between her eyes and mine, talking to me as if I understood. "She never will forgive papa. Not in a million years."

"That gun didn't solve your daddy's problems," I said. "It couldn't really solve your problem with De Shields, and it can't scare this one off. Throw it away. You're strong. You can handle your own problems."

"I am taking care of them, Sassafras. This way I won't be around to shame the inestimable Denbrough lineage with a trial. Norton will be free to live with Rose. And, even better, mama will have all the money she will ever need."

"Girl," Miss Claudette said, a desperate hone to her voice, "in heaven's name, what are you blathering about?"

"Why, mama, how could you of all people forget about life insurance?"

Beatrice wrapped her left hand around her right and fired. The bullet went whizzing past my ear, splintering wood in the railing behind me.

Three revolvers responded in kind.

Clipping from *The Brooklyn Chronicle*, March 20, 1936:

SOCIALITE SLAUGHTERED IN POLICE SHOOTOUT

Fiancée to Dell Joyce-Armstrong Trades
SLUGS WITH COPS

Beatrice Denbrough, one of Manhattan's brightest young cosmopolitans, died exchanging gunfire in her Gramercy Park West home with police officers around 7 p.m.

Denbrough, 23, was being arrested as a suspect in the murder of private investigator Andre De Shields in Harlem Thursday morning.

"She confessed to killing him," Detective Sergeant Stanley Dancer said. "After that she started shooting. She gave us no choice."

Denbrough open fired on a group that included her fiancé, Dell Joyce-Armstrong, son of rubber magnate Colonel Ward Joyce-Armstrong of New York and Manaus, Brazil.

Also in the group were her mother, Claudette, her brother, Norton, and members of the WPA-sponsored Harlem Negro Theater Unit. Rose Ramsey, an actress in the Unit, has been romantically linked to Norton Denbrough.

The gun battle is the latest in a series of bizarre incidents that have recently surrounded the Denbrough family.

Beginning last Sunday...

The Last Chapter

Tuesday, April 14.

Beatrice had lain beside her father in the Denbrough family crypt at Kingstead Cemetery for three weeks. Norton had been asked by his mother to leave the family estate, but not before he withdrew the one hundred thousand dollars from their bank account. Because the newspapers had thoroughly covered the Ben Kanter angle of De Shields' murder, Orson was forced to remove Norton from the role of the Porter. Rose stayed on as Lady-in-waiting. The whole Unit took up a collection to help keep the young couple afloat.

Gradually the tragedy of Andre De Shields and Beatrice Denbrough faded into the background, more and more so as opening night approached.

It started at sunset.

Musicians from the Monarch Lodge of the Benevolent and Protective Order of Elks struck up a tune, blowing their trumpets and beating their drums. Marching in two detachments throughout the streets of Harlem, wearing uniforms of light blue, gold, and scarlet, they followed two huge, crimson banners:

ACT ONE

MACBETH
By
William Shakespeare

The detachments converged on the Lafayette at six thirty, eighty-five musicians flocking around the Tree of Hope, playing for ten thousand people milling along the sidewalks. At the same time a contingent of mounted policemen and beat cops were making a valiant but futile effort to rope off four city blocks directly around the theatre, the officers outnumbered and the excitement too contagious to be contained.

For an hour northbound traffic on Seventh Avenue came to a standstill, with cars backed up ten blocks. Floodlights, mounted in trucks parked around the Lafayette, turned their beams on the dusk to tickle the cloudy sky with lazy, circling strokes.

Newsreel cameras were clicking and clattering away on the surrounding rooftops, recording a hectic scene of first-nighters arriving in top hats, ermines, and jewels, togged as smart as any hob-knobs at any Gilbert Miller opening. Many of these folks were making their first expedition to Harlem and getting quite a reception, struggling past hundreds of bystanders to reach the lobby doors.

The next couple of hours were an exercise in regimented chaos for the Harlem Unit. While Miss Flannagan and Mr. Houseman were giving interviews about the Federal Theatre Project to a swarm of reporters in the Lafayette's lobby, Orson was on a frantic backstage quest for a fresh shirt to replace the one he had been wearing the past twenty-four hours.

"Who around here wears a size sixteen shirt?"

Scrounging one that fit, if you ignored that the sleeves were too short, Welles began concentrating on keeping his players under control. The troupe was beside themselves. All any of them wanted was to bolt out of the chute and start acting. Unfortunately the hoopla outside kept the curtain, scheduled to go up at eight forty-five, from rising until nine twenty-five. But rise it did.

❧❦

The house lights dimmed.

With a wave of his baton Virgil Thomson's diabolical music, jumbling voodoo rhythms with a nineteenth century waltz-melody, seeped out of the orchestra pit.

The stage remained dark.

Thunder drums racked the air, like timbers tumbling across a concrete floor, followed by a rain drum. Then silence.

The act drop rose.

Dafora Horton and company began their chanting, softly at first, then steadily louder, keeping pace with the lights that were creeping up on stage. Act one, scene one was set in the Haitian jungle, trees meeting in a great overhead arch, the twisted trunks suggesting a gigantic living skeleton.

The chanting faded and a vocal solo cued a cellophane rain effect. Enter Macbeth and Banquo, the pair confronted by an array of warlocks and occult acolytes commanded by Hectate, in Welles' production a voodoo priest who curses the Thane to his doom.

As the scenes progressed Orson took advantage of a tower, a bridge, even a gateway to conjure a Dracula's Castle atmosphere for Macbeth's Citadel, thunder and lightning storming ceaselessly in the Haitian mountains.

Without a doubt the showstopper was Macbeth's royal reception following the murder of Banquo. Dozens of couples togged to the dictys in court finery swirled about the stage until a high inhuman scream froze them in their tracks. As awful as this scream was, it paled beside Macbeth's terrified wail as the spirit of Banquo, represented by a familiar skull-shaped green spotlight, flickered and flailed on the battlements to taunt the Thane.

As macabre as the reception was, nothing topped the final act's penultimate scene for audacity. Macbeth is on the parapet. Macduff's forces have him surrounded, and the Thane shoots the "cream-faced loon" who has brought him the news, kicking the body to the courtyard eighteen feet below.

Enter Macduff, a rangy bearded man, thirsty to avenge the slaughter of his wife and boy. Macbeth aims and fires, emptying his gun but missing Macduff, and the enemies clench for the final battle, their struggle carrying them off stage. One moment later Macbeth's head comes careening down the battlements, Macduff's jubilant victory cry following right behind. The final scene, with its dibbing up of Haiti by the victors, was almost an anti-climax as the curtain fell.

And the play was over.

—⁂—

The applause and "Bravos" that followed were outrageous! Salvo after salvo rolled through the air like boulders, a new wave exploding as each actor came on stage for their curtain call. The extolment didn't break until Orson was finally dragged out on stage and forced to take a bow.

By the time the audience finally dispersed and the last musician had marched home it was almost two in the morning. The coast was finally clear for the cast to trot over to Small's Paradise on 135th Street, where reservations had been made for us to commemorate and fret until the bulldog editions came out with *Macbeth's* reviews.

Our party threatened to push Small's capacity cap to its limit. One of Harlem's four best night clubs and the most hospitable to Negroes, Small's management made sure we had a good time, which wasn't hard. The joint was famous for its knockout floor shows, big band jams, and dancing waiters who performed the Charleston full out while balancing trays loaded with drinks on their fingertips.

Chinaman and I grabbed a table together, the Big C feeling warm and cozy after four snifters of cognac. To be honest he was blitzed, happy as a lark that Orson had invited him to join the Unit for the run of the play.

"If the reviews are favorable," he said, "we'll be going to the WPA theaters in Bridgeport, Hartford, Cleveland, Indianapolis, Chicago, Detroit, and Dallas. Isn't life wonderful?"

"Yes, it is." Don't ask me how, but I kept a straight face.

"Mr. Houseman is aware illness and mortality are frightingly high among Negro performers, so he sees the wisdom of hiring an understudies' understudy. Someone who knows all the parts in the play."

He leaned close to me and whispered so no one else could hear him. "Confidentially, Mr. Winters, it so happens I know every damn line in every damn play old Willie Shakiespeare ever wrote. That's why they aren't holding my color against me."

"Yes, Chinaman, I know."

He shifted into high gear again. "Oh, it was a marvelous performance tonight! A marvelous performance! But poor Macbeth." Chinaman started to sniffle. "Driven by fate. Cursed by a demon to a vainglorious doom. All that thunder and lightning buzzing around him to emphasize the corruption of power. It's a wonder he could even think with all that going on!" Now he was bawling. "It's tragic!"

"Yes, Chinaman, it is."

Just like that, though, he perked up. "Weren't the costumes beautiful? Mr. Carter looked smashing on the battlement in his satin-striped red and white breeches and shiny boots. And the ladies! Oh, what glorious silk dresses they had on." He whistled.

"Yes, Chinaman, I know. Chinaman?"

"Hmmm?"

"Have you ever considered the advantages in hiring your own personal valet?"

The newspapers arrived soon after four, heralded by an exhausted Eric Burroughs, who had run all the way from a stand on the corner of Seventh Avenue and 130th Street. Orson, Mr. Houseman, Miss Flannagan, and Jack Carter each grabbed a different edition and read to the anxious actors.

Orson: "'As an experiment in Afro-American showmanship, *Macbeth* merited the excitement that fairly rocked the Lafayette Theatre last night. If it is witches you want, Harlem knows how to overwhelm you with their fury and phantom splendor.' *The New York Times*!"

Mr. Houseman: "Arthur Pollock of the *Brooklyn Daily Eagle* comments on the 'childlike austerity' of the performance. 'With all their gusto, they play Shakespeare as though they were apt children who have just discovered and adore the old man.'"

Miss Flannagan: "'A spectacular theater experience. This West Indian *Macbeth* is the most colorful, certainly the most startling, of any performance that gory tragedy has ever been given on this continent.' Burns Mantle, *New York Daily News*!"

Jack Carter: "Oh, oh. Percy Hammond in *The New York Herald Tribune* writes, 'The Negro Theatre, an off-shoot of the Federal Government and one of Uncle Sam's experimental philanthropies, gave us, last night, an exhibition of deluxe boondoggling. One has to wonder at the inability of so noble a race to sing the music of Shakespeare.'"

"Don't worry about it, Mr. Carter," Chinaman chirped from our table. "Just ask Abdul to put a curse on Mr. Hammond." This was seconded by wild applauds.

After all the papers had been read out loud, the final tally was all but one for *Voodoo Macbeth* as a triumph for the Harlem Theatre Unit.

The newspapers were passed from one eager table to the next, while Orson made the rounds to congratulate everyone. My table was his last stop, Chinaman gone off to read reviews.

"Sassafras, we did it! We did it!"

"Yep. You sure did." To tell the truth, I was glad the long haul was over. I felt numb. Orson, who looked as tired as I felt behind his twinkling eyes, sat down next to me. "I pulled it off!" he said. "In spite of every crazy thing that happened, I actually got *Macbeth* off the ground!"

"And you said it wouldn't fly." I raised my glass to toast him. "I'm glad you're proud. You did nice work."

"Thank you," he said, shifting his eyes away, my sincerity embarrassing him.

I tipped my glass towards Welles and swallowed some soda water.

"So will you be coming on tour with us?" he asked, looking back my way. "We'll play for six weeks in the Lafayette, move to the Aldephi on Broadway for another six weeks, then hopefully hit the road for a couple of months. I'm sure there'll be dangers aplenty for you and me to tackle in every port."

Tempting as it was, it wasn't for me. "No. I'm tired. I'm going home. Drop me a postcard now and then and tell me if Chinaman's taking care of himself."

"But how will I get along without my bodyguard?"

"What are you grousing about? The Communists aren't bothering you anymore."

"And what if somebody gets murdered?"

"Call the cops."

"Fine," he sighed. "Be that way. Perhaps I'll have to solve the next mystery myself."

"I think you're going to be too busy directing *Macbeth*. Forget about mysteries and enjoy your triumph. For Christ's sakes, Orson, Harlem is throwing itself at your feet. Don't you care?"

Son of a gun if it hadn't dawned on him yet. Looking around at the tables, he watched his cast reading and rereading their notices and complimenting each other. In his mind, now and forever, Welles would recall the festivities of April 14th, 1936 as his coming of age, an authorization of his talent. And this was just the beginning. There would be more plays for the director and his Unit, and even more challenges long after the WPA breathed its last. Who knew where this young man's genius could take him? I was looking forward to finding out, but tonight Orson Welles had passed his first trial by fire and proved himself worthy, to both the borough's naysayers and his own doubts. "By God, you're right. I conquered Harlem."

"Yes, buddy, you did." I had to laugh. His pride was a joy to see.

"They've been treating me like a king all night. And I am! I am a king, Sassafras. I really am the King of Harlem!"

About the Author

Steven Philip Jones, a die-hard Chicago Cubs fan, lives with his family in eastern Iowa.

He is the author of the novel *The Bushwhackers*, the novella *The Sceptre*, and several graphic stories and adaptations, including *Nightlinger*, *Tatters*, *Dracula*, and *The Adventure of the Opera Ghost*.

His editing credits include the paperback anthology *Herbert West: Tales of the Re-Animator*.

Jones has a B.A. in religion and journalism from the University of Iowa, and was accepted into Iowa's prestigious Writers' Workshop MFA program. He is also the author of a *King of Harlem* prequel novella, *The Curse of Wrigley Field*.

Printed in the United States
123268LV00003B/64/A